MARK MANNOCK

COUNTERPOINT

First published by Shotfire Books 2023

Copyright © 2023 by Mark Mannock

This novel is entirely a work of fiction. The names, characters and incidents portrayed in it are the work of the author's imagination. Any resemblance to actual persons, living or dead, events or localities is entirely coincidental.

Mark Mannock asserts the moral right to be identified as the author of this work.

First edition

ISBN: 978-0-6489036-4-2

This book was professionally typeset on Reedsy. Find out more at reedsy.com

For Gaye and Denis

Contents

Chapter 1

Damn. What the hell was that?

My head snapped backwards. Like a hammer blow.

A piercing, blinding pain cut through my consciousness.

I squeezed my eyes tight.

But not for long.

The fog descended.

I drifted… into darkness… then into nothing.

I opened an eye. Fatal curiosity.

The white light speared my cornea like a laser.

Then a writhing shape appeared.

A silhouette?

A dementor?

Two eyes open. Another mistake. Twice the light, twice the pain.

Again, the fog came down, swallowing my senses.

With the darkness came relief.

Once more, the light bled into the dusky recesses of my mind.

Lesson learned. I squinted, just peeking into the brightness.

Soft blurred lines, weaving, unidentifiable. A red hue now wept across the monochromatic landscape.

Blood?

Whose blood?

Slowly, the images sharpened, but not enough. I needed clarity.

I tried to lift my right arm. Nothing.

Then my left. Nothing.

Was I unhinged?

I stared straight ahead. My squinting gaze fixed on a receding black dot, fading to a distant vanishing point captured in a gloomy mist.

"Sharp!"

I grunted.

"Sharp!"

I wished he wouldn't yell. Whoever *he* the hell was. My head still pounded like a jackhammer. The yelling didn't help.

Each conscious second offered a chance to rebalance. I'd focus on staying conscious.

"Sharp, there's no point struggling."

That damned voice.

Like a slow drip, each lucid thought emerged... then evaporated.

Stay vigilant, stay awake.

Again, the claggy fog.

Let the darkness roll in.

I thought I'd come around quicker this time. The cognizant thoughts became more frequent. I gave my arms one more almighty wrench.

Shit. Nothing but acute, burning pain.

The voice had said 'no point.'

The voice was right.

I had a sense of sitting bolt upright, tied to a chair. The light, or sun, or whatever the hell it was, smothered my view. The dementors appeared and disappeared, perpetually transforming. But the red hue remained.

Blood red; for life or for death?

I tried to drag a memory to the forefront of my mind. Any memory.

I'd either been drugged or hit... or both. There were waves...

"Sharp, for God's sake, get a grip."

The voice.

"What the hell...?" Words. My words. The sound of my own speech. Good on me, one step forward.

"Sharp."

Stare him down. Eyes wide open. Attitude aggressive.

A torrent of hot pain lashed down. The light rays penetrated my skull like a warhead of four-inch nails.

I scrunched my eyes... and waited.

But I couldn't wait forever.

A few moments on I reopened them, gradually, like someone peering out of a mailbox slit. The lightning bolts remained invasive and overpowering, but they didn't kill me.

"Sharp!"

No sign of the man who spoke. I wondered briefly if his tone rang familiar. Not something to work out now. Maybe later.

The voice came from behind the impenetrable wall of whiteness. He may as well have been a mile away. A one-sided relationship.

Footsteps.

Abruptly, everything turned black again, yet this time I remained wide awake. The figure had stepped in front of the light source, blocking my entire vision.

Then he took a pace back.

I strained my neck upward to stare into his face.

As his features came into focus, the clarity I'd sought became a judgement.

I was a dead man.

Chapter 2

Several years earlier...

The warm river waters lapped against his torso, the splashing disguising the heavy gasps escaping the young Marine's lungs. Beta fought to control his breathing. He'd been trained to be in control of every aspect of his physicality. Easier said than done when you'd just sprinted eight hundred yards through dense jungle pursued by heavily armed militia.

Slowly, the pounding in his chest began to ease. He made out footsteps trampling through the undergrowth, the occasional word floating in the breeze. The harsh tone suggested orders.

"Buscar en la orilla del rio!"

The words proved useless to Beta. He didn't speak the lingo.

Understanding no longer mattered as the footsteps traipsed toward the river... and him. He pressed his body close to the bank and sank further into the water, his mouth and nose barely visible above the surface. His eyes and ears, his only two sources of intel, were now rendered useless.

Beta felt out of touch. He hated being out of touch with

his environment. As a highly trained marksman, any failure to process his surroundings grated. Any small change may affect his mission and his survivability.

Submerged under the flowing water, Beta remained only vaguely aware of the muffled cadence of the outside world, but the pressing on his chest felt very real… and comforting.

His rifle. Standard Marine issue M27. He allowed a hand to drop down to caress the weapon's outline. Aware he was in no position to make a shot, he pressed his torso harder against the rifle and the bank, willing himself to disappear.

The first bullet shattered the Marine's watery fog. He heard the muted thud of gunfire from above just before witnessing a round break the surface fifteen feet from his location. He felt strangely detached. Beta knew each slug would slow down as it drove into the river, only a threat if he lay in the shallows. Grimacing to himself, he gauged the depth of the surrounding water. Too freakin' shallow.

More gunfire, more tiny torpedoes streaking down, searching the depths. The next barrage seemed to be about twenty feet distant. Beta allowed himself a small sigh of relief. They were moving upriver. After several more shots, his world fell into an eerie silence, apart from the sound of running water.

Had they moved on? Would he be safe to crawl out of his hide?

Beta decided to wait two more minutes, just to be certain. He still had a mission to complete, now more difficult because he'd lost contact with Gamma. They needed to re-establish some form of communication quickly, if his partner remained alive.

Beta tensed his muscles in preparation for his extraction from the river. He inhaled a long, slow breath. His left hand was barely an inch from the surface when the crack of a gunshot suddenly pulsed through the water. In the same instant, a bullet shot a trail through the shallows, a deadly missile only two feet from his location. He pulled in his hand as another round entered the stream, right where his fingers had been.

They'd found him.

The barrage fell like a hellish rain, as lead poured down around him. He saved his breath and held it, clawing at the riverbank, pushing himself deeper into the water. He gained little protection, certainly not enough to shield his body from the constant gunfire.

Still, he tried.

Almost laying flat on the riverbed now, Beta wedged tightly into a small crevice. The act seemed more psychological than effective. A bullet could easily find him, and probably would.

The militia men continued their assault, the bombardment from above consistent and confronting. They'd found their man. Beta figured he only had a few more seconds before water replaced the air in his lungs and he'd be forced to dive for the surface. He saw the irony in the fact that his first gasp of air to save him from drowning would also be his last breath — period.

He counted down the seconds until he needed to break for it. The torrential barrage of gunfire continued. The bullets churned up the riverbed as he lay immersed in a bath of brown watery mud. Beta sensed a pull on his sleeve. He knew what it was straight away, a round tearing through his heavy combat utility uniform. Another puff of mud exploded beside his face as one more slug searched him out.

He wouldn't need the five seconds. He'd be dead by then.

Beta braced himself. He'd chosen to be a warrior. He'd known a death such as this may be on the cards. But where in God's name was Gamma?

Suddenly, a cacophony of gunfire exploded, twice as loud as before. They were closer. Even through the river's swirling water, it sounded deafening.

Then, just as suddenly... it stopped.

Beta couldn't believe it. Hell to heaven in two seconds flat. He lunged for the surface, hungrily gasping at the air, letting it give life to his exploding lungs. Still, he remained cautious, certain that the militia must be close by.

He raised his head out of the water. No reaction, nobody shot at him. Slowly, he grabbed at a tree root and heaved himself upward. In a single motion, he fell flat on the embankment, shoving his rifle in front of him. Ready.

Beta scanned the area. Not a soul standing. Then he noticed the first sign. A mangled, bloodied hand protruding from a bush ten yards ahead. No movement.

The Marine inched forward. A small clearing came into view as he slithered along the ground. Blood dripped from the bushes and soaked into the soil. It hadn't been like that moments earlier when he bolted through the clearing on the way to the river. Bodies now lay scattered across the space. Corpses mostly, but not all. A couple of men groaned, their hold on life tenuous as a crimson tide wept across their chests and faces.

The militia.

Beta rose to one knee, his rifle steady and high, ready to fire. He swung around in a one-eighty-degree arc until he pointed back to the stream. There were bodies here on the bank and in the water. They all clutched weapons, some automatic. They had been his death squad.

The snap of a twig breaking on the other side of the clearing caused Beta to swivel around, desperate to get a fix on the source. Most people wouldn't have noticed the sound. Beta had been trained to notice everything.

Two branches parted about thirty yards ahead. Beta squeezed on his trigger but didn't commit. He noticed an arm reaching forward, pushing at one of the bushes. The uniform the arm wore was similar to his own.

Beta held his aim.

The figure, a male, edged partially into a space beyond the clearing. He moved carefully, swinging an L119A2 carbine across his view. When he saw Beta, the man stopped sweeping his weapon and pointed it fixedly at him. In the same second, Beta's rifle returned the challenge.

It was then that Beta saw the soldier's face and noticed the wound on his upper thigh. It bled profusely, clearly restricting his movement.

The two combatants looked at each other. Neither fired.

Beta glanced at the bloodied corpses that lay between them. How the hell had Gamma managed to take out the whole fucking lot?

Beta started to rise to his feet. Gamma's wound needed attending to. His partner raised a flat palm and motioned him back down. He then put a finger to his lips. Momentarily uncertain, Beta followed Gamma's instruction and lowered himself to the ground. Gamma knew the lie of the land, his data current.

Ten seconds ticked past. Neither soldier moved. Beta saw

a slight smile creep onto Gamma's face, or maybe a grimace from the pain in his leg. A second later, it disappeared.

Gamma raised a vertical palm, indicating that Beta should remain still as his partner circled the clearing. Beta sensed a looming threat but had no idea from where.

Two minutes on, seemingly satisfied with what he saw, Gamma nodded toward Beta before retreating back into the undergrowth. It was as though he'd never been there.

Beta prepared to rise, for a second time.

Then all hell broke loose.

Automatic gunfire pulverized the bushes where Gamma stood moments earlier. The shots came from the south. Yet again, Beta began to push up. The staccato of unbridled destruction filled his ears as a hail of bullets shredded the undergrowth surrounding the clearing. Beta had no choice. He flattened himself to the ground.

Suddenly voices. Yelling.

"Buscar en todas partes. Encontrarlos. Matarlos!"

Again, Beta didn't understand, but he knew it couldn't be good.

Seconds later at least a dozen men, all heavily armed with the Chinese Type 56 automatics, blocked the young Marine's escape into the anonymity of the jungle. He contemplated sliding down into the river but decided against it. He wouldn't go through that hell again. Besides, Gamma would need back up.

The militia soldiers seemed focused on the direction Gamma had taken. They offered only a cursory glance around the clearing before pursuing their prey on the run.

Beta risked raising his head, searching for a path of extraction. He'd assumed all the soldiers had gone, but he'd been wrong. One remained. In his fifties, average height with a solid build, unshaven, but not disheveled, he stood tall. The militia man stared down at the fallen. They must have been his comrades. He shook his head before bowing it slightly. His lips moved, as though muttering a prayer.

Beta inhaled sharply as he stared into the man's cold grey eyes.

This was the man he and Gamma had been sent to kill.

As silently as possible, Beta raised his weapon. Abruptly, his target whipped his own weapon upward, pointing it directly in front of him. Before Beta could fire, the man unleashed a curtain of automatic fire across the whole area. The Marine dug himself back into the ground, clawing into the earth. When he looked up ten seconds later, the man had disappeared. The sea of red had become an ocean. None of the shooter's comrades had survived his bloody onslaught.

This was a cold-blooded killer.

Beta heard them up ahead. Although the jungle was thick, their voices cut through the air. If that wasn't enough, the intermittent bursts of gunfire kept him on track. The militia soldiers pressed forward. A good sign. It meant Gamma had got away. Unsure what he might achieve against so many armed men, the young Marine knew that sure as hell he'd try something when he caught up.

Besides, now he'd located and identified his target. He had a job to do.

Branches lashed at him, and the uneven ground remained constantly challenging. Beta held his M27 in readiness, not knowing when he may break out of cover.

11

The yelling increased in intensity. An ominous sign. The tone in the men's voices became agitated, their phrases rushed and urgent. The sporadic gunfire now turned into a constant drone of relentless cracks. Beta pushed forward, fearing the worst.

He came up on the heels of an outlier, obviously there to protect the group's rear. These people may have been blood thirsty, but they were organized. The outlier swung around as Beta rounded a tree behind him. The man started to lift his weapon, but too slowly. Beta shot him in the throat. No one would notice the shot amongst a hundred others, and there would be no calling for help. For his troubles, the militia man would die a silent death.

Beta pushed on. The voices and gunfire sounded close now, but he didn't slow his pace. The thought of Gamma and his target drove the young warrior onward.

As he shoved himself through a substantial clump of bushes, a sharp pain smacked the back of Beta's head driving him face down to the jungle floor. He rolled defensively, uncertain what caused his fall. He twisted onto his back, raising his weapon. Before he got it halfway up, the gun flew from his hands, kicked aside by a towering, muscled soldier, his mouth leering in anticipation.

"You will die now, my stupid friend."

Unmistakable Colombian accent. Unmistakable intent.

As he spoke, the man drew an enormous machete from his belt. Beta kicked up at the man's groin as the blade came down. The blow faltered but didn't change direction. The Marine rolled to his right, face down, as the steel hit the earth next to his head. Hoping his attacker held his weapon tight, Beta unleashed his right elbow in a blind rearward stab. A surprised grunt told him he'd found his mark. As he rolled back, Beta spread his fingers around the man's hands, still holding the machete. He managed to flick the weapon up, spewing dirt into the militia man's eyes.

Marine training taught Beta that a good fight is a fight that ends quickly. As his attacker removed a hand from his weapon attempting to clear his sight, Beta grabbed the handle with full force and swung it round in an arc. The swing ended in a bloody mess, rupturing the man's neck as his head flopped pathetically to one side.

The corpse fell to the ground.

The attacker had lost his life, and Beta had lost time he couldn't afford.

He gathered himself and pressed on, shoving his way through the now constant clumps of foliage, prickles and stubborn branches that tore at his exposed skin. The Marine was about to burst through another clump of bushes when some instinct told him to pause. Raising an arm ahead of him, he gently pulled down a branch. His instinct had served him well. If he'd stepped forward, he would have been in clear view of the militia group, not two hundred yards ahead of him. They perched on the far side of a small tributary of the river he'd just left.

What Beta saw alarmed him.

He noted at least twenty men. The group that he'd pursued must have met up with another team. Each man carried a gun, most of them Chinese automatics. Beta briefly wondered why Colombians were armed with Chinese weapons, but he didn't have time to consider that now. Half a dozen of the men faced outward, scanning for threats. The rest gathered in a semicircle, looking inward. The focus of their attention appeared to be a stretcher that leaned on a forty-five-degree angle against the tray of an aging truck. A makeshift track sprawled ahead of the vehicle. From this distance, Beta couldn't identify the form strapped to the stretcher, but it wasn't difficult to guess.

The Marine detached the sight from his M27, wiped it down, and focused through the glass to get a better look. With so many men gathered around the stretcher, Beta only managed to catch glimpses between the bodies of the gaping militia men. But he saw enough.

Gamma's clothes half fell off him in a bloodied mess. He'd certainly sustained further severe wounds, much more serious than his leg. Beta zeroed in on his colleague's face. Gamma's eyes were closed, and from his current position Beta saw no sign of breathing. The worst-case scenario, Gamma forfeiting his life, protecting him. Before he left, Beta had to be certain. Honor, courage and commitment, the values drummed into him from his first day at boot camp, were now intuitive. His partner, Gamma, displayed those qualities in truckloads, and he wasn't even a US Marine. Not even an American. Beta was aware that the English produced high-level Special Services operators. Gamma came from the SBS, Special Boat Service, and he'd certainly proven the point. Beta wouldn't let him down. No chance in hell, not if there remained any hope at all.

Beta needed to get closer but crossing the tributary would leave him exposed. Aware that he hauled pathetically little firepower against so many well-equipped men, the Marine had to think this through. He needed a plan, a suicide attack would advantage nobody. If he doubled back up the tributary, crossed the water out of sight of the militia and came down on their side of the river, he might find some higher ground where he'd be able to pick the soldiers off and get to Gamma. It wasn't much of a plan, but better than no plan at all.

Suddenly, the mechanical stutter of someone attempting to start the truck's engine shattered the peace of the rain forest. A second attempt and the engine roared to life. Beta's fledgling plan became an instant wipe-out.

The young Marine moved quickly. Gathering up his rifle, he headed downstream, parallel to the water, towards the truck's position. He stayed behind the cover of the undergrowth. As he ran, twigs broke too loudly and birds squawked as they fluttered away. Beta desperately hoped the muttering of the truck's diesel would conceal the noise.

Within three minutes, he drew level with the vehicle... and the soldiers. Beta scanned the area until he spotted a thick kapok tree with low-lying branches. Without hesitation he slung his rifle over his shoulder and sprinted for it, leaping desperately onto the nearest strong bough. He began his climb, limb by limb, no longer paying heed to disguising his movements. Speed was now everything.

The crescendo of the truck's engine increased. It would come down to a matter of seconds before these men, and Gamma, pulled out.

As soon as he sensed he'd made the height, Beta slithered out across one of the branches. As he broke through the foliage, the view down to the track by the water's edge became disturbingly clear.

Two men held the end of Gamma's stretcher, about to slide him onto the truck's tray. Still no visible sign of life from his partner. It seemed odd they were removing a lifeless body

15

that could easily be left to the ravages of the wild, but Beta didn't dwell on the thought. Several of the militia had already climbed aboard the truck, waiting for their human cargo to be loaded. Others clambered up to the vehicle's sideboards to catch a ride. As the troops spread out, two things happened; both were life changing.

Beta looked through his sight, his rifle lying low across the branch. One of the stretcher bearers stepped forward, revealing their leader standing beside him... the man Beta and Gamma had come to kill. The leader appeared preoccupied with the loading of the stretcher, too much so for the loading of a mere corpse. Beta swung his scope towards Gamma's face. Then he had it... proof of life. Gamma's chest rose and fell in slow, shallow breaths.

The truck began a gradual roll forward as the leader strode down the side closest to Beta's position, ready to take his place in the cab. A no-win situation. The Marine would have no chance of taking out the soldiers now, but the leader was in clear shot. But where would that leave Gamma?

For a brief moment, Beta scanned his sight between Gamma and the leader. The chest continued to rise and fall. Yes, Gamma was definitely alive.

Beta decided he'd take out the leader. Despite his orders to extract himself from the area as soon as his mission had been completed, he'd then track down Gamma and get them both out, if they lived. As his own breathing eased, he began to squeeze the trigger gently; death's caress.

Seconds remained. Betta paused his process to scan the area one more time before returning to Gamma's face. He felt himself go numb as his partner stared straight back at him. Beta shouldn't have been surprised. The Special Forces man possessed the eyes of a hawk. There would have been a glint of metal through the leaves, something that would have given Beta away.

Again, he flicked his view back to the leader, now four paces from the cab, not hurrying. A victory march. When it was over, Beta would have to get out of there quickly. His chance of surviving the attack would be minimal. His tree, and those on either side, would be obliterated by automatic fire seconds after he took his shot.

One more quick glance at Gamma before he'd fire his round and escape.

What Beta saw surprised the hell out of him. Gamma was mouthing something, talking to him through a face masked in pain. He couldn't make out the words.

"Something... me? What?"

"Kill me!"

Beta squinted. Gamma knew his chances of being rescued by Beta were almost non-existent. He also knew that if Gamma survived his wounds, he'd probably wish he hadn't.

The leader stepped up to the cab.

Fulfill his mission, or take out Gamma, the man who saved his life. There could be only one shot.

Beta stared through the scope, his hands steady as a rock. He made his decision.

17

Chapter 3

Los Angeles... four weeks before today.

Three gunshots echoed over the clatter of galloping hooves. I needed to react quickly or not at all. Crap… too late. The fanfare of blaring brass reverberated across my bedroom.

"Hi-ho Chen," I chuckled, reaching for my cell.

"Sharp? What's so funny at this godforsaken time of night?"

"A private joke between me and my ringtone."

"Huh?"

"You, the theme from the Lone Ranger, cavalry coming to the rescue."

"Ah. So, you gotta minute?"

"For you, always Detective Chen."

"I've got a situation down here that might interest you. Sniper's work, a badass sniper."

Suddenly, I was wide awake.

"Where are you?"

"Down at the LA Docks. I'll text you the exact location."

"I'm on my way."

"Bring your mate."

"Greatrex?"

"No. Freakin' Tonto. Who do you reckon?"

I hung up.

I slammed my feet onto the floor. Not a great idea. My head pulsed like a kick drum. The night before had been challenging. We'd done a corporate show with Robbie West, aging 80's megastar, to the wealthy. Afterwards, the band headed down to Medina's, the best bar in the world. Between Robbie's amorous stories of a rock star's life and the tales of our veteran bass player, Barry Flannigan, touring with just about every legendary performer in US history, we consumed way too much scotch.

Detective Samuel Chen had helped Jack Greatrex and me out of a tight spot in the Californian desert a while back. If he needed my help, he'd get it. One marksman to another, only this marksman had retired... mostly.

Thirty minutes later, Greatrex and I sat in my none-too-new Jag XJS, rolling down the Seven-Ten toward the location Chen sent us.

"Did he give you any details?" asked the big fella.

"Only what I told you on the phone. Sniper, LA Docks. That's it," I replied.

"Why call you?"

"I guess we're about to find out."

"Nicholas, I have the classic bad feeling about this." He'd still come along for the ride.

"Just a bit of professional courtesy. What could go wrong?"

"Whatever goes right when you get that glint in your eye? You do remember you're a retired sniper?"

"Touché, but being a working musician does allow a little time to help your mates."

We drove on in silence.

Eventually, we swung off the Seven-Ten onto Terminal Island. A skip past the Federal Maritime Commission headquarters, and we arrived at the container port that Chen had identified. An alien planet. Huge containers stacked one upon another formed lanes and streets. This place was a world in itself.

A uniformed LA Port Police officer met us at the gate. We followed his vehicle down several meandering alleys. Eventually we rounded a corner to arrive at a cement square surrounded by containers on three sides. The fourth side lay exposed to the water's edge.

In the center of the square several uniformed and plain clothed cops hovered around a motionless body lying on the concrete. A forensic team appeared immersed in their work, photographing and measuring everything that could be photographed and measured.

Detective Samuel Chen of the Los Angeles Asian Crime Unit looked up as we pulled to a halt a respectful distance from the scene. He greeted us with a wry smile.

"Good to see you again, Sharp, you too Jack." He offered his hand before turning to the woman next to him. "This is Nora Bartel. She's with the Los Angeles Port Police. This is her neck of the woods."

"Pleased to meet you, Officer Bartel." It occurred to me that most men would be very glad to meet Nora Bartel.

"You too, Mr. Sharp. Sam tells me you're a man to be respected. I gotta say, my gut instinct is to discourage anyone who inserts themselves into an investigation of mine." She patted her sidearm as she spoke. "Maybe not this time."

Bartel smiled. I couldn't read it, yet I sensed a cold edge.

Perhaps in the wrong circumstances, a lot of men would be very unhappy to make this lady's acquaintance.

"So, Detective Chen what brings you, and by proxy me, down here?" I asked.

"The first answer is easy, Sharp." Chen bent down to remove the obligatory sheet from the corpse at his feet. "This is Officer Elison Gao. He's one of mine. Nora notified me immediately the body was found."

I grimaced. "Sorry Chen."

"And our involvement?" enquired Greatrex.

Chen smiled. "A little more circumspect. We've been here for some hours. Our forensic team's initial explorations tell us that the bullet entry to the chest indicates the shot was made from some distance away... at a sixty-degree angle."

"And?" I asked.

"Well, here's the thing. Take a look around, Sharp. Can you see any location, more than a mile distant, that would result in a sixty-degree entry wound?"

I scanned the horizon. "A passing boat or ship?"

"Nothing has been past here in the last twenty-four hours. Did you think we didn't consider that?" Bartel was growing impatient. It hadn't taken long.

I eyeballed the area again. The containers were too close to the dead man to allow for that angle of wound. Each stack appeared high enough to prevent a direct shot from anywhere further afield. The bullet came from the seaward side. I glanced at Greatrex. He'd been strolling around, casual to an onlooker, but I knew he was taking in everything, processing.

The big fella stared at me before shaking his head.

"I can't see it, Chen. The forensic guys must be wrong," I announced.

Chen raised his eyebrows. "I doubt that. Think further afield." The detective motioned with his eyes across the water.

"You're not serious," I said.

Chen remained silent.

To the east stood a large crane. Perfect for a sniper's hide. There was only one problem: the two and a half miles separating us. The longest confirmed kill shot in history was just over two miles, credited to a Canadian special forces' sniper. Many experts had called it a fluke. I was undecided.

"Couldn't be done Chen. That's at least half a mile further than the closest confirmed."

This time Nora Bartel raised her brows, turning to Chen. "You said he'd consider it, not rule it out straight away."

Chen turned to face me. "Maybe you're right, Sharp. Maybe we've made a bad read of the whole situation. But bear with me for a second. If your life, or the life of someone you cared about, depended on making that shot, would you give it a go?"

"You bastard, Chen."

Bartel tilted her head, confused.

Chen responded. "I've seen Sharp make a shot the history books wouldn't believe. He made it because he had to. That's my point."

A backhanded compliment if ever there was one. "But I didn't make this shot, Detective. There are several hundred witnesses that can put me on a stage in downtown LA at the time you figure your colleague died."

"Not for one second Sharp, do I suspect that you're the shooter here. But in my experience, the top players in the business tend to either know each other, or at least be aware of each other."

"You're a marksman, Chen," I responded.

"But not in your league Sharp. What I'm asking you is who the hell would have the skill set to do this? I'm certain it was nobody local or known to us. FYI, the reason Officer Gao had been down here - we had intel suggesting an international assassin of some sort may be passing through the port this week. A suggested link to China meant the ACU involvement."

I studied the body lying at my feet, before raising my gaze to the crane, way too far away. My final glance was to Jack Greatrex. He shrugged his shoulders. This would be my call.

I considered everything: timing, prevailing winds, terrain. When I was done, I considered them all again. No one spoke. No one interrupted me.

I inhaled deeply. "There is only one man I know, or I should say knew, who would have had any chance of making this shot. He was the best of the best, but I'm afraid knowing his name will not help you at all."

"Why is that? asked Chen.

"Because he is dead, and he's been that way for a long time."

Chapter 4

"You know there have been rumors," said Greatrex.

"Yeah, I caught a couple of things, but nothing substantial." The Jag raced along the highway back toward my apartment in Venice.

"I heard ex-military, either European or British, highly skilled."

"That narrows it to a few thousand. How can you possibly link this to *him*?" I inquired.

"Well, there's the thing. It seems that for years, this mythical operator had disappeared off the map. Talk was he'd been working for another government."

"It doesn't connect. Whose talk?"

"The general."

My shoulders sagged. A lifetime ago, General Colin Devlin-Waters had been our commanding officer in Iraq. He'd always been a reliable source of underground information. In fact, I'd never really known him to be wrong.

"Well, he's wrong," I suggested, maybe a tad belligerently.

Greatrex continued. "The general stated that a mole in China's intelligence system told him that they had a western player in custody for an extended period. They turned him eventually, then sent him out to work for them. At some point around two years ago, he went rogue."

I pressed down on the gas pedal. Speed, a great distraction. Greatrex just raised an eyebrow.

"I prefer it when you use the piano as your therapist rather than the car, especially when I'm in it."

I pressed harder. The big fella grimaced.

"Why did the Chinese contact give this information to the general?" I inquired.

"Apparently, some people in positions of responsibility within the Chinese government suspect that the assassin may come after them. Retribution. They don't like the idea, accordingly they're happy to have some help in finding this guy."

"You mean killing him," I suggested.

"Pretty much."

I considered Greatrex's words. "It still doesn't add up. There may well be a guy, an assassin, and he may well be a threat to a few corrupt Chinese power brokers, but on no level does that tie into the man we're talking about."

We drove on in silence for several minutes. My mind drifted back through the years to another time, another place. A dangerous place. I'd been in plenty of those, but everyone remembers their first. That was my first.

"No way, not a chance. I virtually saw him die," I blurted out.

"Virtually." Jack Greatrex: infinitely patient man, in most instances.

"Well, he was minutes away from an almost certain death."

"Almost."

"Those smug replies are quite annoying." I glanced across to Greatrex's large presence in the passenger seat as I spoke. He nodded. Infinite patience.

Finally. "There's more," announced the big fella. "Do you want to hear it?"

"Do I?" I noted the first hint of doubt in my voice.

"I guess not, but you should."

"Okay, bring it on." Nicholas Sharp, graceful in defeat.

"The general mentioned that his contact claimed their man had originally been captured in Colombia."

If I could have pushed the gas pedal through the floor, I would have. I satisfied myself by taking a sweeping left-hand bend without slowing down at all. The rear wheels squealed.

"Impressive driving," declared Greatrex. "Except that you just missed our turn."

Crap.

We headed down the highway, wasted miles until we could double back. Finally, we found an interchange and made the move.

Once we'd reversed course, the conversation continued.

"So, keeper of all wisdom, when did you discover this?" I asked.

"The general phoned me two days ago. He wanted to give me a heads up… and keep an eye on you."

"Why the hell didn't he call me?"

"Didn't want to worry you."

"I'm not a child."

"You're driving like a petulant teenager and you're about to miss the exit again if you're not planning on slowing down."

I touched the brakes and swung the wheel right. This time, the squeal became a holler.

"Mmm," Greatrex responded. Patience *and* understatement. "Note to self, don't give Nicholas bad news while he's driving."

I grunted. I *was* being petulant. I trusted Greatrex and the general more than any two people on earth.

We sped towards the beach. I sensed this conversation wasn't over.

"You've spoken to the general again, haven't you?" The big fella flinched. My driving didn't cause the reaction. His guilt did.

"Yup."

"When?"

"This morning."

I glanced at him. If I raised my eyebrows any higher, they'd have grazed the roof.

"I've been waiting for the right time," he added.

I accelerated again, on purpose.

"Turns out this wasn't it," Greatrex smiled as he spoke.

"And?"

"At four o'clock this morning, Washington time, the general received another call from his contact. Apparently, the mole sounded agitated, perhaps even desperate. The Chinese don't like getting things wrong.

"I repeat... and?"

"Nicholas, pull over."

Shit, this wasn't going well. I slammed my foot on the brake pedal and nosed the Jag toward the curb.

Greatrex waited until the car had rolled to a halt. He looked me straight in the eye.

"The general's contact in China had more information. He claimed the person in question, the guy they held captive all these years, and then lost control of, was highly skilled.

27

Allegedly, he came from the British special forces, a trained sniper.

I didn't respond.

"Nicholas, the operative provided a name."

I felt cold. Like ice.

The big fella took a deep breath. "Nicholas, the general was told the assassin's Chinese operational handle—Night Eagle. But the general pushed him for more. Eventually, the source revealed the operator's real name. It was Lachlan Byrn.

If blood could freeze like a river...

Chapter 5

"Their information may have been wrong. They might have latched onto that name from some discarded report. It all happened a long time ago."

"Nicholas," said Greatrex. Stern teacher.

"Hell, I went back to look for him... you know that. I spent three weeks combing every inch of the jungle and the neighboring villages. I established hides, I watched, I listened. I saw no sign at all that he remained alive."

"Was there any proof of death?"

An unconvincing silence.

We sat in my apartment overlooking the beach. The first thing I'd done when we returned from the docks was to pour us both a scotch. Never mind the hour. The day had taken a wrong turn.

"It nearly cost me my place in the squad, taking leave to go back. They said I was being overly emotional... too connected."

Greatrex grunted.

"I was just being thorough," I continued. "I owed him that much."

I watched the waves pound the sand across the road. Relentless. Like guilt.

"You couldn't have done more," said the big fella.

"He saved my life."

"And you tried to save his."

"He didn't want me to save it. That's the point. I always thought he somehow knew he'd survive his wounds, and he knew what lay in store for him if he did," I responded.

"Nicholas, they trained you to hunt down and kill the enemy, not to take the life of a fellow soldier. You reacted as any of us would, except you took it further by returning to Colombia to search for him." Greatrex's words were well-intended but didn't really help.

I stood up, emptied my glass in one gulp and marched to the trolley that acted as my bar. I picked Greatrex's glass up along the way. After topping him up, I filled mine before emptying it down my throat and filling it anew. My drinking wasn't a problem… then again, it probably wasn't a virtue. I seemed to collect guilt like others collected baseball cards.

I passed the big fella his scotch.

"He didn't just want me *not* to save him, he wanted me to shoot him, Jack, as though he were the enemy."

As I spoke, I stared out to the restless movement of the Pacific. And then did it some more.

"There are two things at play here," I began. "First, I must be certain if Lachlan Byrn is still alive. If he is, then we'll need to meet."

Greatrex interrupted me. "I'm thinking that's not such a great idea. From what you've said of Byrn, he wasn't the most balanced of individuals in the first place."

"True. I never really understood how he managed to pass

the special forces entry psychologicals. Certainly, the SBS is the one arm of the British war machine that encourages, if not requires, a certain ruthlessness. But Byrn's profile ran a light year beyond ruthless."

"Maybe he had strong acting skills?"

"Perhaps," I reflected, "or maybe because he was such a good shot, they simply overlooked the dark character traits."

"Either way," said Greatrex, "consider Byrn's state of mind today. The battle in the jungle, years of captivity, consistent torture at the hand of his Chinese interrogators, his escape."

"And his incredibly natural talent as a killer," I added.

"Exactly. How do you reckon he's going to feel about you now?"

"I'm not sure that he feels."

"Do you remember how your anger at Giles Winter simmered and grew over the years? He'd betrayed you, and when he reinserted himself into your world and threatened those you cared about, you didn't hesitate to take him out."

My mind drifted back to the cliff above the Solent, on the Isle of Wight. The explosion in the darkness as I'd ended a very bad man's life without one inch of regret.

I took a slug of my drink. Time to refocus. Too much memory lane stuff going on here.

Greatrex continued. "If you made that kill without blinking, and you're almost a balanced individual, what would a man like Lachlan Byrn be capable of?"

"Thanks for the vote of confidence," I retorted, mildly sarcastic. "But I get what you mean. He probably considers me as the reason his life went to shit."

"Well, you are." Greatrex, never subtle. "I would recommend you keep your distance. Besides, the chances of coming

31

across him are slim, anyway. Now, what was your second point?"

"Helping Chen with his sniper issue," I replied.

"Do you suspect that's related to your first point?"

"Apart from the fact that whoever took the shot at the docks is an incredible marksman, and that there are rumors of a high-level professional assassin on the loose, and that you're telling me the greatest sniper I've ever met survived certain death, and that both he and this situation have a link to the Chinese… I see no connection at all."

"Exactly," Greatrex responded.

Once more, I turned away from my trusted friend and resumed my gaze over the golden hot sands of Venice Beach. The crowds cruising the boardwalk seemed suddenly disconnected from my reality.

The waves kept pounding at the sand. One after another… and always one more.

In an instant, I'd returned to the Colombian jungle, inching my way out of the river. Damn that mission, damn those relentless militias, damn the people who sent us there.

Above all, damn Gamma. Although he couldn't really go to hell because I'd already delivered him there.

Chapter 6

Greatrex had his Nissan packed with keyboards and guitars, about to head down to Medina's. It was Kenny Medina's birthday and a few musician friends planned on getting together to give our benevolent mentor a night to remember. No information had been shared through any social media. We didn't want Kenny to get wind of it, and we certainly wanted to avoid the media picking it up. The long list of people Kenny had helped over the years included a fair few popular celebrities. We wanted to keep the event personal and private, just for Kenny.

I'd reached the bottom of my apartment's stairs when my cell sounded. Chen.

"Detective, what can I do for you?" I replied.

"Thanks for the information you sent through, Sharp. It allowed us to look in the right places. I don't know where you find that stuff out, but your source is gold."

No one ever really understood the resources General Colin Devlin-Waters could muster. I certainly didn't comprehend the full depth of his reach.

"Have you made any progress?" I responded. "Personally,

I'm not convinced it's possible that Lachlan Byrn is still alive. I believe this could be about nothing."

"Oh, it's possible alright."

"You sound awfully confident of yourself, Chen. What's up?"

"Well, I'm not sure whether this will make your day or torpedo it, but you better get down here."

I'd arrived at the car. Greatrex stood impatiently at the driver's door, pointing at his watch.

"I don't really have time for a social visit. We've got a commitment."

"You will want to make time for this Sharp."

Chen was beginning to annoy me. I had a show to do.

"Sorry Chen, I'm planning on catching up with an old friend."

"A prophecy if ever there was one," replied the detective. "I have an old friend of yours in a holding cell down here at the National Center. I'm thinking you may want to catch up with him. He goes under the name Lachlan Byrn."

Greatrex must have read the expression on my face as easily as one of his Jack Reacher books. Concern radiated from his worried look. I placed a hand on the roof of the car, or rather, it placed itself. I found myself starting down at the curb as though it held some profound wisdom.

"Sharp, Sharp!"

"Right here Chen," I responded, "we'll come straight down."

"What the hell is wrong?" asked Greatrex as we both climbed into the SUV. "You look like you've just seen a ghost."

"Not yet," I replied, "but I'm about to."

It was mid-afternoon when we pulled up at 100 West 1st

Street. The Civic Center had replaced the original Parker Center as the LAPD's headquarters. I knew some veteran cops who missed the old place, maybe even shed a tear when they demolished it. But the new complex contained much better facilities.

I called Chen once we'd found a park and reached the front of the building.

"I'm coming down," he said. Apparently we deserved the five-star treatment.

A few minutes later, Samuel Chen appeared through the building's massive doors.

"Come up to my office. They're moving Byrn to an interview room. I'll get you up to speed before you see him.

See him. The last time I'd laid eyes on Lachlan Byrn, he'd been lying semi-conscious on a make-shift stretcher in Colombia mouthing the words 'kill me'.

An elevator and several corridors later, Greatrex and I sat opposite Chen's service issue desk waiting for news. We'd hardly spoken on the way down in the car. The big fella had respected my need to gather my thoughts. Personally, I figured I'd left them scattered all over the sidewalk outside my apartment.

"Walk us through it, detective," I said.

"Well, it all began to come together after you provided Byrn's identity and description. In the age of continual terror threats, our border security is first class."

I interrupted. "Surely he wouldn't have used his own name."

"No, not for a second," responded Chen. "We did manage to get one of our LAPD forensic sketch artists to create a facial image. Coupled with what we can do with digital imaging these days, that gave us a starting point. Our IT crew created

35

an algorithm that searched all incoming ports of entry, air, sea and road. A few years ago, that would have taken weeks."

We both nodded, waiting for Chen to continue.

"Of course, my people, along with Bartel and her team, were working the docks. Over the last forty-eight hours, anyone breathing in the dock area would have seen that picture."

"And?" I asked.

"Good old police work, doing the slog… and we got lucky. A crane driver recognized the image, said a man looking like that had been poking round the container areas the week before. We sensed we may be getting close. But of course, close isn't close enough."

I didn't speak. Greatrex didn't speak.

Chen continued. "It was one of Nora Bartel's men who broke it. He planned to cruise the area between the International Seafarer's Center in Long Beach and the Union Hall in Wilmington. Sailors go there to find work."

I nodded. Chen took that as his cue to carry on.

"Bartel's man had been cruising East E Street when he noticed a man fitting your bloke's description walking somewhat unsteadily down the road. It's an industrial area, and he seemed to be weaving around some large bins parked alongside the road. The cop figured him to be an out of work sailor or stevedore who'd had too much to drink, but thought he'd check him out anyway. The man fled, the cop ran him down on foot and cuffed him. The suspect denied having any ID, so Bartel's man searched him. Came up with a wallet."

"And the ID in the wallet?" asked Greatrex.

"Inconsequential," replied Chen.

"It would be," I added. 'How many international assassins walk around with their real identification on them?"

"Exactly," acknowledged Chen. "Bartel's man intended to take the suspect down to the Long Beach Police on West Broadway. When he decided to pat the fellow down one more time to ensure he had no weapon before putting him in his car, he identified something in the lining of the suspect's coat."

"On the ball," declared Greatrex.

"Yup. He hauled the coat off him. Apparently, both the man and his clothing reeked of alcohol. The cop didn't feel threatened, but because of the nature of our search target, he took precautions. He used a second set of cuffs to attach the guy to the vehicle. He then ripped the lining open and found another set of ID and some pills."

"And?" I grew impatient.

"The pills are being analyzed in our lab. You've probably guessed by now. The ID read Lachlan Byrn with an address in Jakarta, Indonesia.

"That simple," said Greatrex.

"You get lucky sometimes," Chen responded.

I wasn't so sure. Mind you, I wasn't sure of anything I'd heard over the previous few days.

"Let's go and meet the enigmatic Mr. Byrn, shall we?" suggested Chen.

We traversed more corridors, two elevators, and some additional narrow passageways before we stood outside a series of interview rooms. The cop on duty nodded to Chen and buzzed us through.

I steeled myself. However this moved forward, it wouldn't be easy... for anyone.

Three doors down on the left, another cop stood guard. They weren't taking chances. He opened the door. Chen entered the room first. Greatrex stepped back to let me through. I didn't hesitate, but I didn't rush either.

"Mr. Byrn," said the detective.

Stepping out from behind him, I immediately recognized the mane of wavy dark hair. It appeared longer than it had been when he'd been in the forces, and thinner, yet still distinctly familiar. He sat handcuffed in the chair, his face hanging down, his eyes cast toward the floor. He didn't even bother looking up as we strode in. The attitude was familiar too.

"Mr. Byrn," repeated Chen, "we need to talk."

A muffled grunt, almost a low-pitched growl. Disdain.

"Mr. Byrn."

Nothing more.

I took a pace forward. "Lachlan?"

Another grunt/growl. No sign of further movement.

"Gamma?" I tried.

For a moment, there was no reaction. Then gradually the head began to rise. When his face ran perpendicular to the floor, he suddenly flicked his head backward, his hair retreating to reveal a deeply creased expression. Sunken scars framed each side of a nose that had clearly been broken more than once.

I stared at him, my disbelief battling my sense of remorse. It was a face that had probably seen a myriad of battles, both within and without. It bore a demeanor of weary contempt, as if nothing could touch him now. It was a face whose crevices spoke of life and death many times over.

But it was not the face of Lachlan Byrn.

We'd been had.

Chapter 7

The late afternoon sun skipped across the water like a pod of shimmering dolphins. In the distance a silhouetted flotilla of sails cruised toward the marina, pushed ahead by the gentle afternoon breeze. Tranquility at its best... but not for us.

Greatrex and I had our haunts. The Mariasol Cocina Mexicana perched on the ocean end of the Santa Monica Pier had become one of them. The view was calming on a good day. We hoped this would be a good day.

The day before had been mixed. Eventually, the suspect in the interrogation room, the man Chen had identified as Byrn, came clean. He'd been paid five hundred dollars to make his presence felt around the wharfs and the sailors' hangouts for a couple of days. He'd spent most of the money on booze and had no idea why he'd been requested to do what he did. He'd been broke, now he was cashed up. He didn't really care.

Chen had pushed hard about who paid him the cash and provided the coat. When the out of work sailor described his benefactor, he could have been describing himself.

Once the guy had been interrogated, we said our goodbyes to Samuel Chen and drove straight to Medina's. Kenny

Medina had been surprised by the secretly planned show and overwhelmed by the list of well-known faces that had stepped up onto the stage as proud conspirators.

The evening distracted us. After a suitably late wake up, we decided to meet here and refocus. I nursed the cold beer in front of me, letting the breeze clear my foggy brain. The promise of the Mariasol's enchiladas was encouraging.

"The nut at the Civic turned out to be a waste of time. What in God's name would anyone have to gain by setting themselves up, or being set up, as a fake Lachlan Byrn?"

A stunning sloop, it looked to be around forty feet, glided silently past, tilting gently toward the sun. It was fifty yards distant before I answered.

"I've been working on that. I'm not certain, but I've got an idea or two."

"Pray continue, oh wise one." Greatrex.

"I'm still not convinced that Lachlan Byrn is alive," I began. "Before you say anything, I'm well aware I might be kidding myself. Perhaps someone is just trying to mess with my head, or setting up a yet to be revealed scenario, and using Byrn's name as a distraction."

"Mmm," came the reply. Unconvinced. "Who? Why?"

"I have no idea."

Pause.

"All right, ye of little faith," I continued. "Let's suppose Byrn is still alive. Let's take it further and assume he killed Chen's man on the docks."

"Making more sense to me already," replied Greatrex.

"Then we get back to your original question — why the Lachlan Byrn masquerade?"

No response.

"At first I thought that, assuming he's alive…"

"You said that."

"At first, I thought he figured that we'd somehow stumbled onto his existence. He once described to me his habit of observing the reaction to his work… from a distance. He said he liked to see the damage he'd caused and identify his pursuer."

"Interesting idea. Unusual in a sniper," observed the big fella.

"He was unusual, on many levels, but that's not the point. He may have witnessed you and me turning up at the docks at Chen's request. He might have decided to send me a message, indirectly. Hence the 'what will we do with Lachlan Byrn, the drunken sailor?' bit."

"You don't believe that now, do you?" asked Greatrex.

"No, I don't. It seems totally unnecessary and too personal. I worked with Byrn. He'd never waste time on the unnecessary, and nothing was ever personal."

"So?"

"So, if he's alive…"

"Mmm…"

"If Byrn is alive and wanted us to have that knowledge, he would have had a reason for us… me, knowing so. Jack, Lachlan Byrn is a ruthless man, and he lives in a world of machine-like calculation. I'm aware that all snipers process that way on the job, but not to the extent Byrn does. He's not only compulsive, he enjoys it."

"Therefore…"

"Therefore, Byrn not only wanted you and me to know he remained alive and operational, but he needed us here, in LA, chasing him down."

41

"A distraction."

"Yeah, that's what scares the hell out of me. If Lachlan Byrn needs to distract me. What is he distracting me from?"

The waitress arrived with two large plates of the best enchiladas in town. She also brought a couple more beers. A more immediate distraction.

We spent thirty minutes enjoying our meal and exploring our thoughts. That was the thing between Greatrex and me. The communication didn't need to be verbal.

I reckoned I sat five mouthfuls away from satisfaction when Greatrex's cell rang.

"Kaitlin."

I put down my fork. Kaitlin Reed was my on-again, off-again flame, in addition to being the General's stepdaughter. Although our current status was 'on hold', it seemed unusual for her to call Greatrex rather than me. I patted down my pockets. No cell. That explained it. It didn't explain the look of consternation on Jack Greatrex's face as his brows furrowed and his neck muscles tensed.

"We'll be right there," he hung up.

"Is Kaitlin back in town? I understood she'd been visiting her stepdad in Maryland."

Jack appeared preoccupied, as though my question was irrelevant. He pushed his plate away before scrutinizing my face.

"Nicholas, the general's been shot."

Chapter 8

Seven hours later, Greatrex and I stood at the foot of the general's bed at Walter Reed. The great man looked pale, worn out. He'd only been out of surgery a short time. Although his speech was slurred, his mental faculties seemed to be returning at lightning speed.

"Nick, Jack, it's wonderful to see you, but you didn't have to come all the way across the country to check on me."

"There was no chance of us not coming, sir, and I think you're aware of that."

The general began to shrug before a grimace of pain shot over his face. A bullet tearing into your shoulder will do that to you.

"I'm glad you came." Kaitlin Reed stood by her stepfather's bedside. She also looked drawn and exhausted, her long blond hair bound untidily in a ponytail. She wore no make-up and her almost trance-like mannerisms suggested that she may be bordering on shock. Seeing someone you love shot is not an easy experience, even for a person as resilient as Kaitlin.

General Colin Devlin-Waters was a lucky man to have a stepdaughter who revered him so much. That said, he probably didn't feel so lucky right at this moment.

The general turned his head back toward me.

"I'll tell you Nicholas, I'm pretty fortunate."

Well, there you go.

"How so, general?" inquired Greatrex.

"The shot I took came from the shore. There were no boats within several miles of where I'd anchored."

The general had been out alone in his luxurious cruiser. Like me, he'd always enjoyed the water. Once a Marine.

"Makes sense," said Greatrex, "but where does the luck come into it?"

"The round that hit me packed a lot of power and sent me sprawling across the deck. I blacked out for a bit. When I came to, the cockpit was awash with blood. It was lucky I'd been leaning over my tackle box. Had I been standing, the bullet would have ripped through my chest and that, as they say, would have been that."

Kaitlin shook her head, not liking that scenario at all.

"Why were you alone on the bay?" I asked.

"A very good question," interrupted Kaitlin. "My mother is away working in Europe. I told this stubborn fool of a man not to head out on the water alone. I mean… at his age."

As fit as any person in his late sixties could be, if the general wanted to go boating, nothing short of a hurricane would stop him.

"Who had knowledge of your trip today?" I asked.

The general wriggled uneasily in his bed. He wouldn't be resting in comfort for a while.

"I'd told the staff at home, on the property. I didn't tell Kaitlin because I figured she'd make a fuss. Anyway, the boat has a radio, and I had my cell with me."

I decided to reserve my opinion with regard to his luck. More information required.

"So, what happened when you regained consciousness?" I asked.

"Well, it became pretty obvious I needed to stop the bleeding, so I grabbed some towels and plugged myself up."

"No second shot?"

"None. I suspect the shooter had decided he'd taken me out and made his escape."

"Mmm…" Somehow, that didn't ring true.

"I headed the boat back towards the marina and rang Kaitlin on the way. She alerted the authorities. I must say, I began to feel pretty groggy on the return journey. It was a relief when the Marine Police showed up."

"It was dark when they brought him back to the dock," said Kaitlin. I waited for him along with the police, coast guard, FBI and whoever else you can think of. The night lit up with more red and blue flashing lights than you'd find at a rave."

Not only incredibly stubborn, the general was also a very important man. The authorities don't like it when assassins go around shooting important people.

"What's the prognosis?" asked Greatrex. "Are you going to be alright, sir?"

"Don't ask him," said Kaitlin. "He'll just say everything is fine. The bottom line here is that my stepfather lost a great deal of blood. He almost didn't make it. The bullet missed every vital organ, although I'm not sure how. Complete recovery will take a long time."

Kaitlin shifted her gaze from her stepfather to me. I'd have put money on what came out of her mouth next.

"Nicholas, you've got to identify this person, the shooter.

Once they become aware that my stepfather is still alive, they'll come after him again. We need to find out who wants him dead, why he's a target and, above all, stop them before he or she succeeds."

I tilted my head slightly. She continued.

"The authorities will be on it, of course. I've even had a call from President Blake. I'm certain he'll make sure they throw everything at this, but we must do more. *You* must do more."

Kaitlin's eyes started to water up, tears were seconds away. Kaitlin Reed is not a person who cries easily. She's also not a person who finds it easy to ask for help.

"No."

Kaitlin's mouth dropped open; she balled her fists in frustration.

"If my stepfather means anything to you, if I mean anything to you, Nicholas Sharp, you'll step up and find out what the hell is going on."

"No."

On the other side of the room, Greatrex glanced down. I figured he might have an idea where this was going. The general reached out and took Kaitlin's hand. For a man who appeared only half-awake, his eyes opened wide with surprise. Perhaps he was perplexed, perhaps disappointed.

"Again, no." I stared into Kaitlin's eyes before looking at the general. "I won't look into this because I don't need to. I know who shot you, general, and I know why."

An uncomfortable silence.

"There was no second shot because the shooter didn't want you dead. Every critical organ was missed because the shooter engineered his shot that way. The result is exactly what he intended. And I'm reasonably sure the shooter didn't intend

46

to make a clean escape."

"What was his intention, Nicholas?" asked the general.

"To be honest, sir, I can't give you precise details, but I can tell you this. This man wanted to get my attention. He also wanted to send me a message, letting me know he could take out any person I cared about any time that suited him."

"What are you saying, Nicholas?" asked Kaitlin, her voice now coldly calm.

"I'm saying that I won't need to find the shooter because he is going to find me."

I glanced at Greatrex. The frown told me he wasn't happy.

"Jack, I was wrong. Lachlan Byrn is capable of making a personal statement, and it doesn't get more personal than this."

The big fella shuffled uncomfortably on his feet, understanding what came next.

I continued. "Right now, I'm a target, and the man who is targeting me is one of the most perilous killers on the planet. Accordingly, as is obvious from today, I'm a very dangerous person to be around."

I paused to catch my thoughts.

"To put it simply, I've got to do this alone, for all of our sakes."

With that, I strode across the room, threw the door open, and marched through the doorway, before I changed my mind.

Chapter 9

LACHLAN BYRN

Lachlan Byrn peered through his binoculars toward the hospital's front doors. The floodlit entrance allowed him to identify people moving in and out of the building, despite the surrounding darkness. He'd blacked out the van's windows with heavily tinted glass. No view in. A clear view out.

Almost an hour after he'd taken up position, Byrn saw Sharp burst through the facility's glass doors. As a sniper, Byrn had been trained to read body language like a book. Sharp's long stride, brisk pace and hard-set jaw spoke of anger, frustration.

That was good. In fact, Sharp's demeanor brought a slight grin to the edges of Byrn's mouth. His prey within his sights, a kill imminent. What could be better?

For Lachlan Byrn… nothing.

He lay the binoculars down on the metal floor next to him and rubbed his eyes. He hadn't slept for two days, but his little helper, the Night Eagle, kept him awake and alert.

Better known in the US as Modafinil, he'd first taken Night Eagle during his time in the Special Boat Service. His British masters didn't really care how he got the job done, so the 'go pill' had been tolerated, as long as he remained effective.

Byrn was always effective.

He supposed he'd become mildly addicted to the drug. Then again, he supposed any addict thought of their addiction as only mild. It didn't matter because he maintained access to an endless supply through his Chinese connections.

Byrn refocused on Sharp. Clearly lit up by the streetlights, the former Marine headed up the sidewalk toward the parked van. Not a problem. As tempting as it was, Byrn wouldn't take Sharp here. Too public. Besides, he remembered Sharp as being pretty good in a close scrap.

In Byrn's mind, Sharp was a dead man walking. No target had yet survived his attention. Although sitting there in the van, with his mark now only yards away, Byrn surprised himself, realizing some indecision regarding Sharp's fate lingered within him. Perhaps too many questions needed answering. Blank passages of time to fill in. A lot of blanks.

The assassin rubbed his dulled gray eyes again. His expression rested in a permanent state of disappointment. Disappointment with humanity, with himself, with life, and today, particularly with Nicholas Sharp. When Lachlan Byrn was disappointed, invariably someone would pay...

After scratching at his pupils until they stung, Byrn reached his right hand into his coat pocket, grabbing a small plastic vial. He emptied out two pills, threw them into his mouth, and swallowed. He checked his palm to ensure neither pill remained lodged in a crevice. He had plenty of crevices, some natural, some not so much. The assassin raised his left hand and stared at his blotched and discolored palms.

At first, he'd been surprised they hadn't crushed his hands.

It turned out his captors understood he'd need them to retain functionality. He'd provide a useful skill set for later use. The burns didn't impede that. He gazed at the scars. Each one a story, a memory.

A reason for revenge.

The damp ceiling was lined with endless cracks. Byrn tried to follow each crack, imagining each one as a road to freedom. They weren't, they were just cracks. He didn't look anywhere else, just straight up to the roof, the road map.

He lay shackled to a wooden board, its edges digging sharply into his back. The shackles' heavy metal cut into his wrists and ankles. A cross beam supported his arms. He'd overheard the guards describe the irons around his extremities as 'Hell's Shackles' and the plank as the 'death bed'.

Death would be good right now. He'd welcome it.

A muted scream filled the room as the guard ground his cigarette firmly into Byrn's palm. The special services operative didn't plan to scream. He never planned to scream. Despite his haunting cry, the burning flesh of his hand wasn't the worst bit. His dread lay in the anticipation of what came next.

He'd been here for months, many months. He'd figured out his jailers' routines. He knew they wanted him to understand their processes. With understanding came anticipation. The knowledge of imminent pain was often worse than the pain itself.

Byrn started to shake... trepidation. He gazed at the map. Perhaps one of the roads led to the sea. He used to like the sea....

He smelled it before he felt it. The bucket of burning, filthy water. Suddenly a flash of pain become a cloak of agony. Could something be sudden if you expected it? The agony became suffocating, unbearable. Byrn knew he'd pass out. Fine. The trouble was he also knew he wouldn't die; he'd be back. Back here.

  Screw the motherfucker who put him here.

Byrn decided to follow Sharp. He'd do it on foot, at a distance. Aware he'd need the van later, he didn't want Sharp recognizing it. The assassin understood there'd be a risk. That was okay, he needed some element of danger. He found it motivating. For a moment Byrn checked himself, recognizing the mistake of needing anything, including emotional release. He'd transcended the attributes of enjoyment, sadness, empathy. The best he could manage was a detached satisfaction.

He waited until Sharp had traveled two hundred yards down the road before he heaved open the vehicle's door and climbed out onto the sidewalk.

Ten minutes later, Byrn decided that Sharp strode with intent, but he noted no sense of directional purpose. Sharp just walked, angry, shaking himself loose.

That suited Byrn. Angry men made mistakes. Byrn had transcended anger, too.

He didn't make mistakes.

Chapter 10

NICHOLAS SHARP

I pounded the sidewalk in fury. The situation was unacceptable. I was bitter because I placed people I cared about in danger. My rage at General Colin Devlin-Waters being shot for no reason other than to gain my attention was beyond words.

Lachlan Byrn was a madman. He'd been on the edge when I'd known him years earlier. Whatever had happened to him since had clearly sent him into another realm. He obviously blamed me. I supposed that in some distorted way he was right. I couldn't change that, but I could find him.

Originally, I'd wanted to talk to him. Now I just craved to kill him.

Jack Greatrex would come after me. The man had had my back since they assigned us together in Iraq, but I would not let him put his own life in needless jeopardy. Byrn wouldn't hesitate to cause some collateral damage to get to me. Not going to happen.

I reached into my pocket and powered down my cell. Off

the grid.

I focused on each forward step, nothing else. Some physical distance between me and my friends was paramount. The streetlights guided me. Somewhere.

I avoided the Capital Beltway and headed toward the river. Perhaps a visit to the parkland near the Potomac might provide some thinking time.

An hour later, I leaned with my back against a tree, searching through the darkness, watching the water ripple under the moonlight. It was a far cry from the Pacific Ocean at Venice Beach, but it would do. The sign said Little Falls Reservoir. In my march here, I'd passed both the Intelligence Community Campus-Bethesda and the International School of Music.

Irony.

Planning time. With my lone wolf status now established, my priority was to locate Byrn. Easier to say than do. If I'd been correct in not needing to find Byrn because he would find me, so much the better.

However, given that scenario, our meeting would be on Byrn's terms, not mine. Not a good idea. The fact was, I needed to draw Byrn out, place myself in a location where I'd be able to control events. This would be all about control.

I also had to stay alive until that moment. If Byrn had eyes on me, he'd have his scope on me as well. Sitting alone in a park may not have been the smartest move, even at night.

Nicholas Sharp… deer in the crosshairs.

Five minutes later, as I made my way back into a more populated area, it dawned on me. If Lachlan Byrn simply wished to take me down, I wouldn't be breathing right now. No, he wanted a confrontation. I'd given him all the chances in the world for a straight kill.

A confrontation. Bring it on.

Chapter 11

BYRN

What the hell was Sharp doing?

Byrn had followed him to a wooded area down by the river. Sharp offered him any number of clear shots, but that wasn't the assassin's plan. His target appeared either exceedingly brave, or just too stupid to understand his predicament.

From experience, Byrn knew that Nicholas Sharp was not stupid.

Clearly Sharp had him figured. He'd exposed Byrn's method as more complex than a simple kill. Smart. For a moment, Byrn considered changing intentions in order to remain one step ahead. Just taking the shot would be easier. It would certainly be quicker.

No, there needed to be more.

Byrn fidgeted. He was focused but edgy. The pills had kicked in, and his senses ran on full alert. Once he'd established Sharp's direction, he'd retrieve the van and make his move. Everything else had been prepared.

Bullshit… Sharp now headed backward, retracing his steps.

Byrn watched his former ally pause under a streetlight before raising his hand to hail a passing cab. That put paid to any attempt to bring the van back into the game. Byrn ran towards the roadway, eyes peeled for another cab. He saw nothing.

The assassin ran onto the road, well aware that it may be a careless move and Sharp might see him. A required risk. Sharp had climbed into the cab and was pulling out from the curb. Byrn glanced behind him. Still no second taxi.

Up ahead a man, gray hair, slightly rotund, mid-sixties, crossed the street. He walked purposefully towards the car park adjacent to the street. Probably finishing a late shift in the building opposite.

Byrn followed.

Clearly illuminated in the floodlit car park, the man pulled out an electronic key, pointed it and clicked. A small Mazda's taillights flashed. That was all Byrn needed. He jumped the garden bed and bolted the ten yards between him and his newfound target. Taken completely by surprise as Byrn grabbed his shoulder and swung him around, his mark dropped his leather briefcase. He opened his mouth to yell. One swift chop to his pharynx rendered the man silent. The assassin shoved him to the ground. As the man struggled, gasping for air, Byrn reached down and yanked his keys away. Killing his victim was unnecessary… as long as he cooperated. Byrn raised one finger, indicating that the man should remain still.

The man lay motionless on the concrete. In doing so he saved his own life.

56

Chapter 12

SHARP

"Head toward the marina district," I instructed the cab driver, an idea slowly forming. Byrn had been a Special Boating Service operator, a sailor through and through. There was a certain poetry in using the water to draw him out.

As the cab sped off, I glanced out the rear window. For a split second, I thought I caught sight of a man matching Byrn's current description jumping into a small car. The cab flew around a bend and the image disappeared. Despite what I'd described to Samuel Chen, I hadn't laid eyes on Lachlan Byrn for years, and the darkness didn't help. What would I know?

Yet perhaps this created an opportunity.

"I've changed my mind," I said to the driver. "Please head back toward the beltway."

The driver rolled his eyes but did what he was told.

"Feel free to take a scenic route. I'm in no hurry."

Encouragement. Dollars in his pockets.

Every few bends, I turned around to check the road behind.

The first two times I saw nobody. The third time, it was there. The small Japanese car I'd noted previously, now positioned a hundred yards back.

Promising.

Ten minutes on, I'd only seen the car once more. My pursuer was efficient, utilizing the darkness to his advantage. I expected nothing less.

"Okay, back to the marina," I told the driver.

After the obligatory eye roll, we headed south.

I needed to find a boat... in Washington DC... at night. How hard could that be?

Chapter 13

BYRN

Byrn knew Sharp was trying to lose him. It figured. Sharp may or may not have seen him commandeering the car, but either way, he'd be on the lookout for a tail. Byrn decided to hang back, touching base with his quarry only when he needed to.

By nature, Byrn was not an improviser. From what he remembered from Sharp's skill set, that method of operation seemed more up the former Marine's alley. Byrn liked to plan, methodically and meticulously. Right now, he was winging it and he didn't like it. On the other hand, he'd broadened his skills since his days in the special services. He'd live with the situation.

He needed to figure out where Sharp was headed. Playing ahead of the game, Byrn could anticipate and rearrange. Sharp's cab had turned, now heading down Wisconsin Avenue, toward the Potomac.

The water, always a great equalizer. But would Sharp lead him onto his own home turf? Byrn appreciated the irony in the expression, but it didn't help him. Sharp had been a Marine, he would be comfortable on water, too. What the hell was he thinking?

Byrn lacked his long-range weapon. That may be a problem. He'd left it back in the van. In the scenario he'd planned, it acted only as backup, anyway. He had a Black Star pistol in a holster under his shirt. The Chinese knock off of the Soviet-type Tokarev TT-33 wasn't his preferred choice, but it was disposable and easily replaced. Byrn remained a Sig-Saur man through and through. He decided he wouldn't need the backup. He'd stay a step ahead of Sharp.

The water. What would he plan if he led a hunter to the river's edge?

Chapter 14

SHARP

Plenty of boats called the Potomac home. Equally important, I'd find adequate sea room once the river led out to Chesapeake Bay. The key would be getting Byrn onto the water before the assassin caught up with me. I had no weapon, and my pursuer would certainly be armed. If I could lure him seaward, the chances might even up. The looming question, how do I create a delay between me accessing a boat and Lachlan Byrn doing the same?

We were almost at the end of Wisconsin when an idea hit me.

"Make the turn onto Massachusetts Avenue," I ordered.

"That won't take us to most of the marinas."

"But it will take us to where I want to go. Capitol Cove."

"The navy yard? They won't let you in."

The Capital Cove Marina on Giovannoli Street formed part of the Joint Base Anacostia-Bolling. I should have thought of it sooner. The general kept his boat there. You needed military or veteran identification to get in.

I had that, and I was pretty certain Lachlan Byrn didn't.

Chapter 15

BYRN

Sharp headed over the Navy Yard Bridge to Anacostia.

Lachlan Byrn possessed an astounding capacity to control his mind in order to focus on the problem at hand. It had always been a strength, but his time in captivity required him to develop the skill further, pushing his psyche to its limits in order to survive, and to stay sane… if that's what he was.

As he swung onto the Anacostia Freeway, Byrn's instincts regulated his driving. The rest of his brain began the analysis, searching for possible locations and conceivable outcomes. He contemplated Sharp's likely actions and reactions based on the knowledge of the man and this environment. He'd had a long, long time to consider what made Nicholas Sharp tick. Now for the payoff.

Sharp wasn't making a run for it. Not in his nature. Byrn had originally thought water, but now Sharp bypassed most of the marinas. The assassin's brain kept calculating, weighing the variables.

Most of the marinas, not all. That was it. Sharp intended on heading to the remaining boatyard in this area. Capital Cove. He would figure that Byrn couldn't get through the gates and would have to double back to another marina to source a boat. That would give Sharp an opportunity to scope things out, perhaps set a trap.

Clever.

With air support out of the question, Sharp would figure his hunter must find a way to keep his prey within reach. On water, that meant a watercraft of some sort. Byrn felt himself being dragged into a scenario of Sharp's making. Not going to happen.

Byrn understood the training, so did Sharp. There would be no alternative strategy... unless you already knew where your quarry was headed.

Sharp had almost been right. Byrn's instinct *was* to grab a boat and follow Sharp down the river. The difference between Byrn and most men was his ability to temper his own instincts. In fact, he shaped them, as many victims had discovered just a little too late.

If Sharp planned to corner him, Byrn would work out how. With that calculation completed, the rest would be easier.

There would be no boat. Lachlan Byrn was back in control.

Chapter 16

SHARP

The cab stopped at the front gate. I flipped my ID to the guard on duty. He didn't seem that interested. Military personnel came and went at all hours. Strolling down Chappie James Boulevard, past the myriad of base housing, there were few lights, and barely a sound. I attempted to appear comfortable and relaxed in case anyone peered out a window. A quick glance rearward to the main gates by the visitor's center revealed no sign of my tail.

Strange. I guess I expected something. Even a flash of passing headlamps.

I edged into the darkness as I passed the coastguard station. When stealing a boat that most likely belonged to a military person, it seemed best to do it quietly. For a brief moment I considered the many armed personnel nearby. Perhaps this wasn't such a good idea.

Too late to go back. Besides, retreat just wasn't my thing.

Capital Cove was a relatively compact facility, yet there appeared to be plenty of craft to choose from. I spied a small runabout, about nineteen feet long, tied to a pontoon near the breakwater. That should do the trick.

Clinging to the shadows, I inched my way toward the vessel. The car park was well lit, but the boats sheltered in a gloomy dimness. Five minutes later, I clambered off the pontoon onto the runabout's deck. The craft dipped to one side under my weight. I crawled forward to the driver's seat, easing myself under the wheel housing. Two minutes later, I had the ignition hot-wired. The low burble of the inboard engine throbbed to life.

I'd stolen a boat once before, in Venice, Italy. I seemed to be getting pretty good at it.

I slipped the ropes and moved quietly onto the river, the water splashing gently on the craft's hull. If anyone heard me, I hoped they'd dismiss the vibration as an early morning angler heading out toward Chesapeake.

The waters of the Potomac widened as I eased down on the throttle, but there was no hurry. Byrn would be some distance behind me. I needed to think my plan through. Refine it. I always liked to have a plan.

Chapter 17

BYRN

Sharp was trying to turn the situation around.

Byrn decided that if he'd been in Sharp's position, he'd find a boat, get a decent head start, and then search for a location to create an ambush. Plenty of tributaries ran into the Potomac, places where Sharp could lie in wait, his vessel concealed from anyone heading down the main channel.

If their positions were reversed, Byrn would choose a spot where the river narrowed and wait. As his opponent passed, he would charge out into the open water. If he managed to avoid being shot in the period between exposing himself and the point of contact, a collision would level the playing field. Then there would be a scrap. It would be messy. Sharp may even believe he would have the upper hand in that situation.

Of course, he'd be wrong. Over the preceding years, Byrn had honed his skills in numerous ways, including water-based combat. There would be no upper hand. Sharp would also be wrong because there would be no collision. With Sharp's intentions now clear in his mind, the assassin would plan for something completely different.

Byrn pulled off the road and studied the Google Earth app on his phone. He traced the Potomac down to the Point Lookout State Park, where the river fed out onto Chesapeake Bay. Sharp would surely plan to strike before that point. Further downstream the water became too wide. He used the app to follow the river slowly back toward DC, calculating every distance, every turn.

He planned Sharp's attack as though it was his own... because now it was.

Chapter 18

SHARP

The plan clear in my mind, I motored toward my destination. I'd been boating with the general and his family several times and knew the river well. I remembered one spot that fitted all my criteria.

The night wind fired tiny, chilled arrows into my face as I steered the boat through the darkness. With my running lights turned off, it was difficult to see far ahead. Fortunately, the bright moon identified enough landmarks to find my way.

Once in position, I'd wait. I'd been trained to wait.

A sniper's routine. Planning, patience, implementation, death.

Before the sun rose, Lachlan Byrn would be dead.

Chapter 19

BYRN

The way forward was now obvious. Byrn had doubled back to the street near Walter Reed, dumped the Mazda, and picked up his van. That also meant he had his rifle, an AW Convert. The AWC could be broken down into parts and carried in a suitcase, making it ideal for Byrn's purposes.

The gun was an integral part of his new plan.

Feeling more secure in his intentions, Byrn cut south to the 301. The van's engine revved loudly as he pushed it along the road, his focus entirely on placement and timing.

Lachlan Byrn fully intended to be in the right place at the right time.

After parking the van in the bush near the western end of the Governor Harry Nice Memorial Bridge, the assassin allowed himself a small grin as he stared at the sign. Irony.

Certainly, no-one had ever called Byrn 'nice'.

The wind whistled northward, up the river from Chesa-peake. Byrn found it invigorating. He clambered down to the water's edge and sheltered behind some scrub. He wouldn't make his shot from there, but he would take his cue. He huddled down and waited. He knew how to wait. He knew how to listen.

Chapter 20

SHARP

It took longer to get to the location than I expected. Twice along the way, I cut the engine, just drifting, listening for the sound of a marine motor across the water.

Nothing.

It didn't matter. I knew he'd come. In his shoes, I would have come. Always the hunter.

The shadow of the headland loomed as I motored down the channel. I planned to wait on the exposed side of the land mass, to the south. They'd be no shelter from the wind, but I'd be hidden from anyone coming down the river.

The engine died as I parted the wires that I'd hot-wired together earlier. After slowly releasing the line that eased the boat's small anchor into the cold water, I found a knife in a fishing basket under the bow. When the time came, I'd use it to slash the anchor rope. At that point, speed would mean everything.

The river water lapped incessantly at the hull, like a child's hands slapping gently on the fiberglass. Almost soothing. I reached over the side, cupped some water in my hands and splashed it on my face. Being caught off guard was not such a good idea.

I sat back in the craft's driver's seat and waited.

Thirty minutes later, I was questioning my own judgement. Thirty minutes after that, when no boat had passed the cove, I knew I'd got it wrong.

Maybe Byrn wasn't following me, maybe he couldn't access a boat. Yet neither scenario rang true. The man was clever and resourceful. If he wanted a boat, he would have found one. I remained certain he'd been watching me, but my plan to lure him out onto the water hadn't worked.

Why?

I ran a couple of hypotheticals over in my mind. Could he still be covering Walter Reed? Perhaps I'd slipped out of there unnoticed. Unlikely. Byrn was far too observant to have missed me, and once I had his attention, he wouldn't want to lose me. Giving up just wasn't in his DNA.

After a further forty minutes, I saw no point in hanging around. I'd head back into DC and regroup.

No need for further stealth. I rewired the ignition, pulled in the anchor, dropped it into its housing, and shoved the hand throttle fully forward. The powerful engine roared, sending the boat into an almost vertical position before the hull settled onto a plane across the waves. As I left the cove, I hauled the wheel to port, ready for the journey back up the river.

Byrn had out maneuvered me and that made me pissed.

Chapter 21

BYRN

And there it was, the thundering howl of a marine engine shattering the near silent marine environment. Byrn had heard Sharp's boat pass almost two hours earlier. He didn't act then. The assassin wanted his prey heading up-river. Credit where due, Sharp had waited patiently for Byrn to turn up. Of course, that would never happen.

Byrn couldn't see Sharp's position from where he now waited on the bridge, but he could hear him coming.

The assassin stood up and placed his bipod carefully on the bridge's railing. He took a deep, slow breath.

It was time to reintroduce himself to Nicholas Sharp.

Chapter 22

SHARP

The first shot ruptured the boat's plexiglass windscreen, piercing through to the throttle. The lever virtually disintegrated under my hand. Instantly, I ducked down, tugging the wheel to the right. At least I still had steering. To keep heading toward the bridge would be suicide, like running naked into a kill zone.

A second later, another round smashed the marine radio to my left. It missed the top of my head by less than an inch. As it turned, the boat keeled up on its starboard side, sending me hard into the hull. In the same moment, torrents of water swept over the bow, drenching me. My hand slipped on the wheel and the runabout turned itself back up the river. Staying low, I wrenched the helm back down. A millisecond after I heard the third shot, fragments of metal, fiberglass and plexiglass showered across the cockpit. Like a cluster bomb.

The fourth round impacted directly behind my seat. I had now lost complete control of the momentum of the craft. With no throttle to temper its forward motion, it remained set at full speed. The bridge was still far too close and despite the darkness the luminous spray kicking up around the boat framed me like a target.

My only hope was distance, as much as possible, as soon as possible.

For a moment, I thought he'd stopped shooting. Then three cracks of gunfire in quick succession peppered the boat's transom. It was amazing the engine wasn't hit, or the fuel line. The craft plundered onward, half in control, half runaway, as it headed down the Potomac toward Chesapeake Bay.

Every second that passed offered hope. Then two more rounds through the rear seats muted my optimism.

Chapter 23

BYRN

Job done. Lachlan Byrn bolted back to the van. Without bothering to stow his weapon, he threw it behind the seat, climbed into the cabin, and flicked the ignition. His face set in grim determination, the assassin pressed hard down on the gas pedal. The vehicle lurched forward.

It was time to close the deal.

Chapter 24

SHARP

The boat surged forward. There was nowhere else to go. As I rounded the Point Lookout Lighthouse, the swell began to build. Chesapeake was in a mood, and I had no way of responding. After several failed attempts to disengage the gas line that passed under the deck, I'd given up. Only managing seconds at a time away from the helm, my efforts became futile. The craft wouldn't slow down until the fuel ran out.

To swing right towards Norfolk and the open water beyond would invite disaster. The swells would increase. The boat barely made it from wave to wave as it was. No. Left it would be. Toward Baltimore.

As the winds picked up, the waves grew white frothy tops, challenging the runabout to pass across each foaming crest. Sometimes the craft would jump the top of a wave and land sideways on the next, digging deep into the water. Each moment seemed like an eternity before the boat righted itself and resumed its journey.

I sat on the back of the seat, the cockpit in ruins. As I

wrestled with the wheel, I strained through the darkness to make out each approaching wall of water. Every single peak passing under the hull seemed a small victory.

One looming question remained, and it had nothing to do with the fact I'd been completely outthought by Lachlan Byrn. I'd grudgingly accepted that. The problem was I didn't know when I would run out of gas. The gunfire had destroyed the fuel gauge, and I couldn't begin to even contemplate abandoning the wheel to investigate the tank in the boat's stern.

Would I make Baltimore? Maybe, maybe not. In the meantime, if I tried to beach the speeding craft, it wouldn't go well. An image of shattered fiberglass, blood, and bone filled my mind.

There was no choice... just hang on for the ride.

Chapter 25

BYRN

Byrn drove like a madman, pushing the black van beyond every limit as he hurled north along the 301. He turned west at the 50, bypassed Annapolis, and made the Chesapeake Bay Bridge with almost no time to spare.

He faked a breakdown on the bridge, lifting the hood and throwing a large flask of cold water on the engine block to emulate steam. Anyone passing by would assume an overheated radiator.

The first rays of dawn were revealing themselves over Kent Island as he cast his eyes south. The assassin was surprised how easy it was. Ten minutes after stopping, he saw a dark speck driving across the water. Five minutes later, he determined it to be a small pleasure craft. Sharp's boat. It was running fast and being thrown around mercilessly by the waves, but each minute it drew closer, the bucketing receded as the vessel entered waters calmed by the leeward side of the island.

Byrn took a risk and withdrew his scope from under his

jacket. He identified a clear image of Sharp sitting on the back of the skipper's seat, clutching the wheel and peering into the rising light. He put the scope away.

Before long, Sharp's craft passed underneath the bridge, leaving a wide white wake behind it. Byrn did nothing to impede its progress. He had something else in mind.

As the boat disappeared northward, Byrn watched it arc to the left, heading toward the Patapsco River and the Port of Baltimore. The assassin almost felt a sense of joy when he heard a faint splutter of the engine in the distance.

It was time to make a phone call.

This couldn't have been more perfect.

Chapter 26

SHARP

It couldn't have been more perfect. Despite the hellish ride, the motor conked out just as the Port of Baltimore came into sight. I tried my cell, but it was out of charge. Not to worry, as the sun continued to rise, the boat traffic would increase. Someone would notice the runabout drifting aimlessly and come to my aid.

I wondered what Lachlan Byrn figured he would gain from the situation. Perhaps the human calculator had miscalculated. Then it occurred to me that numerous dead people had probably thought the same thing.

Best to stay alert.

It took around forty minutes before a small boat headed in my direction. As it neared, I made out a man waving on the foredeck. I waved back, relieved rescue appeared imminent.

As my rescuers drew closer, I figured the craft to be a working boat, possibly a ship's tender of some sort. When they reached a hundred yards north of my position, they waved again.

"Nihao, do you need help?"

"Yes," I responded. "I'm out of fuel."

"We'll come."

As the tender drew closer, two crewmen stood, bracing themselves on the starboard gunnel, beaming from ear to ear. "You are lucky we saw you. It would be easy to be run down by a big cargo ship in this channel."

"Thanks for stopping," I replied.

"We were out fishing, catching some fresh breakfast for the rest of our crew, when we caught sight of you. It didn't seem right."

From both their appearance and accents, I assumed them to be from a ship of Asian origin. The Seaport of Baltimore harbored many such vessels.

"Do you have any spare fuel?"

The shorter crewman threw out a rope as they swung their boat alongside. With the swell a lot more forgiving here, it was an easy maneuverer.

"We will tow you," explained the taller of the two men. "We have fuel on our ship. I'm sure the captain will spare you some."

The second man didn't seem as outgoing. His eyes ran the length of the runabout, surveying its condition.

"Your boat is damaged."

I nodded. "Bad storm."

He shook his head but said nothing more.

Taking the rope up to the bow, I tied a knot around the front cleat. The taller man in the work boat secured the other end to a cleat on its stern. The second man moved forward and applied some gentle power. When the tow rope sprang tight, he gave it more throttle, and we headed into the port.

Nicholas Sharp in calmer waters.

The tow gave me the opportunity to find a toolkit under the bow. I pulled out a screwdriver and performed some makeshift repairs on the throttle. By jamming it deep into the mechanism, I could hopefully maintain some regulation over the boat's speed. Using pliers, I also managed to smash away the layers of jagged fiberglass that had prevented me from reaching my hot-wiring system. Now at least I'd be able to turn the engine on and off.

Having some element of control gave me confidence. I scanned the stern of the craft where the petrol tank hid under the back seat. I felt fortunate that none of the gunshots had ruptured the tank or hit the engine.

Then I considered Lachlan Byrn's accuracy with a rifle. Perhaps 'fortunate' was not the right word.

Twenty minutes later, a substantial cargo freighter towered over our tiny flotilla. As we rounded its stern, I viewed the name *Beijing Pearl* in large red letters. Underneath in small writing appeared a single word: *Tianjin.*

The ship appeared old and unkempt. Streaks of rust cascaded downward over the black hull. The vessel didn't look particularly generous by international standards. I estimated approximately four hundred feet long. It stood decked out to carry containers, but certainly wasn't one of the huge modern freighters.

We edged our way to a point amidships where a gangway had been lowered to water level. The taller of my two rescuers tied the work vessel to the gangway while the other man kept up some power, keeping the tender in position. Once secure, they hauled my boat in and tied it alongside theirs.

"Come," instructed the taller man. "We will go find the captain."

I clambered across the combined gunnels of both craft before reaching the base of the gangway. Ahead of me, the shorter of the crew reached a hand down to help. As I stepped onto the gangway, I glanced back toward the deck of the work boat that rescued me.

Strange. I couldn't see any fishing gear.

Chapter 27

BYRN

Lachlan Byrn gazed across the bay. The sun, now well entrenched, cast a myriad of colors over the waves. Since he was a kid, the water had besotted him. The sea, rivers, lakes. For most of his life, water had represented a calm, settling influence.

And then it hadn't.

His shoulders ached, as though nails had been driven through every muscle... but there were no nails. Three feet above his head, Byrn's wrists pulsed in agony, bound tightly to the bars of the metal cage. He thought he'd been in that position for at least twelve hours, although he couldn't really be sure of any single passage of time.

The dank smell of the swamp below him devoured his senses, cutting through his pain. As ever, the anticipation hung over him like an acid filled cloud.

The water started to lap at the soles of his feet. He sensed its intrusion only seconds earlier. He knew what would happen the moment he heard the brittle screech of the chain grinding above him. It was an odd sensation. It felt more like the water rising than the crate being lowered.

It lapped around his ankles now.

Byrn knew he would count out two minutes before his knees disappeared into the cold murkiness.

A minute after that, the process abruptly stopped.

The first time that happened, he'd allowed himself a glimmer of hope. Not now, not anymore. Hope was a term he no longer entertained.

Around twenty minutes later, the water rose again. His groin, his chest, and then his neck. Suddenly, the machine jerked the crate to a halt, just as the stale water began to slap at his chin. Finally, a fraction of an inch at a time, the crate was lowered further. Water trickled slowly into his mouth. An unwanted poison.

He strained his neck upward, craning for any air he could find. When he sensed a gap between the tiny waves that rippled against his face, he drew a deep breath. Invariably it was followed by gagging as a flood of rancid liquid replaced the air. Still, he had to try.

The chain stopped cranking. Now the water enveloped his mouth, teasing mercilessly at his nose. Any movement of his head caused more waves. The waves intruded into his nostrils like an invading army.

Every part of Byrn's body stretched tight. He fought against any reaction his aching muscles demanded.

He wondered if he would survive this for another twenty-four hours. Maybe it would be better just to submit.... and die.

Chapter 28

SHARP

The breeze slapped at my face the moment I stepped onto the ship's deck. Cables, machinery, and rows of stacked containers filled the space.

"This way, we must report to the captain," said the taller of my guides. I accompanied him along the deck, past some containers that offered temporary relief from the wind, until we came to the vessel's imposing superstructure. The crewman tugged on a handle and a heavy metal door swung open.

Inside, the atmosphere changed completely. Warmth replaced the bitterness of the weather. The wind had given way to the quiet, consistent drone of machinery vibrating through the deck's metallic floor.

An elevator stood on the left side of the corridor we'd entered. Our guide picked up a phone beside it. He spoke briefly, not in English.

"The captain will see you now," he announced, before pressing the open button and ushering me in. The second crewman followed.

The elevator hummed and clanked as it rose several stories. When it finally jerked to a stop, the first crewman reached forward and slid open the door. The view was instantly breath taking.

The Port of Baltimore appeared before us in a flowing, majestic vision. The long expanse of the Patapsco River gave way to a remarkable array of dockyards surrounded by towering city buildings. The city's impressive foreshore beckoned in the distance.

"It's quite something, isn't it Mr.… er?"

"Sharp, Nicholas Sharp." I reached out my hand to the rather stocky, broad-shouldered man before me. His neat, uniformed attire suggested he was the ship's captain.

"I'm Zhào Dingxiang, the commander of this vessel. I see the surprise on your face. The bridge of a ship is as high as most skyscrapers. When we are in port, as you have found, the view is inspiring. It's another matter when we're amid a storm."

The captain offered a warm smile.

"Thank you for your help," I began.

"It is not a problem. I understand your boat has sustained some considerable damage. I'm afraid all we can do is offer you some fuel and send you on your way. We'll be setting sail soon."

"That would be fine, thanks."

Captain Zhào smiled, but I suddenly felt no warmth.

I sensed the two crewmen stepping up on either side of me. Before I could react, they each grabbed an arm. The captain stepped forward, reaching into his coat pocket. He withdrew a syringe. I struggled, trying to shake free, but the men held firm. The man on my left yanked up my sleeve as the captain plunged the needle into my skin.

It was all too quick. Within seconds, the room wobbled, slowly fading in and out of focus. I could barely make out the captain's next words.

"It would appear that you are amid a storm right now, Mr. Sharp, and for me, that is certainly no problem. On the other hand, for you..."

Then the world went dark.

Chapter 29

Today

As his features came into focus, everything became clear. I was a dead man.

The hair appeared longer and more unruly than I remembered, just like the impostor. The face bore a wild intensity, but not his eyes. Normally anger came from the eyes. It was impossible to read what lay behind that dull, gray mask. His emotion came from the tension that drew his skin tight, fighting with the lines, crevices, and scars to dominate, intimidate. His jaw set firm, but the edges of his mouth expressed a mild amusement.

"Sharp."

"Byrn. It's been a long time."

"No shit Sherlock. I suspect you're wishing it could have been longer."

I pulled at my wrists. The bindings wouldn't budge.

"Pointless Sharp."

"Yeah, you said that."

Fear, shock, rage. Call it what you want, the result remained the same. My senses came barreling back.

"You've proved your point, Byrn, but there was no need to shoot the general. I would have come."

"You ignored my first invitation, you disbeliever. I had to make it clear. There could be no other option for you."

"But you didn't kill him."

"You can thank me for that later."

I struggled again, muscles tight with fury. Nothing. Byrn inclined his head, as you would to a child.

"Speaking of not killing someone Sharp. Think back a bit. Do you have any idea what you did to me?"

"I allowed you to live."

"You allowed me to die a thousand times, in a thousand ways. That's a debt I intend to repay… today."

"You've lost perspective, Byrn."

A muted chuckle.

"I never really had much to begin with, did I?"

I didn't answer. There was no point.

"I suppose you'd argue that it wasn't your fault, what they did to me. But you have no idea. None at all."

"I'm not presenting a case to you. Go screw yourself."

"You say that to the man who saved your life?"

I paused, my eyes focused on his. Blankness.

"I'm grateful for what you did. It won't matter, but I went back. I looked for three weeks. You'd disappeared."

For less than a second, a flash of surprise crossed Lachlan Byrn's face.

"You obviously didn't search hard enough. The day after you abandoned me, they took me to a facility in mainland

China. I remained there for two years."

More silence.

"Do you know what they did? Do you have any idea what that can do to a man?"

"Yeah, I can see it right in front of me."

The backhander across my face took me completely by surprise. I lost focus as the pain shot through my temple and across my forehead.

"Point made," I observed. "Mine, not yours."

"You've got balls, Sharp, I'll give you that."

I was done being the victim.

"Byrn, if you're going to kill me, just get on and do it. If you have a speech to make, make it and then pull the trigger. You or me, I don't really care which."

"Not so soon Beta. We still have things to talk about."

"What things? What could we possibly have to talk about?"

Byrn returned to his position behind the light, the loss of his shadow blinding. I squinted. Once more, everything seemed blurred.

A minute later, he returned with a chair. After sitting opposite me, he reached down, flicked a switch and the light went off.

"Story time," he announced.

I almost wished he'd just pull the trigger.

"Before I begin, I've got to thank you, Sharp, for making my job a whole lot easier."

I didn't respond.

"I planned to pull you off the street at an appropriate time. There was a van waiting, and as you just experienced, a syringe full of good stuff, ready to go. To be honest, the plan worried me slightly. I remembered that despite your marksman elitism, you don't mind a bit of a street fight, so I needed to be careful with regard to the timing and location. As it turned out, you solved my problem for me."

"The boat."

"Exactly. It was a nice move to draw me out onto the water. I suppose you figured I couldn't resist, and you were almost right. Until I thought it through. My plan had always been to get you onto this ship. You virtually drove yourself here."

"So, the bit on the bridge over the Potomac was designed to keep me moving along in the right direction?"

"Some encouragement."

I cursed myself for feeling relieved when no bullet had ruptured the boat's petrol tank. I wouldn't underestimate Lachlan Byrn's' guile or accuracy again. Then again, I probably wouldn't have the opportunity.

"So, you're working for the Chinese?"

"The ship seems like a bit of a giveaway, doesn't it? But in fact, no, I'm not. It would be fair to say I have a good working relationship with some sections of the Chinese intelligence community, and I've done some jobs for them. But no, I don't work for the government. I understand some of them are rather scared of me... and quite rightly so."

"It sounds complicated."

"Everything in my life has been complicated since we last met Sharp." Byrn closed his eyes and inhaled deeply. "But I'm working on simplifying it. Truth be told, now that I have no chain of command to report to, I'm really enjoying my work."

Byrn could have been talking about digging ditches rather than graves. His intensity and his nervous and agitated mannerisms led me to suspect he'd descended to a place no man should be.

"What about the man you killed on the docks in LA? I assume that was your work."

"Yeah, a hell of a shot, wasn't it?" Byrn replied. "I did it more for the challenge than the money. I could have taken him out twenty different ways, but that shot seemed more fun."

"You shot a cop. He worked for the LA Asian Crime Unit."

"Do your homework Sharp. Officer Elison Gao was as corrupt as all hell. He'd been embedded within one of the Chinese triads in LA for some time. He's been passing on information regarding the operation of the ACU to his masters. Ask your pal Chen how many times an investigation ran off the rails because of intel leaks. Gao had his hands buried in a sea of activities, including illegal importing of amphetamines, prostitution and people smuggling, and let me tell you, he didn't give a monkey's ass if those people lived or died."

"Can you prove that?"

"I don't have to. I'm sure the appropriate authorities will uncover the facts in due course."

"So, who do you work for?" I asked.

"Whoever the hell I want. You can also interpret that as I kill whoever the hell I want if you like. I wouldn't expect a man with your naïve sense of morality to understand."

I'd been called many things, but never naïve.

"Now, the story of the day," Byrn continued. "How much do you know about our mission to Colombia all those years ago? Did you ever do any ferreting around?"

"It was a mission. It succeeded. Beta made the kill; Gamma was killed or MIA… so I presumed."

Byrn let out a low, guttural laugh, although it seemed to express more pain than humor. For a couple of seconds, he turned away, lost, probably in the Colombian jungle. Eventually, he returned his gaze to me.

"Yes, Beta produced the kill, didn't he? You're a boy scout, Sharp. The mission at all costs, to hell with the collateral expense."

"If you're referring to yourself, you knew the risks going in. You were a professional. Besides, I don't think too many people would call me a boy scout now. I'm out of the service."

"Yeah, I heard that. Figured you for a lifer, family tradition and all that. Who knew?"

I didn't reply.

Byrn sat back in his chair and took a deep, tired breath. He then leaned forward, his face inches from mine.

"You should have bloody looked into it. I had a long time to think about that mission. Years, in fact, working it over in my mind, at least in the periods my mind remained functional. It didn't make sense. The lack of back up, the limited intel and the very small circle of people aware of it. Truth be told Sharp, it wasn't a mission at all, it was a bet."

The assassin leaned back in his chair once more. His eyes squinted, but it had nothing to do with the light. His jaw sagged, just for a few seconds.

"We were totally played Sharp. You and me."

I had no idea what he was talking about.

"You're mad Byrn. Maybe no one can blame you, but you've gone right off the rails."

Byrn shook his head. "I didn't believe it myself at first. But eventually it began to ring true. It started at a dinner, in DC, military folk only. Some middling and senior officers followed it up with a poker game." Byrn paused, then repeated the same guttural growl. "Turns out we were the chips."

The rails looked further and further away with each word he uttered.

"In the end, four of them remained at the table. All Marine and British special forces officers. Like any boy's night, with too much alcohol, it turned into a pissing contest. Who was better in the field? A special services marksman or a Marine Scout Sniper. The idiots decided to put it to the test. To put us to the test."

I struggled to comprehend what I heard.

"They managed to dream up some obscure militia leader in Colombia. I believe you met him. Then they chose two rookies straight out of sniper school, told them they formed a team, working with each other. But they weren't working together at all."

"The mission was a competition?" I asked. My voice tremored slightly as I spoke.

"Yup, some perverted form of 'Hunger Games', and you won Sharp. Turns out I lost… big time.

A story beyond belief… almost.

I attempted to collect my thoughts. They were a little hard to locate. Eventually I refocused.

"Who was at the dinner… the game?"

"Well, I start with my side first. Captain Simon Rogers and Major Tim Knight. You can trust me that within a month, both will be dead."

Byrn clearly meant what he said.

"What about the Marines?"

"Initially, I thought Devlin-Waters had been there. He was in your direct chain of command."

"It wasn't him."

"How can you be sure?"

"I'm sure."

"Well, you're probably right. That turned out to be a bum steer, still, he got a bullet in the shoulder just in case."

I felt my rage swell.

"So?" I demanded.

"Two officers. One, a man called Giles Winter. I understand he was a lieutenant back then. Do you remember him?"

"As though it was yesterday." Hearing that name echoed through me, like a repeating electric shock.

"And the other?"

Byrn looked quietly satisfied with himself as he returned his face to a position an inch from mine.

"General Thomas Ireland."

Impossible.

It took me a moment to process the words.

Byrn nodded. "And I can promise you, both of those men will be dead within a month, too."

At least for one round I would have the upper hand.

"You'll have no need to kill Winter."

Byrn tilted his head yet again. A habit. He also ground his teeth together, as though anticipating a meal.

"Why?"

"Because I've already killed him."

For the first time since we'd reengaged, Lachlan Byrn looked openly surprised.

"You sure?"

"Yes, I'm sure. I can give you the location on the Isle of Wight, the date, the time, and the caliber of the freakin' bullet I used." The anger swelled in my voice as I spoke.

"Impressive Beta, impressive. You've saved me some work, but it won't change the bigger picture."

The bigger picture was what really worried me.

"You're going to take out Ireland."

"Count it as a certainty."

Apart from my own immediate well-being, I saw a problem. A huge problem. The Thomas Ireland this madman intended to assassinate, was currently the United States Secretary of Defense.

A cold, brutal silence hung in the air for at least a minute. I could do nothing that would change what was about to happen.

Lachlan Byrn stood up and pulled his jacket straight. He reached his right hand inside and retrieved a large pistol. I recognized it as a Chinese Black Star.

"It's time we parted ways Sharp."

Byrn's voice had developed an icy tone. Void of any emotion.

"I'm almost sorry, except that I'm never sorry."

The assassin raised the gun. He held it ten inches from my sweating brow. I watched the muscles in his forefinger tense as he began to squeeze the trigger. If we were parting ways, I had no doubt Lachlan Byrn's way would be much better than mine.

I heard the beginning of a loud explosive crack, then the lights went out.

Chapter 30

"Are you all right? Sir? Are you okay?"

Once more, I began hearing voices, seeing shadows, and wincing under a blinding light. But this time, it seemed different.

"Sir?"

As my vision cleared, one fact became apparent. I was alive. How the hell did that happen?

"Um, yeah, I think so. Give me a minute."

A concerned looking face, wrinkled in all the right corners, appeared in front of me. It belonged to a woman in a gray uniform. Silhouetted behind her was a fair-sized police boat.

"Sir, are you hurt?"

"No, not really." I felt fine apart from my throbbing head. "Where am I?" It seemed an obvious question.

The officer's tone changed on a dime. "It's not so much about where you are, rather than where you're going. I'm placing you under arrest for the willful damage and theft of a vessel."

With that, she flipped me over onto my stomach, grabbed my wrists, and cuffed them together. All this while her partner read me my rights.

Great to be alive.

I felt myself being hauled upright before being yanked over the gunnels of both boats and into the police launch. The officer's partner turned out to be an enormous black man built like the side of a barn. He seemed no more friendly than the woman, but stronger.

It became clear I'd been back in my boat. Well, not really my boat, as the officer had just pointed out.

Sitting in the cruiser tied up alongside the runabout, I noted the word 'Police' plastered along its cabin. Next to it was the Maryland Transport Police badge. As the world continued to refocus around me, it wasn't hard to figure. We had to be somewhere in the middle of the river.

"The Beijing Pearl, it's a ship. I was on board. Where is it?"

The female officer stared at me with an expression bordering somewhere between pity and contempt. "Tell it to the sergeant." I suspected it wasn't the first time she'd used that line.

An hour later, I stood at the booking desk at the MDTP station. I began 'telling it to the sergeant'. The veteran cop looked like he really didn't give a damn. He had a boat thief caught in the act. A solid arrest.

"Sergeant, I implore you. Please check on the whereabouts of the Beijing Pearl. It sails out of Tianjin in China. I've been held captive on it for…." Hell, I didn't even know how long I'd been on the ship.

The Sergeant offered me a pitiful smile just as the officer had earlier. Maybe it was department issued. My arresting officers stood behind me, chuckling quietly.

"Okay, let's play along. When did you escape from this

pirate ship?"

A sarcastic cop, great.

"Er... I don't know." This wasn't going well. "Sergeant, this is important. Lives are at risk. Please contact General Colin Devlin-Waters at..." I stopped mid-sentence. Of course, the general remained in a bed at Walter Reed, incommunicado. I racked my brain for someone else with a bit of clout who might get me out of this. "Perhaps if you called Jefferson Blake..."

The Sergeant behind the desk chuckled.

"So sorry, the President of the United States no longer accepts my personal calls." It became too much for him. He erupted at his own wit. "Maybe you'd like me to give the pope or Jack Sparrow a call. I'm sure they'd love to hear from you."

Funny guy. Everyone in the room thought the comment hilarious. The sergeant was almost in tears. I saw their point.

I took a deep breath, as though I could inhale credibility.

"I get it, officer, I understand. Will you do me one favor? Please check the harbor manifests for the Beijing Pearl? If it has been in port in the last forty-eight hours, can you at least do me the courtesy of calling a number I'll give you?"

The chuckling cop replied, "Okay, okay, I can do that much."

He marched off to the back room. The female police officer and her offsider had their eyes glued to me, looking more amused than threatened.

The sergeant returned five minutes later.

"Apparently, a small container ship, the Beijing Pearl, registered out of Tianjin, was in port for a week." He appeared surprised.

"Was?"

"It left yesterday."

I'd been adrift in that tiny boat longer than I thought.

"Can you return my phone to me, please? I'll give you a number and a name."

The officer nodded before reaching into a bag and producing my cell phone. It had been charged. They'd probably been checking it for ID. He passed it over the counter. I scrolled through until I came to a name I thought would help. I gave the phone back.

"Just press dial."

The policeman studied the name on the screen and then did as I asked.

"Abe Peterson please," he said, as someone on the other end picked up. The sergeant identified himself and asked, "Please tell me your occupation and in what capacity you know one Nicholas Sharp?"

The Sergeant suddenly went quiet. He even straightened his back. I wondered if a salute may be out of the question.

"Yes sir… definitely sir…" He explained about me, the boat, and my story. "I fully understand, sir." Then a small, now familiar chuckle. "I'll arrange that immediately."

After returning my phone, the sergeant stared me directly in the eye.

"The Head of the Secret Service. Really?"

"I told you that you should have called The President."

Chapter 31

The black Chevy Suburban pulled up outside the MDTP station. A tall man wearing a dark gray suit and an earpiece climbed out of the passenger door before ascending the steps to the front entrance. After bursting through the doors, he stopped, turned, and cast his gaze across the room.

"Mr. Sharp?"

I got up from the seat where I'd been waiting. "That's me."

The man nodded his head in my direction, walked up to the counter, and flipped an ID wallet out of his coat pocket.

"He's all yours, my friend," said the sergeant, probably glad to see the back of me. The agent nodded and ushered me out to the car.

The driver had the rear door open by the time we reached the vehicle. I climbed in, feeling a little relieved. The two agents got in the front, and the SUV sped away from the curb. The agent in the passenger seat withdrew a phone from his pocket and pushed dial.

"We have him." He listened for a moment before replying, "Yes sir."

He then turned and passed the phone over the seat to me.

"It's for you."

I pressed it against my ear. "Sharp."

The only sound I heard was a low chortle.

"Stealing a boat from a Navy marina in the middle of the night, destroying it, and then being found snoozing in the center of Chesapeake Bay." More chortling. "Holy hell, I've really got to hear this one. The president is going to love it."

"Abe, nice to talk to you."

Abe Peterson was the Head of The Secret Service. Previously, he had been the longstanding Head of President Jefferson Blake's security detail. We worked together to support President Blake when he came into office under the most unusual circumstances. The situation which began in Sudan, had nearly cost the President, Jack Greatrex and me, our lives.

"So, walk me through it, Nicholas? It doesn't take much to figure out that this may have something to do with the attempt on General Devlin-Water's life."

"It has everything to do with it, Abe."

"Hmph. Before you continue, you need to know that Greatrex and Kaitlin have been turning this city upside down looking for you. I've called to tell them you're okay."

"Thanks Abe. The MDTP wouldn't allow any calls until your men showed up. Just being cautious, I guess."

"All right, what gives?"

I told Abe Peterson the whole story, starting with Greatrex and me visiting the docks in LA up to my last conscious moments on board the Beijing Pearl.

"It sounds like this Lachlan Byrn is quite a piece of work. Given your history with him, I'm surprised, and don't take this the wrong way, that you're still alive."

"That makes two of us, Abe, and I'm not really sure why. The issue now is getting protection for the people on Byrn's hit list."

"If what Byrn told you about your mission all those years ago is correct, I reckon no one could blame you for not rushing to their aid."

I stared out the window as the traffic flashed past. We headed down the Baltimore Washington Parkway, our driver intent on overtaking every vehicle ahead of us.

"In all honesty, Abe, I wouldn't waste my time spitting on them."

Peterson grunted. "I'm not sure about the Brits, but the one remaining American on that list is the United States Secretary of Defense. You're aware of that, right?"

"I refer you to my previous statement."

Peterson grunted again. "Between you and me, the president isn't too keen on Thomas Ireland, either. He was a hangover from the previous administration, and Blake kept him on to satisfy the naysayers at the Pentagon."

"Makes sense. Either way, SecDef needs to be made cognizant of the situation, and they must bolster his security."

"Keep up Nicholas, I've emailed his team as we've been talking. His security head is heading over here now."

I should have known better than to underestimate my old friend.

"What about the two Brits?" I asked.

"I'll get in contact with the authorities in London. They'll see to it."

"Once again, Abe, I don't want to tell you your business."
"But?"

"But when you speak to them, please make certain they

understand that Lachlan Byrn is beyond dangerous. He's driven, possible slightly psychotic, and definitely one of the most ruthless killers on the planet."

"I hear you, and I'll pass it on."

"Can you give me an update on the general's condition?"

"Yup, he sure is a stubborn man."

No surprises there.

Peterson continued. "They've released him home under Kaitlin's supervision on condition he stays immobile and has daily visits from a nurse. He's on his way to that palatial spread of his as we speak. I understand he was extremely relieved when we located you."

"Abe, I think I better come to you. There is a lot to talk about."

"Not going to happen, Nicholas. You're being taken straight down to the general's place in Maryland. We can catch up later. Besides, I've got a bunch of stuff to do here, setting wheels in motion. Unlike some other people I know, I understand how to follow orders, and they were my orders."

"From the top?"

"It gets no higher."

I hung up. It seemed best to sit back and enjoy the ride... by presidential decree.

107

Chapter 32

"I thought they confined you to bed rest, sir."

I stood in the luxurious lounge room that was the center-piece of General Devlin-Waters' sprawling mansion. The general sat awkwardly in one of his Chesterfield chairs. Heavily bandaged, skin still pale, the great man's square jaw set in grim determination.

"And I... we, thought that you wouldn't be so stupid to run off fighting a one-man battle with a crazed killer," he responded.

I cast my eyes across the room. Greatrex had ensconced himself in the other lounge chair beside the fireplace while Kaitlin perched bolt upright on the couch. No one smiled. It was almost as though they'd been rehearsing how to greet me.

"Point taken, sir." I looked across at Kaitlin and the big fella. "Point taken, all of you."

If I had time over, I would do the same thing. Ironically, they would know that.

Appearing suitably admonished, I searched for somewhere to sit. The drawn look on Kaitlin Reed's face made the couch next to her less than inviting. The only available candidate, a wooden chair in front of the writing desk in the corner.

It appeared the Spanish inquisition was imminent.

"You'd better tell us everything Nicholas," said the general. "Please leave no detail out. When you're done, there will be a change of clothes and a warm shower waiting for you upstairs."

That sure would be in contrast to my cold greeting.

I began my story from the moment I took off from the hospital, leaving nothing out as instructed. When I was done, I sat back as comfortably as possible in my chair. I wondered if the atmosphere might ease, or would it just be the inevitable barrage of more questions?

It was the questions.

"Forgive me for being slow into the game here," declared the general. "You're saying this man Byrn wants to kill you because you didn't kill him?"

"No, not quite, sir. If he wanted to end my life, I'd be dead."

"And something you said to him created doubt in his mind. But what?" asked Greatrex.

"I've been thinking about that on the way down here," I replied. "It could be two things. Either Byrn appreciated I returned to Colombia to search for him, or he liked that I killed Giles Winter."

"Which one?" asked Kaitlin. For a second, I imagined a slight softening in her expression.

"I'm going with number two," I responded. "Although he seemed surprised I'd gone back for him. I don't figure he's the sort of man that would forgive what he perceived as my initial weakness in not shooting him that day in the jungle. The fact I returned to Colombia wouldn't be enough. I reckon he had respect for my action in killing Winter. Plus, it saved him the trouble of doing the job himself."

"So, he let you live. That shows a certain morality to the man," declared the general.

"A moral assassin," added Greatrex, "that sounds a little familiar." For the first time, I saw the big fella smile.

"Now don't go getting carried away," I said. "You know as well as I do that since I left the Marines, I've only killed when I've had to. Byrn is different. He chooses to kill.

Silence.

"Killing is his happy place."

Kaitlin's sharp intake of breath echoed across the room. "That's terrible, frightening."

"Well, it is for the people he's pursuing," said Greatrex.

"Let's move on," suggested the general. "If Byrn is right about that mission in Colombia being a poorly considered bet, I certainly didn't know of it."

"No sir, I wouldn't have believed for one second you would. I figure Byrn had mostly convinced himself about that, too. The bullet in your shoulder was aimed at drawing me out. That it was you he shot was just a bonus, in case he'd made the wrong judgement."

At my words, the general slumped back in his chair. "Astounding."

I continued. "Tell me about Thomas Ireland, sir. You served with him."

Temporarily lost in thought, the general gazed into the fireplace. Eventually he replied.

"Tom Ireland was always an asshole. He spent his whole military career putting himself before those serving under him. He talked up the few positive things he'd managed to achieve, and blamed others, usually underlings, for his failures."

"How in God's name did he become a general?" asked Greatrex.

"Ireland always had one particular talent: making connections. I was never really sure if it was because he worked hard to ingratiate himself within the political power circles of Washington, or whether he had inappropriate information on others." You could feel the bitterness in our former leader's words.

"Like Hoover," observed Greatrex.

"Exactly," replied the general.

"Abe Peterson told me that Jefferson Blake doesn't have much time for Thomas Ireland. He only kept him on for political expediency," I added.

The general nodded.

"One more thing, sir," I continued. "If Byrn was correct, and our mission resulted from a drunken bet between those who should have known better, is it really possible that the politician who is now the US Secretary of Defense could have been responsible?"

The general didn't rush to answer. It was a big question. I speculated how much time a man in his position would need to pass such judgement on a former colleague.

Turns out it was two minutes.

"Absolutely, and without a doubt, yes."

We sat in stunned silence. Inside my pockets, my fists balled in tension. My thoughts took me back to a river in Colombia, cowering underwater, desperately needing to breathe, but realizing if I surfaced for air, that one breath could be my last.

I'd always harbored a huge animosity toward Giles Winter. He'd been my immediate superior in Iraq. What he did to

111

me and others there, and later on after I quit the Marines, required his life to end... in order to save many innocent lives. Finding out he'd been the officer who sent me on the fake mission to Colombia shortly before we moved out to the Middle East exacerbated my rage. Although the man died at my hand, my hatred of him hadn't.

Now the hatred had company. Thomas Ireland.

I stood up and walked to the window. A good view usually helped me think. The green rolling pastures of the general's Maryland property should have acted as a panacea. They didn't.

I considered Thomas Ireland.

I sensed the others' eyes boring down on the back of my head, awaiting a response. I suspected they wouldn't like the question on which I fixated.

Could Lachlan Byrn be right?

An hour later, I was upstairs in the small bathroom next to one of the general's guest rooms. I stood in the shower, letting the spray rain down on me like a comforting warm blanket. The constant tension that had permeated my body over the previous forty-eight hours slowly relinquished its hold.

I jumped as I felt a hand squeeze tight on my shoulder. A split second later, I flipped around.

Apparently, Kaitlin and I were back on.

Chapter 33

"How do these people end up at the top of the tree?"

Greatrex looked at me quizzically. I suspected he considered my question naïve.

"Do you really need me to answer that?" he responded.

"No, I suppose not. It just seems that for every General Colin Devlin-Waters, there are two Thomas Irelands. Not only here in the US, but in bureaucracies around the globe."

We sat in the general's morning room, sipping coffee after a breakfast that could have fed a dozen. There were three of us. Jack, Kaitlin and me. The general took his breakfast in his bedroom. A small compromise to his wounded state.

"There are a lot of leaders who don't understand the 'serve' bit when it comes to leading others or serving our country," declared the big fella.

"Too damn right," I concurred.

"Now boys, you two are way too young to develop grumpy old man syndrome. Can we move on to the task at hand, please?" Kaitlin's instruction was firm.

"And what precisely is the task at hand?" I inquired.

"We need to make sure the Secretary of Defense is adequately protected," announced a gruff voice.

I hadn't heard the general enter the room.

"Good morning, sir," responded Greatrex and I as we stood up together. Old habits die hard.

"Please sit down. You do realize I haven't been your commanding officer for some years, don't you?"

We sat.

"With respect general, the SecDef has the US Army Criminal Investigation Division agents to look out for him. In comparison, what are we?"

"Good point Nicholas. Yet I would wonder if Jefferson Blake held the same view on his return from Sudan. Anyway, the fact remains you probably know how Lachlan Byrn thinks, more than any man alive, at least in the western world. And that sort of intel is a huge benefit."

"I get it, general, and I'm happy to talk with anyone from CID, the Secret Service, the FBI or even the Boy Scouts if you believe it will help. But that's about it, I'm afraid."

Nicholas Sharp making a stand.

The general didn't give up.

"I'm getting the impression that you may not be overly concerned about Thomas Ireland's wellbeing. Am I wrong?"

"Well, no sir, you're pretty much spot on." I replied.

Kaitlin chipped in. "If what Byrn said is true, you can't blame Nicholas for not wanting to step up with his usual bravado to protect a man who nearly sent him to his death for a bet."

"Fair enough, my dear, except for one thing."

"What's that?" asked Greatrex.

The general continued. "I've been on the phone most of the morning. In a week's time, SecDef is due to fly overseas as a special guest of Future Nucleus, an international conference looking at warfare in the digital age."

"Sounds like an Iron Man convention," I responded.

"Maybe so," replied the general. "But after talking with Ed Chelton, the head of the Army Criminal Investigation Division, I'm concerned. He considers that it's more likely that Byrn will go after Ireland when he's out of the country, figuring that security services are more stretched when playing an away game."

"He's probably right," said Greatrex.

"So, get him to cancel the trip. Stay home," I replied.

"That would be the sensible thing to do," said the general, "but everyone in this room knows that politicians don't always do the sensible thing."

"I don't suppose President Blake would cancel a trip because he was at risk. He wouldn't even postpone a state dinner," added Greatrex.

"Completely correct Jack. Blake is persistent in his view that the US should never cower when under threat."

I sensed the general hadn't finished, but I interrupted anyway.

"So, Thomas Ireland holds the same view?"

"Outwardly, yes," said the general, "but Ireland suspects his term as SecDef is coming to an end. He correctly figures that Jefferson Blake has just about had enough of him. It appears even his supporters at the Pentagon won't be able to save him when the axe falls."

I wondered where this was going.

"There will be high-level representatives of every major defense corporation in the world at that conference. Ireland is planning on networking himself into a high paying consultancy."

"Selfless to the end," I said. My disappointment in humanity was boundless, at least Ireland's type of humanity.

"Again, with respect general, I ask, how does that involve us... me?"

"Well, here's the kicker Nicholas. You know I don't like to ask favors, particularly in situations like this."

I waited.

"There is a modest contingent of loyal US personnel who are going to be part of Ireland's team. Many of them are digital specialists, experts in their field, of course."

"Where exactly is the conference, sir?" asked Greatrex.

"Jack, the conference is in Rome. And for the record, my dear wife Cassandra, Kaitlin's mother, is one of those specialists. Despite my protestations, she'll be at Tom Ireland's side for most of that week, working for our country, not for him. And, before you ask, she's of the Jefferson Blake school of thought. My wife is in Italy already, and she won't pull out."

Goal kicked.

Chapter 34

One reason I'd left the Marines was so I could control my own choices. This wasn't one of those times. If Cassandra Devlin-Waters, Kaitlin's mother and the general's wife, was anywhere near Lachlan Byrn's firing line, I needed to be there.

Rome. I'd never been to the Italian capital, but it certainly seemed like it was the most likely place for Byrn to make his play. We had time to prepare, since Ireland wouldn't head over for another week.

As ever, I'd automatically assumed the 'we' part. That wasn't really fair.

"Jack, there's no need…"

"Shut up Nicholas, I'm coming."

There you go.

We spent the next couple of days scoping out our ideas. The general seemed to have an infinite source of information. That really helped. That our plans involved anticipating the intentions of a deranged madman didn't help… at all. The only saving grace was that Byrn and I had similar training, allowing me a glimpse into his method of operations. I'd mentioned that to Greatrex on the afternoon of our first day of planning. His response had been blunt.

"You don't figure two years of imprisonment and constant torture may have had some effect on the way Lachlan Byrn does business?"

He had a point.

On the morning of the second day, Greatrex and I sauntered around the general's extravagantly manicured garden. We debated the advantages of tagging ourselves to SecDef's team versus a more distant approach. The environment was relaxing, the discussion wasn't.

"The only advantage I see in attaching ourselves to Ireland's team is preventative," I suggested. "In normal circumstances, letting an assassin know you were onto him should send him on his way. Regrouping for another attack would be appropriate."

"In normal circumstances," Greatrex repeated. "Do you really believe seeing you at SecDef's side is going to put Lachlan Byrn off his stride?"

"Not in the slightest, if fact, he'd view the kill as more of a challenge."

We stopped at the front steps leading up to the veranda.

I turned to the big fella. "Is there a chance Byrn is angry, but just shooting off hot air? After all, he didn't kill me."

As I set my foot on the first step, the door opened. The general strolled out. He'd regained his color, and although moving gingerly, he showed some spring to his stride.

"Good, found you. You're both aware that we put the word out to our colleagues in the UK that Simon Rogers and Tim Knight were the focus of a professional assassin's attention. It appears the former Major Tim Knight had retired and was living a quiet life on the southern coast of England. Previously

Captain Rogers is now Major Rogers and is still active within the military. In fact, he commands a Special Boat Service squadron."

"Sir, you just said Knight *was* living a quiet life," I interjected.

"Nicholas, Jack, I've received information that yesterday afternoon, retired Major Timothy Knight was involved in a dreadful car accident in Cornwall. His vehicle went off a cliff. The Major was killed."

I looked over to Greatrex. "Belay my last statement. Lachlan Byrn clearly meant every word he said."

The general had obtained a copy of Thomas Ireland's itinerary while in Rome. We huddled around his large desk in the center of his study. It was an imposing place, filled with classic furniture and bookshelves lining the walls. I'd been in the room before, meeting some very interesting people.

SecDef's itinerary was laid out next to a copy of the general's wife's schedule.

"To be honest, I don't like it. Cassandra is with Tom Ireland way too often for me to be comfortable about this. She can't stand the man, and is only doing this out of duty, but I'm worried."

I replied. "General, we'll do our very best to ensure Cassandra's safe return to you. I won't make any promises, but Jack and I will do everything we can."

"Yes, I know that Nicholas, and I appreciate it."

Greatrex added, "Sir, there is one simple way to avoid all this. If you could persuade your wife to come back home, there would be no issue."

The general looked up at Greatrex as though he spoke in tongues.

"You've met my wife, Jack?"

"Yes, sir."

"Did you get the impression that she would either a: follow my advice unquestionably or b: retreat from a fight?"

"No sir, neither sir."

The general added. "You see why we have a problem?"

Suitably chastised, the big fella resumed studying the two itineraries on the desk. I joined him. We had to figure out where and how Byrn would strike.

It would have been easier to read a crystal ball.

An hour later, a thought occurred to me.

"General, has there been any word from our friends in the UK regarding the whereabouts of Major Rogers?"

"It's odd, really. They didn't appear too worried about Simon Rogers' immediate wellbeing. Apparently, he's currently on base with his squadron. Those we spoke to believe it would be impossible for anyone to breach the base's security arrangements. They likened it to leaping into a nest of vipers."

I considered the general's words. "They would be mostly right. Infiltrating the Special Boat Service headquarters would seem like a suicide mission to almost any sane person. But of course, Lachlan Byrn isn't just anyone."

Greatrex leaned forward over the desk before looking up at me. "And is he sane?"

Chapter 35

LACHLAN BYRN

The thunderous roar from the clouds was distracting, but it made no difference to Byrn. Neither did the torrential rain that hammered the already soddened earth.

It was ironic how Simon Rogers would die. The very skills the SBS officer had taught Lachlan Byrn would cause his own demise.

The assassin lay flat on the ground. The hole he'd dug was deep enough for two men, although it wouldn't be that crowded for long. Two inches of soil rested on the chicken wire mesh secured over the dugout. Byrn's first job when he began digging the hole had been to carefully place the rough turf from the surface to one side. Later, with the rest of the work completed, he sprinkled it back over the structure. It would be difficult for someone to notice the hide.

The same system of camouflaged construction had worked for the Special Boat Service operatives for decades. During the Falkland war, Argentine soldiers had walked within a few feet of these hides while the SBS and SAS teams inside them remained undetected for days on end.

Byrn was certain it would be a long wait. It had been a long wait before he even started digging the hole.

Years.

Darkness eventually subdued the overcast day. The limited vision wasn't an issue. Byrn didn't have to see far. He knew the area like the back of his hand. The Brecon Beacons in Wales had been the training ground for SBS and SAS commandos for decades. Byrn had been out here studying the landscape well before he applied to the SBS. Preparation is everything.

Ninety percent of the young recruits who got this far in their instruction made it no further. They were returned to their units almost immediately. Being banished back to their previous units with their tails between their legs was a humiliating experience. That hadn't happened to Lachlan Byrn. He wouldn't let it.

The candidates out of SENTA, the Sennybridge Training Area, had been passing by for almost two hours. Byrn had positioned himself a short distance before the end of their course. This was their big day. The 'long drag' was the climactic event after several extended hauls through the hills and mountains laden with their entire rig. Their heavy rucksacks, weapons and bulky uniforms took a toll. The 'long drag' ran for nearly twenty-five miles and had to be covered in less than twenty hours. The men were tired when they began and frequently delirious when they finished… if they finished. Three men had died on the trail a few years earlier, after attempting to complete the course in horrendously hot conditions.

Now it was freezing cold and wet.

The British Special Ops was never beholden to the weather,

no matter the cost.

Lachlan Bryn knew how Major Simon Rogers operated. The SBS man would wait until the final hour of the training task, before driving a Land Rover up to a location just around the hill from Byrn's current position. The struggling tailenders weren't destined for the greatness of Special Ops, so Rogers took sadistic delight in patrolling the last couple of miles alone, eliminating and humiliating the remaining candidates, the weak links.

Byrn's research had taught him that despite rising in the ranks, Roger's MO hadn't changed. No surprises there.

Once a bully, always a bully.

Forty minutes and three sapped recruits later, a familiar figure loomed into Byrn's view. The assassin immediately sensed from the man's stride that this was not a candidate. He noted no struggle of effort in his walk, only the proud jaunt of an arrogant officer.

Byrn unknowingly ground his teeth. The pills and his anger had kept him awake.

For this moment.

Rogers stopped less than ten yards from the hide. Byrn paused. Despite lying still for hours on end, his muscles tensed, ready to pounce. The assassin raised the roof of the dugout minutely, to verify the distance.

Without warning, Rogers spun around. Byrn froze. If Rogers had noticed something, Byrn needed to figure out what. A second later, another contender staggered into sight, unsteady on his feet and clearly exhausted. A bigger man may have shown some empathy.

Rogers showed the opposite.

The soldier spied Rogers through the rain lashed darkness.

He attempted to draw himself upright.

"Sir?"

Rogers yelled to be heard.

"You're weak and pathetic, candidate. Give up now. You have failed, you have no chance. It's over."

Byrn eyed the flash of teeth in Rogers' sneer.

"Sir. I will get this done. Sir."

"Give up you fool, you'll never have what it takes to make Special Ops."

The soldier hesitated for a second, swaying. Byrn thought he would collapse. He didn't. Without another word, the man arched his back, before willing himself on, around the bend and up the next hill.

Byrn returned his gaze to Rogers. He wasted a few seconds imagining the man in a completely different setting. A dinner in Washington, a few drinks… a bet. The stakes: Lachlan Byrn and Nicholas Sharp, both too young and stupid to know better. The eventual price? Well, Byrn couldn't consider that right now.

Using his shoulder, the assassin raised the roof of the hide further, and slithered out across the mud.

A brief glance back down the track. No one in sight.

In less than three seconds, Byrn was on his feet and within reach of his prey. A second later, he prodded Rogers in the spine with his pistol, while whipping his arm around the Major's neck. He pressed his Gerber Knife to the man's neck.

"Not a word," Byrn spat into Rogers' ear. "Step slowly backwards, don't turn, don't reach for a weapon. That would be a life ending mistake."

Acutely aware that the man he threatened was a highly trained killer, Byrn sensed his victim tense up, preparing to retaliate.

"Forget it. You'd have to reach across at least six inches of space. I'd only have to squeeze a trigger or press this blade a little harder. And don't even consider the head-butt. I'm at the wrong angle. Thanks for teaching me that."

Reluctantly, Rogers stepped backwards towards the hide. Byrn's gun remained tightly wedged into his captor's back as his blade scraped across the man's skin. When they got to the hide, Byrn stopped.

Reaching down, the assassin used his gun hand to strip the SBS officer of his pistol and knife, throwing them into the mud. Byrn's own knife didn't falter.

"Turn around, get in."

Weaponless, Rogers turned. His steely expression reminded Byrn that no SBS man was ever completely unarmed. It was simply a question of degree.

Rogers squinted through the rain, water pounding his face and eyes. But he'd seen enough.

"You."

"Yes me, Rogers. And by the way, Nicholas Sharp says hello."

Bryn had expected the next move, or at least it was one of the five options he'd anticipated.

Rogers lifted his right leg, his knee instantly jabbing up towards Byrn's groin. As impressively quick as it was, by the time the knee connected with Byrn's jeans, it was intercepted by a downward slash of the Gerber. Blood sprayed into the air as the blade ripped across the skin and through to the bone.

Rogers staggered backward.

"You idiot."

"I don't think so," replied Byrn. "Now crawl into the hide."

Rogers didn't move. Byrn raised the knife again. To his

surprise, the SBS man remained motionless.

"Fair enough," said Byrn.

He then lifted his pistol and shot Simon Rogers in the kneecap. The SBS man went down in a heap.

"Jesus freakin' Christ. You're insane."

"It's been mentioned. Now get in the hole."

Rogers crawled through the gap Byrn had left open for him, twisting onto his back. Byrn immediately followed, leaning all his weight on Rogers' chest.

"I built it regulation size, just for the two of us. You really were an excellent teacher."

Rogers attempted to struggle, but his pain was obviously overwhelming.

"Are you going to try to stop the bleeding?" the SBS man asked.

"I see little point."

Even in the dimmest of light, Byrn noticed the fight abandon his victim's eyes.

"Now we'll have some fun. Turn onto your stomach so you can watch the next candidate pass."

Byrn leaned back before heaving Rogers over. The SBS officer screamed in pain. Byrn pressed himself to his captive's body once more.

"Let's wait, but don't talk... yet."

For fifteen minutes they waited in silence, the rain beating down outside. Amid his strained breaths, Byrn knew Rogers was trying to stifle the sound of his agony. He mostly succeeded. Byrn could almost respect that. Almost.

"Here comes one now."

Both men glared out the hole as another candidate rounded the corner. If anything, he labored more desperately than the last, spending as much energy staggering sideways as he did forward.

His mouth an inch away from Rogers' ear, Byrn whispered. "Now look at that man. Twenty minutes ago, his friend was the pathetic butt of your ridicule and humiliation. If I hadn't been here tonight, I'm sure this poor fellow would have suffered the same fate. But things have changed, haven't they, Simon?"

Rogers grunted.

"Yes, they sure have," continued Byrn. "This warrior is now your hero. He is the only one that can save you. Ponder that for a moment. Pathetic one minute, heroic the next. Who would have thought?"

Rogers started to yell, attempting to get the young trainee's attention. Byrn pushed his blade harder into his back. Enough to silence, but not kill him. Rogers winced.

"Now, now. That's not in the rules. Let's wait and see if your hero notices you. Maybe he'll look over and spot the hide. Maybe he won't. He's armed. If he does notice us, he might have a shot at saving you… or he might not."

Byrn waited as the candidate staggered past, before pressing on down the trail.

"Too bad, Simon. That's rotten luck. No one came to rescue you." Byrn pressed his mouth hard against the lobe of Rogers' ear and whispered. "Now you know what it's like to wait for a rescue that doesn't come."

The assassin forced the Gerber harder into Rogers' torso. The major moaned. Byrn was aware that Rogers' pain would be almost unbearable.

Time to eliminate the 'almost'.

"Simon, this situation is alarming you, and here I am,

making our outing seem like some innocent game."

Silence.

"You appreciate a game, don't you, Simon? I'll tell you what. Let's have a wager on the outcome here. Will you live or will you die? What do you reckon, Simon? I've heard you like to bet."

Rogers struggled as violently as his wounds allowed him. Byrn pressed down harder with the weight of his body.

"We didn't think any harm would come of it, Byrn," he gasped. "How could we know you'd be taken prisoner? No one knew anything."

"Don't demean yourself with lies, Simon. Even if what you say is correct, you didn't try to fix it, did you? You made no effort to search for me. At least Sharp came back. But when he alerted your side, you blocked him, so no one was interested."

"We couldn't do anything. No one knew where you were, and we couldn't tell them."

"Be careful with your choice of words, Simon. There's a big difference between *couldn't* and *wouldn't*."

Byrn's patience ran out. He pressed the knife firmly between Rogers' shoulder blades. Two inches in. The man screamed.

It didn't matter now. The rain pounded loudly around them.

"Now one last thing, Simon. I've discovered that for me, it's important that when somebody has done something bad, I mean something really terrible, it's vital that they take responsibility for their actions. In the long run, it's better to understand why you're going to die, don't you think?"

Rogers breathed heavily but didn't speak.

"In my profession I'm not always able to provide that opportunity, but I'm glad I can do this for you Simon."

"Freakin' madman," spluttered the SBS officer.

"Now relax Major. I'll give you a choice. You have two possible pathways out of this world, you shitfaced asshole."

Byrn raised his right hand and used the knife to dig into the soil beside Rogers' head. He'd dug a drain two inches deep when a torrent of rainwater cascaded into the hide. A small surprise he'd prepared earlier. The water began flooding the deepest area of the hole, immediately below Rogers' face.

"Now, here are the alternatives, Simon. Death by drowning or death by a blade in the back of your neck. Your call, Simon, but you haven't got long to decide."

Byrn pressed Rogers' face deep into the rising water. After sixty seconds, he grabbed the SBS man's hair and yanked his head out. His victim sucked in the night air, frantic to breathe.

"You need to understand that I faced this same choice for a long, long time, in fact several times a week for over two years... just because you *couldn't* tell."

Chapter 36

NICHOLAS SHARP

The Swiss Air Lines, A321, circled in a holding pattern, twelve thousand feet above Leonardo da Vinci International Airport. The big fella and I sat towards the front of the bird in business class. The general had deep pockets.

The empty seat between us held a laptop with the Secretary of Defense's amended schedule on the screen. Tom Ireland had refused to cancel the trip. No one believed his decision was based on purely altruistic reasons. Aware that a professional assassin had him in his sights, he had allowed his security team to make some modifications to his itinerary but permitted no change that prevented press or networking opportunities. The general got the word from an insider that SecDef's people had requested they step up the protection of other key members of his party. Apparently, Ireland responded with something along the lines of 'No need. If they're coming after me, then you should put all your resources into my personal detail.'

The general was livid.

It had been a long flight, including a short stop in Zurich where we transferred from United to Swiss. The thought of standing on solid ground again was appealing, as was the anticipation of a good sleep.

We'd arranged to arrive in Rome a couple of days before Ireland's team. I wanted to scope out the sites for a potential attack. Getting some visuals on where each event and meeting was scheduled to take place would be vital. Greatrex and I also needed to catch up with Cassandra Devlin-Waters. I respected her reluctance to leave the conference and return home, but we had to make her appreciate the level of danger she faced. We couldn't let her become collateral damage. Much to his chagrin, the general's doctors had forbidden him from traveling. Kaitlin remained in Maryland, looking after her stepfather. Her last words to me before we took off from Dulles International were, 'If you need me, call. I'll be there within hours.' I didn't doubt it.

Aware we'd need some local knowledge, I made a call to an old friend, a Rome native. Izzy Galante was now a major pop star in Italy and across many parts of Europe. I'd met her in England, when I'd backed her in her London debut at a small club in Soho. Everyone knew that the young artist would do something big… and she did. Izzy seemed delighted to hear from me. She promised to show Greatrex and me 'her' Rome. I hoped we had time.

In the meantime, our plane powered through the European skies.

"I don't enjoy being out of touch. The whole scenario can change in a matter of hours while we're sitting up here," I said.

"Agreed," Greatrex responded.

He wriggled in his seat. Airline seats just weren't made in

his size.

"I also don't like that despite just about every agency in the free world looking for Byrn, we've heard nothing about his whereabouts," he said.

"And we won't. The next time we hear about Lachlan Byrn will be when another corpse shows up."

"You seem sure about that."

"Remember, I've seen him operate close up. He's a machine."

"You know Nicholas, it's not unusual for you to respect your enemy, but you've never really spoken in terms verging on fandom before."

"It's not fandom. He shot the general for no satisfactory reason, for God's sake. He's just that freakin' good, and he's not on our side," I responded.

Greatrex pushed his point. Not always a positive thing with me.

"Now don't go overreacting on me, but do you think in another time, another life, you could have been Lachlan Byrn?"

I glared at him. He went on.

"Perhaps Byrn could even be the darker side of your soul."

I continued glaring, mainly because my greatest friend in the world was probably skating too close to the truth.

As soon as we left the aircraft, I flicked on my cell. Da Vinci was a maze of activity and action. As we boarded the rail car back to the main terminus, my phone came to life.

It was the general's number.

"Nicholas, I've been trying to get hold of you."

"What's up, sir?"

"Simon Rogers' body has been discovered."

I drew a sharp breath.

"I thought they said he couldn't be got at."

"They were wrong," replied the general.

"Where was his body found, sir?"

"It was located some hours after the estimated time of death. He was in a small two-man hide in the Brecon Beacons hillside in Wales."

"The British Special Ops training ground," I responded.

"Exactly."

"I suppose there's a certain poetry in that."

"If you look at it that way," said the general. "Personally, the only thing I take out of this situation is that it doesn't bode well for us, or rather you, Jack and Cassandra."

"Yes sir, you're right. It also doesn't bode well for Thomas Ireland."

"Do I sound like I give a flying fig about that moron?"

That was as close as I'd got to hearing Colin Devlin-Waters swear. I wouldn't have blamed him for going a whole lot further.

"Don't worry, sir. We'll look after Cassandra and bring her home."

I sounded more confident than I felt.

"Thank you, Nicholas, and please pass on my thanks to Jack as well."

"We'll call you when we know more."

I hung up. Greatrex watched on, his face drawn tight.

"News?"

"Yup," I replied. "We're next on the shopping list."

"Shit."

133

"Nicholas, Nicholas…"

I looked up at the sound of my name, my eyes searching the crowd as we cleared customs.

"Nicholas."

There she was, Izzy Galante. Her long auburn hair flowed freely, falling recklessly onto her shoulders. Her mile-wide smile fought for attention with her large green eyes almost popping out of their sockets. She jumped up and down on the spot, waving frantically.

I stepped forward. She hugged me warmly, reaching over the barricade.

"Izzy, it's so good to see you."

I glanced around as I spoke. Clearly, a lot of other people seemed glad to see Izzy as well. Their cells were out, held high in photo mode. I'd forgotten she was a celebrity.

"It's wonderful to have you here, Nicholas, and you, Jack."

Izzy released herself from my grip to give Greatrex a big bear hug. He looked suitably embarrassed.

"And I'd like you to meet my boyfriend, Alessandro."

The tall, broad-shouldered young man, dark hair carefully brushed off to one side with a beard styled to within an inch of its life, stood beside Izzy. He reached out his hand.

"It's an honor to meet you sir." His smile radiated sincerity. "Izzy has told me all about you."

I grimaced, stuck on the 'sir' bit. Izzy and her man would have been early twenties at the oldest. Should I reach for my cane?

"A pleasure," I replied before Greatrex and I made our way around the barrier.

"Where are you staying, Nicholas? Alessandro and I will drive you there."

"We can catch a cab," I offered.

"You are in my city now, Nicholas Sharp. I shall be your host."

I smiled, but my heart sank. I should never have told Izzy that we were coming to Rome. I wondered if my thoughtlessness might put her in danger as well.

Nicholas Sharp... reckless fool.

I gave in too easily, letting Izzy lead Greatrex and me to her late model four-door Alfa Romeo.

"So?" she asked.

"The St. Regis. Do you know it?"

The young singer whistled. "You are certainly traveling in style, Nicholas Sharp. I have had some success, but even then, I would think twice about paying the fees they charge."

"We have a rich uncle," said Greatrex as he squeezed into the rear seat next to me.

The truth was that the conference was based at the St. Regis. Although we had decided not to sign on to Thomas Ireland's team, we still wanted to be accessible. The general hadn't balked at the expense.

Izzy floored the gas pedal. The front tires screeched in protest, as she swung out of the parking space, cutting off a black Mercedes with no warning. Horns blared, fists waved.

I'd survived many life-threatening situations over the years. Yet each experience faded into obscurity as I sat in the Alfa's rear seat hanging onto any and every bit of plastic or metal I could cling to, while Izzy exploded into the Roman traffic.

When there was no leeway between cars, Izzy forced one. When there were oncoming cars approaching, Izzy overtook the vehicle ahead. Six inches between her bumper and the car in front seemed an extravagant waste of space to the young singer. I'd never really had my life flash before my eyes when looking death in the face, but I sensed the slideshow beginning.

When in Rome...

Chapter 37

The St. Regis was a world within a world. We'd stayed at some amazing hotels on tour, but this place stood out. The huge lobby was light and airy. Ornate rugs covered vast sections of the black and white patterned tiled floor. The architectural landscape seemed to extend forever. The ceiling was high, and the enormous chandeliers glimmered above us. Greatrex and I were clearly out of our league.

After check-in, we headed upstairs.

The king-size bed beckoned me invitingly as the portiere showed me in. The luxurious suite contained a sitting area leading to two large windows.

"Quite a sight," I suggested to the portiere as I strolled over to take in the view.

"Si Signore. That's the Fontana delle Naiadi that you can see."

I would have liked to say it reminded me fondly of Venice, but I had very few 'fond' memories of my time there. Instead, I just tipped the portiere a few American dollars.

"Grazie signore," he responded, slipping out the door.

I slipped off my boots and lay on the bed, focused on pushing thoughts of Lachlan Byrn from my mind. Appreciative of the fact I'd survived Izzy Galante's driving, I drifted off to a lazy sleep.

The chirp of my cell woke me. Glancing at my watch as I reached for the phone. Two hours of sleep was better than nothing.

"Nicholas, it's Cassandra Devlin-Waters. Are we able to meet?"

The general's spouse had a reputation for speaking directly.

"Cassandra… yes, sure," I replied, trying to wipe the fatigue away. "When?"

"I'm downstairs in the lounge now."

I abandoned the promise of more rest.

"I'll be down in fifteen."

"Wonderful. You will bring Jack, won't you?"

"Of course." If I had to function on minimum sleep, he could do the same.

Twenty minutes later, I'd retrieved Greatrex from his room next door, and we strolled through the lobby into the hotel's lounge. It was as spectacular as the rest of the place.

Cassandra Devlin-Waters sat nestled on a sofa at the far end of the space. She was a strikingly elegant woman. I presumed her to be in her mid-fifties. She held her outward beauty as though it was effortless. I already knew of her inner resolve. I couldn't help but think of her as a cross between the Hepburns—Audrey and Katharine.

She stood as we approached.

"Nicholas, Jack, wonderful to see you."

"Cassandra, it's a pleasure."

Hugs all around.

"I know Colin was fussing about all of this, but I'm really not sure that you needed to come all this way," she said.

The idea of the general fussing amused me.

"Sit down please, Cassandra," I said. "It's important you realize the extent of the threat Thomas Ireland, and by association you, are facing."

"Surely the chances of just one operator infiltrating all the security arrangements that Ireland's people have put in place is extremely unlikely," she said.

"With respect, Cassandra, that's like saying Katrina was 'just one hurricane.'"

I filled the general's wife in on almost everything I knew about Lachlan Byrn, including his latest kill list.

"Oh, my goodness," she exclaimed when I'd finished. "He sounds like a real piece of work."

"He is," I replied. "He's also a brutally efficient killer, not to mention the fact that, historically, I owe the man my life."

"So, you'd rather not take him out?" Cassandra asked.

I supposed being married to the general for so long had acquainted her with direct 'military speak'.

"The jury is out on that one," I responded. "After all, he shot your husband."

"Perhaps I should eliminate him," she replied.

For a split second, I thought Cassandra Devlin-Waters was genuine. Then she started laughing.

Greatrex spoke up. "Cassandra, we don't want Byrn anywhere near you... not if we can help it."

"You're not particularly worried by all of this?" I enquired.

Cassandra sat upright and placed her hand on her knees.

139

"I was totally distraught when Kaitlin called to tell me Colin had been shot. I wanted to come straight home, but my stubborn husband wouldn't have a bar of it. A few days later, when he rang and suggested I return because of this man Byrn, I refused to cower."

"And now?" I asked, reaching forward and taking both her hands in mine. "Would you consider returning home now?"

This amazing woman stared me down before following through with a smile and a chuckle.

"Why would I? I have you and Jack to look out for me. I've never felt safer."

My shoulders sagged. It had been a small chance.

Greatrex grinned. "I see why you and the general belong together, Cassandra."

The general's wife released my hands and sat bolt upright. "Now gentlemen, let's get down to business."

We went through Cassandra's schedule, marking down the occasions she would spend time in Thomas Ireland's company.

"I don't like it," I announced. "There are too many events you're attending together."

"*You* don't like it?" she exclaimed. "The man is a weasel. I would prefer not to waste one more minute with him than I have to. The trouble is, we've reached a point of negotiation with at least three tech companies that require the secretary to approve further momentum. SecDef knows I have the relationship with the people we're dealing with, and he wants in. Without doubt, he also intends to claim credit for what we are achieving."

We returned to studying the program. Fortunately, most of

the conference agenda would take place within the hotel. The St. Regis had a myriad of meeting rooms, all of which had been booked out by this event. I remained more concerned about the exposure at proceedings outside the building. Those would be the times when security was stretched, and Lachlan Byrn would sense vulnerability.

"Let's go through the external events, one by one," I suggested.

Greatrex began. "It's not external, but in two days-time the conference begins with the opening gala dinner. It will be in the hotel ballroom. There'll be a lot of people attending, but I reckon the chances of a strike are limited. There are only so many entrances and exits and they'll all be heavily manned with security."

"Agreed," I responded.

"There may be a small problem there," Cassandra chirped in. "I overheard Ireland tell his people he wanted a big photo op to kick the conference off. He wants all the CEOs and, of course, himself to be shot in front of the Fountain of Moses just outside the hotel entrance. He said something about it giving him a chance to talk about Moses' parting of the Red Sea. He views himself as parting the sea of convention as he leads us all forward to a new world of military warfare techno-capability."

"The guy is delusional," said Greatrex. "Maybe he thinks he's Tony Stark?"

I smiled.

"Now Jack, be respectful," said Cassandra. "You're referring to the Defense Secretary of the United States of America." Her eyebrows furrowed as she spoke. The stern schoolteacher.

"Sorry…"

"But he is delusional, and to be honest, a complete tool." Direct. "That's why both Colin and the President wanted me here to monitor him, and perhaps temper his '*toolness*'."

Laughter.

"Cassandra, the fact is if SecDef wants to be shot with Moses, he may get his wish. There would be hundreds of possible sniper hides along that street. There's no way his security could cover them all," I said. It was a sobering notion.

"Can we talk him out of the photo op?" asked the big fella.

"That's like asking if we can talk him out of his heavily inflated ego. Not going to happen. His people tried and failed," replied Cassandra.

"Well, if this guy has a death wish, it's his issue," I said. "Can you at least make sure you are far away from him at the shoot?"

"He's requested me to stand beside him."

I raised an eyebrow.

"Eye-candy?" asked Greatrex.

Cassandra chuckled.

"No, but thanks for the thought, Jack. My eye-candy days are long gone, but apparently, I'm a career appropriate co-hostess for SecDef. Truth be known, he probably hopes standing next to me in the photo will quell the current rumors of his after-hours liaisons with an eager young female intern. Everyone knows he'd never make a move on me, or Colin would come after him like a runaway truck. Go figure."

For a second, I hoped that Lachlan Byrn might find a way through, but I stopped myself. Unpatriotic.

There were few other events scheduled outside the hotel walls. A visit to a factory and afternoon tea with Italy's Prime Minister at his residence. Both should be reasonably easy for Ireland's security team to cover, particularly when working hand in hand with the local authorities.

"It's this one here that worries me," I added, pointing to the second last event on the scheduling document.

"Too freakin' right," agreed Greatrex.

"Why in God's name are all the key figures gathering at the Palatine Hill. From what I've seen online, the place appears to be a sniper's fairground. Ireland couldn't have picked a better spot to take a bullet if he tried. Does he *want* to get shot?" I asked.

Cassandra swept her gaze from Greatrex to me.

"Nicholas, Jack, you need to understand this man. Tom Ireland is not brave, but he's desperate. He knows his authority is eroding under Jefferson Blake's presidency. He craves power, and he'll do just about anything short of assassinate the president to hang onto it. He intends the Palatine Hill to be the sight of his victory speech. He'll celebrate the success of the agreements reached at the conference, assume the credit for all of it, and ensure his power and influence well into the future in one photogenic moment."

"But why there?" asked Greatrex. "Why such an exposed position?"

"It's all about that particular location and the optics that go with it," Cassandra responded. "The Palatine Hill is the center most point of the Seven Hills of Rome. They say it's known as 'the first nucleus of the Roman Empire.' It's basically where our civilization began. The Secretary of Defense plans to make a speech suggesting America is leading the planet into a new empire, a technological beginning where the US will have the military might to return to its rightful position as the policeman of the free world. It's no coincidence that this conference is titled 'Future Nucleus.' Thomas Ireland intends to be the modern-day emperor at the heart of that power, be it working for the United States government, or at the top of the corporate tree."

"He's mad, insane," said Greatrex.

"He's also extremely intelligent and very capable," replied Cassandra.

"If he makes a speech on that hill," I added, "he will also be dead."

Chapter 38

That evening, we headed off to dinner with Izzy and her boyfriend Alessandro.

"We'll swing by the hotel to pick you up," she offered earlier.

"Thanks, but Greatrex and I could do with the exercise," I declined.

It's a survival thing.

Our walk felt like a scene from an old classic movie. We followed Izzy's directions to a small ristorante on the edge of the Piazza Navona. It was dark, but the famous square was lit not only by streetlamps but also by the many cafes and ristorantes surrounding it. Locals and tourists alike thronged over the space. Three fountains spread across the length of the square, but the one in the center caught my eye. Underwater lights turned the waters a vibrant blue, beaming upward towards the ominous figures rising up from the deep.

Izzy and Alessandro sat waiting at an outside table. They rose to greet us, handshakes and hugs.

Greatrex ordered a beer, I went for a martini. It seemed like the Italian thing to do.

"It's quite an atmosphere here, Izzy," I said, sweeping my

hand across the view of the piazza.

"Rome is my home," she answered. "You can live here for years and not encounter all its secrets and delights."

"Rome is also a perpetual mystery," added Alessandro, "both present and past."

Izzy giggled. Like *she* had a secret.

"I know I've seen that fountain before," I continued. "It's famous for something, I presume?"

Izzy looked to Alessandro to respond.

"That is Fontana dei Quattro Fiumi, the Fountain of the Four Rivers. It was commissioned by Pope Innocent X and designed covertly by Gian Lorenzo Bernini. It was not a popular decision, as poverty and famine wracked Rome at the time. In 1651, the people wanted bread to eat, not fountains to look at."

Alessandro knew his stuff.

"And it's fame to the rest of the world?" I asked.

Alessandro continued. "Apart from being a well-known tourist attraction, the fountain has featured in many films. Perhaps the most recent is the Dan Brown thriller Angels and Demons."

"Of course, wasn't there a scene where Robert Langdon saved a priest chained to the bottom of the fountain?"

"You are correct Nicholas. In that movie, the Fontana dei Quattro Fiumi was listed as one of the Altars of Science. The fountain represented the path to illumination."

Angels and demons. Sometimes it seemed hard to tell the difference.

"Izzy, I think you've got some fans," said Greatrex, changing the subject.

A small gathering of young girls stood several feet away,

outside the perimeters of the ristorante. They smiled and giggled at first. A minute later they'd rearranged themselves to take selfies with Izzy Galante clearly in view over their shoulders.

"I'll ask them to move on," said Alessandro.

"No," replied Izzy. She pushed her chair back and stood up. "Un momento."

She walked around our table and out the entrance of the eatery. A few seconds later we heard squeals of delight from the youngsters as Izzy posed for a photo with each of them in turn. After a quick chat with her fans, she returned.

"That was impressive," said Greatrex.

"A tiny effort, some very happy girls. I hope they remember me when my star wanes," replied the young popstar.

I wasn't convinced Izzy's star would ever wane.

I sipped my martini, carefully considering how much I would say to her.

"Izzy, as you've probably gathered, we're here on some business," I began.

"Is that music business or something a little more sinister?"

When I first met Izzy in London, it had not been a trouble-free environment.

"Sadly, it's not music related," I responded. "I don't want to say too much, but it relates to the conference that's about to begin at the St. Regis."

'You mean 'Future Nucleus'?" she asked.

"Yes. You're aware of it?"

"More than that," she replied. "It's meant to be a well-kept secret, but I'm performing at the opening gala dinner. I understand I'm the Italian government's cultural contribution."

"Well, there you go. That's wonderful."

147

I was lying. All I could see was another target I cared about in Lachlan Byrn's sights.

"Our job is to provide a little extra security for the Secretary of Defense and some of his personnel," I said.

"Doesn't he have his own team for that?" asked Alessandro.

"Yes, he certainly does. We're here as a personal favor to an old friend," I responded.

There was no point in telling them about the looming threat that was Lachlan Byrn.

"One of our tasks is to scope out the areas where the conference leaders are planning to make appearances outside the St. Regis," I said. "Most of the locations are straightforward. The Prime Minister's residence, the Palazzo Chigi, is well secured, but the location that is troubling me is the Palatine Hill and Roman Forum area."

"Why would they go there?

"Optics," chimed in Greatrex.

Alessandro sat back in his chair and released a deep sigh. He compressed his lips and shook his head slowly.

"I'm sorry to tell you this Nicholas and Jack, but the Palatine Hill and Roman Forum would be one of the most difficult places in Rome to make secure. It is an exposed open space with a thousand nooks and crevices for someone with nefarious intentions to hide. And that's not even including the network of tunnels that hides beneath."

"Tunnels?" I asked.

"I'm afraid so. There are numerous entrances, rooms, and tunnels under the Palatine. The emperors had various ones to take them to different places. They date back thousands of years. Some of them have a dark history attached to them. The emperor Caligula was murdered in one," said Alessandro.

"Incredible, but this doesn't help our job at hand," said Greatrex.

"Helpful no," I added, "but informative, yes."

"I would suggest that you go back to the people who make these decisions and highly recommend an alternative location," suggested our new young friend.

"Suggested and rejected," I replied. I looked across the table to Izzy, who had remained quiet during the conversation. "Izzy, I was going to ask you if you knew anyone who was familiar with the area who might give us some background information on the site, or even a personal tour. Now I'm thinking the answer may lie closer to home."

"You'd be right," she replied. "My lovely Alessandro is, in fact, doing a thesis for his doctorate. His specialties are Roman history and archaeology. You would be hard pressed to find someone more knowledgeable."

"Every now and again you've got to get lucky," declared Greatrex, grinning widely.

Alessandro nodded. "If it's any help, I've supported my studies through university by guiding tours through many areas of Rome, including the Palatine and Roman Forum areas. I would, of course, be delighted to assist you."

"Thanks so much Alessandro. Will tomorrow work for you?"

The young man nodded again. Greatrex and I glanced at each other. First problem solved, although I had the sinking feeling that we now had more questions than answers.

Chapter 39

Greatrex and I began the day staring at the Fontana dell'Acqua Felice, the Fountain of Moses, just outside the St. Regis entrance.

"Quite something," said the big fella.

"Indeed."

Moses, with four sculptured lions ready to defend him, loomed high over the Via Vittorio Emanuele Orlando. We strolled the few yards to the point it intersected with the Via Venti Settembre. None of what I saw pleased me.

"If he makes his play here, Byrn will have more opportunities than John Wick," I said.

"Hundreds of rooms, hundreds of windows, hundreds of escape routes. This would be the smart move."

"Yeah, it would," I retorted. "And it would take a hell of a lot more than those four lions to protect Thomas Ireland if he did."

"You know what's worrying me?" asked Greatrex.

"I've got a feeling I'm about to find out."

"I'm as patriotic as the next guy, but the thought of laying my life down for Thomas Ireland, US Secretary of Defense or not, makes me want to puke."

"Puke if you have to," I replied, "but neither you nor I are placing ourselves in harm's way because of that, er…."

"Tool."

"Yeah, tool," I smirked. "We're here because of Cassandra Devlin-Waters, Kaitlin and the general. The thing that makes me sick is the idea of Cassandra standing next to Ireland on the footpath while Lachlan Byrn bears down on them."

"Maybe we should take Ireland out beforehand. Preventative measures," suggested Greatrex.

For a split second, I thought my friend was serious. His face showed no sign of humor.

"If the story Byrn told me is correct, and Ireland is one of the perpetrators who sent the two of us to Colombia, then I should be the one to take him down."

For a split second, I thought *I* was serious.

We both shook our heads, knowing it didn't work that way.

"Moving forward, all we can do here is to ensure that the CID people, and the local authorities, place snipers across these rooftops ready to act if needed." I said.

"Any idea how a couple of civilians such as our good selves are going to influence decisions such as that?" asked the big fella.

"Well, yeah. The general has arranged a meeting between us and Major Wyatt Davis, head of SecDef's CID security detail. He's in town twenty-four hours ahead of Ireland to check the arrangements," I responded.

"Thanks for mentioning it."

"I just did."

Greatrex rolled his eyes. "And when do we meet?"

"In thirty minutes, in one of the conference rooms they're

using as their detail HQ at the hotel."

"Anything else up your sleeve?"

"Nothing worth mentioning," I replied. "Let's go grab a coffee before we make contact."

We headed toward the hotel door.

As we headed up the steps I turned to the big fella. "Jack, let me do most of the talking with this guy. You have a tendency to get impatient with people that put protocol before practicality."

"Hmph."

Thirty minutes later, we were shown into a middle-sized meeting room in the heart of the St. Regis complex. In contrast to the elegant hotel décor, banks of black road cases sat on two large tables in the center of the room, laptop computers interspersed amongst them. Half a dozen men in dark suits were monitoring the devices, each focused on a screen.

Mobile command at its best.

"Sharp and Greatrex, I presume?" A middle-aged man in a black suit that matched his colleagues, albeit with a slightly more expensive cut, looked at us over the table. His hair was graying, and his figure suggested a lack of fitness that contrasted with the others in the room.

"Major Davis?"

"Yes, come with me."

The major headed towards a double door at the far end of the area. He opened it without waiting for us to catch up. The doors revealed an adjoining space with a desk and a small lounge.

"This place acts as my office and conference room," announced the major. "Please sit down."

He strode behind the large desk and waved us towards two chairs that sat opposite. Not the lounge. Perhaps he'd already decided this was not to be an encounter on equal turf, or perhaps I was being cynical. I checked myself.

"Now, how can I be of service, gentlemen?"

Better.

"Major, I'm assuming that you're aware we've been requested to add an extra layer of backup to the already well-managed security arrangement for the conference. Our focus is the wellbeing of Cassandra Devlin-Waters," I began.

Nicholas Sharp... diplomat.

"I'm aware that some people pulled strings to get you here."

Deep breath.

"We wondered if it would be possible to have a look at the measures you have in place, particularly concerning the external events. Unlikely as it is, there is a possibility we may be able to make some small suggestions."

Diplomacy personified.

"No."

Diplomacy fails.

The major leaned forward in his chair, mildly aggressive stance.

"Mr. Sharp, Mr. Greatrex. You are sitting in this room right now because I have no choice in the matter. My orders were to meet you, not to follow your so-called advice."

"With due respect, major, we have some experience regarding the threat you're dealing with. That experience could prove valuable..."

"I'll stop you there Sharp. I'm fully aware that the two of you are *ex*-military."

He seemed to place a heavy emphasis on the 'ex'.

"I know also that you have reasonable records in active service. That is why I've allowed this interview to continue for more than thirty seconds. I do, however, want to make myself clear. My team are professionals and *current* in their skills. They are highly trained to deal with any external threats regarding the United States Secretary of Defense. We do not need, nor will we tolerate, outside interference from amateurs, no matter how well connected." The major's skin color began turning to a mild crimson.

I held my breath. Staying calm and making a friend was the best strategy.

"I fully understand, major, and in your situation, I would probably feel the same way." I responded.

"Well, that's good. I'm glad we're seeing eye-to-eye on this. You can tell your friends that we've met, and everything is just hunky-dory. Then I'm sure you'll manage to amuse yourselves for a few days on your friend's expense account while my team of professionals does what we're trained to do."

Another deep breath.

"Again, with respect, major. What do you know about Lachlan Byrn and his ability to penetrate the arrangements you've made?" I asked.

"We know enough Sharp. Byrn is just another disgruntled ex-special forces op with a grudge. We deal with people like him on a daily basis. We see nothing extraordinary going on here," replied the major.

"You're wrong."

Damn, I forgot to take the breath.

Greatrex chuckled quietly.

Davis straightened himself and pushed his shoulders back.

"For your information Sharp, we've already advised the secretary to cancel the conference's external events. He's chosen not to. As a true patriot, Thomas Ireland is putting American interests before his own personal safety."

"But it's not only his safety we're dealing with here, is it?"

Breathe man, breathe.

"The threat in this situation is to SecDef, nobody else. There is little to be gained by over-reacting."

"Surely a good leader considers the security and wellbeing of those who surround him."

Davis stood.

"Let me be perfectly clear. I've known Tom Ireland for years, in fact decades. It was he who put me into this role. If he views this Byrn as nothing more than a minor threat, then so do I, despite what some overblown ex-military people back in DC may think. Now, this meeting is over."

I stood up, but not to leave.

"Have you ever been in combat, major? Have you ever really stared death in the face?"

"Irrelevant Sharp. My career has been more focused on administrative leadership, and I'm exceptionally good at it."

Davis started to lean across the desk, but then seemed to reconsider.

"Well, let me tell you something you pumped up little bureaucrat turd." I shoved my fists hard down on the desk and leaned heavily into the major's face. "If something happens to Cassandra Devlin-Waters or anyone else on that team because you wouldn't listen to or take advice from people who could provide vital intelligence, I will personally come after you. Take it as a threat or a promise. I don't really give a fuck, but I can tell you this. Not only will you see death close-up, but it will be the last thing you ever see!"

I turned and marched toward the door. Greatrex followed.

Clearly, someone on the other side had been listening in. The double door swung open before we reached it. I continued the march through the ops room, vaguely aware of several sets of eyes penetrating the back of my head.

It wasn't until we'd made it halfway down the corridor that I spoke.

"I think that went well."

"Terrific," replied the big fella. "Sure am glad I let you do the talking."

Chapter 40

We crossed the Via di San Gregorio and headed up the sidewalk to a gate just below Domus Augusta Palatino, the home of Augustus. The Colosseum towered behind us, an iconic signpost to Rome's rich past.

Alessandro waited at the entrance.

"Welcome to Palatine Hill and the Roman Forum. There are many elements to see and understand, but more to the point, there is a lot just to feel." This young man clearly loved his Roman history. He paused before continuing sheepishly. "I'm sorry, I'd ramble on about this wonderful place forever, but I expect you want to get down to business."

I felt like I cheated myself when I replied, "Sadly, we must, Alessandro. Perhaps we could return another time when matters aren't so pressing."

"I understand Nicholas. Follow me, I'll take you to the places you'll find most relevant to your task. Forgive me if I mention a couple of interesting titbits as we stroll along."

"Of course," I replied. "Thank you."

The night before, we had told our young expert of the place we expected Thomas Ireland to hold his press conference.

We wound our way around the side of Palatine Hill, once the most elite section of Rome, now a tumbled mess of ruins, each with a story dating back thousands of years.

"The first people of Rome lived on this hill," Alessandro began. "The palace over there was named after Augustus Caesar."

We wandered on for a few moments, the smell of history enveloping us. I walked over to the edge of a rock wall and peered over. I gazed down at an enormous field.

"What's that?" I asked our guide.

"Oh, nothing much," he responded, smiling. "That's the site of Circus Maximus."

"You mean…?" began Greatrex.

"Yes, it's where two hundred and fifty thousand people used to gather to watch the chariot races. Think Ben Hur."

The big fella whistled.

I stood in stunned silence. Suddenly weasels like Thomas Ireland faded into the footnotes of irrelevance.

Shaking ourselves free of our eyeglass to the past, Alessandro led us further around the hill toward the Forum. My mind wandered. The morning's disastrous encounter with Major Wyatt Davis had been my fault. Greatrex tried to persuade me that it had been a no hope situation from the beginning, but I knew I'd blown it. Now we found ourselves banished from the security arrangements that would protect the secretary and Cassandra Devlin-Waters.

In Davis's mind, Greatrex and I were two loose cannons. I supposed he was right. On the other hand, when the military hierarchy is pointing all the cannons in the wrong direction, a couple of loose ones may just hit the spot.

Either way, my outburst had made our primary role of

protecting the general's wife more difficult.

"We are now walking the Via Sacra," Alessandro informed us. "This was the main street of ancient Rome. The triumphant processions of victorious generals took this route as they paraded through Rome. They would march past the Colosseum and across the Roman Forum crossing under the Arch of Titus."

Suddenly Thomas Ireland's nod to history made a modicum of sense. He would probably think of his press conference in the Forum as a salute to the military victories of a time when one county's influence dominated the world.

As we stood there, besieged by the beginnings of our own civilization, my focus gradually shifted from tourist to potential sniper. We didn't know the exact location of the press conference. That was privileged information, and we were out of the loop, but we knew it would be somewhere close by. What I saw was alarming.

There were hundreds of nooks and crannies where a shooter might conceal themselves. There was also plenty of open space. Anyone perched high enough would have a clear shot of ninety percent of the area. To make things worse, the escapes routes for a sniper seemed limitless. So many corridors, pathways, and ruined buildings to hide their retreat.

To top it off, the secretary's security team would have extremely limited lines to extradite their man from a potential kill zone. There was no immediate vehicular access. The roads where SecDef might have his bullet-proof car waiting were some distance away. Foot was the only approach. There were walls and half-walls they could hide him behind, out of range, but you'd have to pick carefully.

What if there were two shooters?

"What's that big white building off in the distance, up there?" asked Greatrex, pointing to the west of us as he spoke. "The one that looks like, er…"

"A wedding cake?" Alessandro interjected.

"Exactly."

'That's the *Monumento Nazionale a Vittorio Emanuele 11*, the Victor Emmanuel 11 National Monument." He replied. "It's actually nicknamed the wedding cake because that's kind of how it looks from a distance, and you can see it from many locations around Rome. It's a three-level building designed to honor…."

I'd stopped listening, distracted by the large, white three-story building with more potential sniper hides than you could count.

"Are you all right Nicholas?" Alessandro asked.

"Sorry Alessandro, yes, I'm fine. I'm just not liking what I'm seeing."

"I told you that it would be difficult to secure this location."

"Yes, you did, but sadly, you were wrong, my friend. It's not difficult, it's impossible."

Greatrex nodded.

Alessandro continued. "I understand. Perhaps I should show you the Cryptoporticus?"

"Say again?" said Greatrex, his face wrinkled in concern.

"The Cryptoporticus, the tunnel where the emperor Caligula was murdered. As I mentioned to you last night, the leaders had many tunnels and rooms built under and around the hill, so they could travel in secret and safety."

The tunnels, crap.

Our young guide tried to placate me.

160

"Don't be too alarmed Nicholas, the underground passages can be difficult to locate. Many have not yet been found, never mind excavated."

I stared ahead up to the Monumento Nazionale a Vittorio Emanuele 11, then shifted my gaze to the buildings and ruins that surrounded us. There were too many possibilities to begin to compute them.

Greatrex and Alessandro peeled their eyes off me and surveyed the surroundings. I was certain Alessandro was imagining his beloved Roman history springing to life around him. Greatrex's vision would be closer to my own.

The United States Secretary of Defense was about to saunter into a sniper's paradise and there was a better than strong chance he'd never leave. Worse still, standing right next to him, equally exposed, would be our good friend, Cassandra Devlin-Waters, the general's wife.

"Jack, we've got to stop this," I said. "It simply can't happen."

Chapter 41

"Mr. Sharp, I have virtually no interest in having a conversation with you. I've only granted this audience because Cassandra Devlin-Waters insisted it would be a good idea. My head of security, Major Wyatt Davis, suggested that you and your friend are more of a threat than an asset in terms of my personal safety."

That was a lot to unpack in a single statement. *'Granted an audience.'* Who did this guy think he was, the King of freakin' England?

Secretary Thomas Ireland was around five foot six tall with dirty gray hair brushed back and styled carefully to appear thicker than it was. His pot belly protruded through a light blue suit that probably cost more than an average American's month's wage. His skin tone spoke of more holidays than work, and his voice wreaked of fake sincerity. A man of no substance pretending he had it all.

We perched on a lounge in Ireland's sprawling suite at the St. Regis. It was the morning after our visit to the Palatine Hill. The general's wife had worked hard to get us a meeting with SecDef shortly after he arrived on site. Two CID agents stood at the door, another behind the couch. They looked like dark suited cougars ready to pounce.

"I'm sorry you feel that way, Mr. Secretary, but it was important that we meet with you," I began.

"You have two minutes."

"Mr. Secretary, the operative that's pursuing you is an extremely capable killer. It's our belief," I nodded to Greatrex, who sat beside me, "that he will do whatever it takes to bring you down. He has the means, and the skill set."

"Powerful and influential people are frequently the target of individuals. I'm sure my security team can handle one more freak from the lunatic fringe."

"With respect sir, this is not an outlier. He's a highly trained, resourceful, and determined assassin."

"My team will sort him Sharp. Davis knows his job. When this killer of yours finds that I'm too difficult a target, he'll move onto somebody else. Davis told me he was certain of that."

"Davis is a fool." Greatrex's first words to the US Secretary of Defense drove straight to the point.

"I beg your pardon," Ireland responded.

My turn to be diplomatic.

"Mr. Secretary, this man is coming after you, nobody else."

"And why is that?"

"Do you recognize the name Lachlan Byrn?"

"Apart from the major mentioning it earlier, no."

"Are you sure, sir?" I pressed harder.

"Of course I am, man. Now if you're done, I believe I've acquiesced to Cassandra's wishes, so you can leave."

Ireland had shown no recognition of my own name as we'd entered the suite. I wondered if Byrn had this all wrong.

"Mr. Secretary, do you have any recollection of a clandestine mission several years ago that began with a bet between two allied branches of the military?"

"Don't be absurd."

"Well, Lachlan Byrn considers it to be true. Everyone else who was supposedly in the room at the time is dead. Two out of three of them died by Byrn's hand," I said.

Ireland paused before speaking, a first.

"And the third?"

I stole a few seconds to consider my response.

"I killed him."

The secretary pressed back into his seat before catching himself halfway. The three CID agents visibly tensed. The fellow behind Ireland's couch reached his hand under his coat.

"This meeting is over Sharp. Please leave before I have Davis remand you into custody. I don't care about your military record. You and it are irrelevant. Get out."

I shrugged my shoulders. This was pointless from the beginning. Still, we had to try.

Greatrex rolled his eyes. Ireland caught it. He balled his fists before standing up, incensed.

"Let me be explicit. I expect to see nothing of the two of you during this conference. You are to remain well clear of me and my people."

"I'm sorry, sir, we can't do that. General Devlin-Waters has requested we watch out for his wife's welfare and safety," I replied.

"My people will take care of that."

"Our understanding is you have tasked your team to protect you, not those around you," said Greatrex.

That did it.

"Get the hell out of here now." The man was boiling over, his face deep red with rage. "Do you think someone in my position wouldn't have the best protection? I command the entire US military, for God's sake. I will not cower to an empty threat from a delusional nutcase hallucinating about some deployment in Colombia years ago. You two wannabes can just leave."

Ireland nodded to the agents by the exit. One opened the door while the other approached us. He raised an arm, obviously intent on guiding Greatrex out. A glance from the big fella indicated that may be a bad idea.

We exited the room. Discretion.

Halfway down the corridor, Greatrex smiled without slowing his pace. It was a smug, crooked Cheshire grin.

"Did you get it?"

"Yeah, I got it."

Angry men make mistakes and Thomas Ireland just made a big one.

Neither Greatrex nor I had mentioned Colombia.

Chapter 42

We walked.

It was a pattern for Greatrex and me. If there were issues to consider, problems to solve, we'd get up and go. Escaping the St. Regis was the priority. Since the US Secretary of Defense had taken up residence that morning, the security had tripled. Apart from Ireland's own CID team, the Italian authorities had ensured that their own presence was effective and noted. The politics of protection. It was all getting a bit claustrophobic.

We had no particular destination in mind. Strolling southwest down Via Venti Settembre, we held only the vaguest notion of moving towards the water, the River Tiber. The streets were busy. It was late afternoon. The Romans were heading home from work, enjoying drinks with friends, strolling, or preparing for an evening out in one of the most vibrant cities in the world.

Amongst the chaos, the ambient mood was style and sophistication. The Romans knew how to dress. As Americans, we often seem to think our country is the center of the globe. When it comes to fashion, the Italians don't even regard us as a competitor.

We crossed the Piazza Venezia, where the drivers seemed focused on their intent to kill either us or each other.

"Coffee," I said to Greatrex.

"Read my thoughts."

We walked a while longer before heading down some smaller streets that ended in the Campo di Fiori. The small square opened up before us, an oasis in the mayhem.

A sea of cream canvas covered the middle of the piazza. Market stall holders bargained with tourists and locals alike to sell their produce. A smattering of ristorantes and cafes lined the sides of the square. We skirted the market and headed over to a ristorante on the far side. Our own temporary sanctuary.

"Well, how do you reckon we're doing?" I asked after we sat down at a table.

"Couldn't have done worse if we'd tried," he replied.

"You mean apart from making a lifelong enemy of SecDef's head of security, offending the great man himself and identifying at least two sites that are an assassin's dream, we couldn't have done anything worse?"

Greatrex did his head tilt thing and offered half a grin.

"I suppose we could have saved Lachlan Byrn the trouble and shot Thomas Ireland ourselves."

"Don't think it didn't cross my mind," I replied. "The man is a creep and I suspect a sadist. Makes you speculate how someone like that gets to that level of power."

"I stopped asking myself those sorts of questions years ago, about the time we left the Marines," replied the big fella.

Point taken.

"Yeah, you're right, there's not much point dwelling on it. For every stand-up guy like Jefferson Blake, there seem to be half a dozen blood suckers intent on clinging to power as though it was a birthright rather than a privilege. I still wonder how Blake tolerates him."

"Politics," said Greatrex. "Blake's smart enough to know that if he removes Ireland, a lot of skeletons may come jumping out of closets. The careers of a number of good people could be affected."

"Despite that, the general indicated that Blake's about taken all he's going to from his secretary of defense," I added.

I gazed across the piazza. More folk were arriving, settling into the bars and restaurants. The market was thriving. A city relaxing. The tourists stood out dressed in their practical travel clothes while displaying a mildly hesitant demeanor. The Roman natives oozed confidence and chic. This really was Izzy Galante's town.

The big fella changed subjects. "So, where to from here? We've established ourselves as outsiders, we'll get no help from the authorities, and we don't seem to have a clear plan of how to protect the general's wife."

"Always with the plan," I countered. Greatrex knew I preferred a strategic approach in any potentially dangerous situation just as much as he did, but it was amusing to annoy him.

I leaned forward in my chair as our coffees arrived. "The only plan I have is to be there, ready to react."

"It's not much," declared Greatrex.

"It's less than not much," I responded. "After the way Ireland spoke before throwing us out of his suite, I question to what extent we'll be allowed anywhere near the conference delegates and any of the events. If he actively blocks our presence, we're done."

"Not our best work so far," observed Greatrex.

"No, it's not."

My phone chirped to life. One of Izzy's songs.

"Izzy," I answered.

Five minutes later, Greatrex stared at me across the table as I hung up. A question expecting a response.

'Well, it's all in the timing really,' I announced.

"Pray continue."

"Izzy is insisting that I play a few songs with her at the opening gala tomorrow night. She won't take no for an answer," I told him.

"Nicholas Sharp, you have a tin ass," came his response.

"I suppose something had to go our way, despite our efforts to hinder every opportunity."

"Hmph."

"Well, we're in," I continued. "The thing that worries me is that by performing with Izzy, I may set her up as an ally of mine in Byrn's eyes. That makes me uncomfortable."

"You have a point," Greatrex replied, "but I suspect we have a more pressing issue."

"Go on."

"While you were on the phone, I spent a few enjoyable moments people watching. I'm seeing tourists, I'm seeing locals and I'm seeing those two men sitting at a table under an arch at the ristorante on the other side of the market stalls."

"Problem?"

"The problem is they're seeing us, at least focusing on us. When I look at them directly, their eyes leave our table."

"Interesting. Do you believe Ireland would have bothered to monitor us?" I asked.

"I wouldn't have thought we'd be important enough for that.

He's a busy man. He wouldn't care about two ex-marines with a crazy assassination theory."

"Unless?"

"Unless he knew it wasn't such a crazy theory."

"What about our new friend, Major Wyatt Davis?"

"Now that's equally likely," Greatrex responded. "He's a little man, and I reckon he could hold a pretty big grudge if he put his tiny mind to it. As enjoyable as it was, the show you made as we left his office might just have been enough to tip him over the edge."

"You can't say I'm not thorough," I said.

"Hmph."

I was trying to see the two men across the piazza. Greatrex was right. I caught them staring at us several times over a three-minute period. Although they weren't wearing the staple somber suits of CID operatives on duty, they somehow didn't fit in. Their casual jackets were too neat, the T-shirts underneath them too pressed, the dark glasses too clichéd. Of course, their standard military 'high and tight' haircuts didn't help them either.

My final glance saw both men standing up.

"They know we're onto them. They're either heading off or changing location," I said.

"Time to move?"

"Exactly. Let's go divide and conquer. It's an oldie but a goodie," I replied.

Greatrex nodded.

I continued. "If they leave the square together, we follow, but I don't think that's going to happen. If they leave the ristorante simultaneously, but then split up, we give them a few minutes to relocate."

"At that point we withdraw and separate."

"Exactly. You exit the square through the street beside us." I nodded toward the alleyway next to our restaurant. "I'll stroll the length of the piazza and head down the road at the north-western end."

"Done. Let's give them fifteen minutes to get comfortable," said Greatrex.

Almost immediately the men shifted to new locations. One stood at an outside bar, the other wandered through the market stalls.

Fifteen minutes later, we stood, readying ourselves to leave.

"Keep your cell handy, Jack. Just in case."

"You expect trouble?"

"Not in the slightest."

Turned out I was wrong.

Chapter 43

The two men fell into line, one following each of us. I planned to head down towards the river, find a recessed doorway to step into, and then come up behind my man. It had worked in hundreds of movies; I couldn't see why it wouldn't work for me.

It didn't.

The taller of the men clearly had me in his sights. He may have been a good CID agent, but he was not particularly talented at covert operations. Between catching him in the reflections of shop windows and the odd glance behind, I made him easily.

I led him on a journey down several narrow streets and a couple of even narrower laneways, searching for the right spot to make my move. Whereas the crowd at the piazza had been thickening when we left, there were now fewer people on the pavements and even fewer cars.

Turning right, a quiet street with several shops butted together presented the perfect location. Up ahead on the left stood a small fruit and vegetable shop. I saw no one enter or leave. All the fresh produce action was back at the Campo de Fiora. As I strolled past the shop's deeply recessed entrance, I stepped quickly into the shadows, concealing myself from the view of anyone rounding the corner behind me. James Bond would have been proud.

All I had to do was wait.

So, I waited… and waited.

No one appeared. Certainly not my overly neat shadow with the military hairdo.

After ten minutes, I stepped back out onto the street. I was sure he could have kept up with me. I retraced my steps back two streets before calling Greatrex.

"How's it going?" I asked.

"He's still on me. I'm working my way toward the St. Regis. When I find an opportunity, I'll have a little chat with him. How about you?"

"I've lost my guy. Didn't mean to," I replied. "Next time I'll let him go first."

"What's the plan?"

"I'll head in your direction. Call me when you're speaking with your guy. I might be in the neighborhood."

"Will do." Greatrex hung up.

It was perplexing, but no big deal. As darkness fell, the streetlights flicked on. I headed toward the piazza, planning to retrace our route back to the hotel.

All good plans should be adaptable.

I'd made it about halfway down a narrow laneway that ran between two wider streets when I felt the jab in my kidneys. I swung around, clenching and raising my fist in a move so lightning fast I was certain to surprise whoever stood behind me.

He moved faster.

173

The blow to the side of my head sent me to my knees. The fierce jolt in the middle of my back dropped me face first into the gutter.

The first thing that came to me was the efficiency of the attack. I'd totally underestimated the guy who'd been on my tail. Rookie mistake.

I rolled over, looking for an opportunity to land an early blow as the next kick connected with my ribs, then another. I curled up to protect myself. The man attacking me was tall, broad shouldered and clearly in good physical shape. But he wasn't the man who had followed me. I could see from his clothes that he was a new kid on the block... even with a balaclava over his head.

He kicked me again, in the stomach. Fighting an urge to vomit, I rolled over on my side toward him. Clearly, this individual enjoyed repeating himself. I waited until his foot was inches from my groin before grabbing his ankle and twisting. He faltered but didn't go down.

Following the direction of my twist with his torso, he flipped around and connected a backward kick hard into my arm. This guy knew some martial arts. It had been a clever and well-executed move. Sadly, the crushing pain made me release my grip on his ankle.

As my attacker found his footing, I leaped to my feet. In reality, it was a painful clamber rather than a leap, but I still got there pretty quickly.

We stood there, face to face, well, more like face to balaclava, but at least now I was in with a chance.

For a few seconds we danced the dance. Each waiting for the other to move. Acutely aware that my opponent had conducted himself as a professional, my nerves drew tight.

He'd caught me off-guard in a darkened alley, and waited until I'd checked in with my partner before attacking. Professionals plan. Amateurs get caught off-guard.

Several seconds into the dance, I tensed, preparing for my move. Expectant. I decided on a high kick to his chest, followed by a sharp elbow jab straight into his face. Two classic dishes from the menu. Normally, one combatant can sense when the other will pounce. There are tiny tells in the body language, the clenching of a fist, a heightened intake of breath. It was almost impossible not to give yourself away to someone who knew their craft. The idea was to attack faster than your opponent could defend.

As I surged forward, my opposition's lack of reaction momentarily surprised me. The heel of my boot was an inch from his chest when I realized why.

He didn't need to react, he just needed to execute his plan. In fact, their plan.

Pain exploded through my skull as some sort of heavy cosh slammed down onto the rear of my neck, sending me spiraling back down into the gutter.

With my face pressed hard against the cobblestone, the barrage of kicks sent waves of agony through every part of my body. Three times I tried to get up but was stopped by a boot at the center of my spine. In the end, I gave up trying.

Two men. That seemed like cheating.

Chapter 44

I hadn't lost consciousness, but I kind of wished I had. Somewhere in the recesses of my mind, I searched for the steamroller that ran over me. It hurt to breathe; it hurt to move. Stubborn to the end, I did both.

Using a nearby street sign as a prop, I climbed to my feet, slowly, hand over hand. Feat completed, I took inventory of the damage. From my knees to my neck, my body had turned into a living tribute to how much pain one human can sustain without passing out. My ankles and feet seemed fine and strangely enough, so did my head and face. This had been a targeted attack. They'd hit the parts of me that weren't on public display.

I took my first tender steps. Although functional, the walking wasn't any easier than the breathing. 'Would sir like his ribs bruised or broken?'

Once I'd gathered a small amount of momentum, and it really was small, I reached into my trouser pocket for my cell. I needed to call Greatrex. If the same fate hadn't befallen him, he would come and get me. If it had, we'd commiserate together.

The phone wasn't there. I searched the stone roadway until my eye caught a brief glint from the gutter. The phone. Smashed to uselessness. I gathered it up, hopeful the SIM card could be saved.

Twenty minutes later, I'd made it to a busier street where I could find a taxi. I'd copped a few strange looks along the way. Scruffy clothes and a hesitant gate will do that. The driver gave me the once over as he pulled to a stop. He didn't look happy.

"It's all right," I said. "I had a fall."

His foot looked destined for the gas pedal, so I added, "The St. Regis Hotel please," That appeared to placate him.

"Si signore."

It was an exercise in pain management as each weave and turn pressed me against the door. The taxi driver seemed oblivious to my condition. I suspected he just wanted me out of his cab.

The doorman at the hotel was just as reluctant when we arrived. He glanced toward the security guard on duty.

"It's okay," I said. "I'm a guest." After waving my pass card in their faces, the doorman stepped forward and did his job.

"Welcome back sir. Can I help you?" Unconvincing.

"Yes please. Have a bottle of Johnny Walker Black sent up to my room."

I gave him the room number before commencing my painful meander across to the lifts.

Ten minutes later I half lay, half sat on the comfortable sofa in my room, only it wasn't comfortable now. A knock sounded at the door.

"Come in," I yelled without moving. I hoped it was the scotch.

"Don't you ever answer your cell... crap... what the hell happened to you?" said Greatrex.

I lay there with my shirt undone. The bruising and swelling had already begun, clearly appearing obvious to him.

"I made some new friends," I responded.

"Are you all right? Well, I mean, obviously you're not, but do we need to get you to a hospital?"

"Not necessary. I'll work through it. To be honest, I'm glad a similar thing didn't happen to you."

"Just an easy stroll to the hotel. I lost my man a few minutes after speaking with you. I doubled back to find him, but he'd disappeared," said the big fella.

I told him my story. Identical beginning, different end. There was a second knock on the door.

"Ah, the medication. Would you mind getting that?"

A porter appeared through the doorway with the best-looking bottle of scotch I'd ever seen. Greatrex tipped him, poured us both a drink and sat down on the foot of the bed.

"I'll run you a bath," he offered.

"Let's work toward that," I replied. "First, we need to figure out what in God's name happened here."

"Any thoughts?"

"Process of elimination. I don't think either of my two playmates was Lachlan Byrn. As efficient and professional as they were, Byrn isn't a team player. He would have come at me alone, and without a balaclava over his head."

"What about the pair watching us?"

"That would be my initial instinct, but no. We'd already seen them. The disguises were pointless. Besides, they'd split up. One with you, one with me."

Greatrex responded. "My guy could have doubled back to

join his pal before they took you down."

"Possibly, but the clothes were different. I doubt they had time to stop and change."

Greatrex appeared lost in thought. I knew the look, the squinting forehead, eyes downturned in concentration. "So, the first two guys were the spotters. They had their eyes on us. When we split up, they stepped back and let the attack team do their thing."

I nodded. "And what a thing it was."

I drained my glass and offered it to Greatrex for a refill.

"They didn't want to kill you," he said, passing me back a filled glass.

"No, they were calculated and careful. No face or head damage. Nothing that would cripple me, no broken fingers."

That thought alone was unnerving. The idea of fingers being damaged was a nightmare for a musician... or a sniper.

I continued. "Let's take this as a warning. The question is...."

"A warning from who?" interrupted Greatrex.

"Who indeed?" I continued. "If not Byrn, then who else? Before you say anything, I know the most obvious answer. Wyatt Davis, or perhaps even Thomas Ireland, spring to mind."

"Is that really their style? What would drive them to such a clumsy action?"

"That's what bothers me as well. At a stretch, I could see a man like Wyatt Davis reacting hastily, maybe sending a couple of his CID goons out to convey a message. Remember the military hairdos?"

"Okay, yeah, that's a possibility," replied Greatrex. "But I can't figure the US Secretary of Defense getting involved in this shit, even if he is a complete twat. He has too much to lose."

"Agreed. The most likely candidate is Davis. But if he knew anything about you and me, he should have realized a street beating, as bad as it was, wouldn't stop us looking out for Cassandra Devlin-Waters."

A spasm of pain shot through my ribs, as though reacting to Greatrex's words. Time to drain the glass again.

We sat there, our thoughts racing.

A loud thud hammered on the door.

"Another scotch delivery?" asked Greatrex.

I glanced at the now third-empty bottle. "Not a bad idea, but no. I haven't ordered anything else."

Greatrex strode forward, opening the door with his usual gusto.

A second later I saw him tense, shoulders set back, chest up. His left hand still on the door handle, he tried to slam it shut. It wouldn't close. I heard raised voices. Then Greatrex stepped backward into the room.

Two men followed. One stood tall, wide, and extremely fit looking. He wore a neat parka jacket, and an equally neatly pressed T-shirt underneath. I immediately recognized him from the Campo de Fiora. His forward demeanor and legs apart stance suggested controlled aggression. His shorter offsider was uniformly threatening. He held a military issue Beretta M9 in his right hand. It pointed directly at Greatrex's gut.

He waved the big fella around to my end of the room. Greatrex reluctantly did as instructed. The larger man closed the door behind them before pulling out his own weapon and pointing it at me. Professionals, covering us both while they gauged the lie of the land.

"Mr. Sharp, Mr. Greatrex," he began. "We really do need to talk."

Chapter 45

"You have a problem, Mr. Sharp," said the taller of the men.

I nodded. Greatrex had slammed himself down next to me on the sofa in a manner suggesting he was totally pissed.

"And we have a quandary," stated the second man.

"That's a clever word for a thug with a gun," I responded.

Nicholas Sharp, witty to the end.

The tall man looked at the shorter, who gave a slight nod in return.

To my surprise, both men slipped the guns back into their jackets.

"Sorry about the weapons," began the shorter man. "We couldn't afford a scene out in the corridor. It seemed the only way we could ensure a quiet entry into your room."

"I'm Andrews, this in Djenovic," said the tall man.

They didn't offer to shake hands, nor did we offer them a drink. An unresolved relationship.

"You clearly have a purpose for being here," said Greatrex.

"May we sit down?" asked Andrews.

I pointed to the remaining vacant lounge chair and the bed. Andrews sat on the bed, Djenovic on the chair. They both perched bolt upright, as though they had a rod up their backs. Military through and through.

"We owe you an explanation," began Djenovic.

I nodded.

"We're both CID," said Andrews. "We're part of the Secretary of Defense's security team."

"Well, that comes as a real surprise," said Greatrex. He did sarcasm well.

"We're what you might call members of the outer circle," added Djenovic.

"Outer circle?" I queried.

Djenovic continued. "SecDef has a regular security team who cover him at the Pentagon and around DC. When he travels, more people are brought in, usually seconded from other duties. We're part of that extra team."

"Yet you're close enough to Thomas Ireland to follow us through the streets of Rome and then arrange to have me beaten to a pulp," I observed, my anger simmering. Future of relationship in doubt.

Andrews gave Djenovic a sideways glance. Another nod.

"We didn't do that," he said.

"Don't be ridiculous, man. We saw you, both of you, at the Campo de Fiori," I responded.

"Yes, of course we were there, and it was no coincidence because we'd followed you every step of the way. What Andrews means is that we didn't arrange the attack on you," said Djenovic.

"That was a different operation of which we were unaware," added Andrews.

The tag-team answers these two supplied were smooth, almost convincing. The trouble was my body, wracked with pain, swelling and bruising told a different story.

"So, you're saying Ireland sent you to follow us, and completely separately sent another team to deal with me? It doesn't make any sense," I said.

"You're absolutely correct," replied Djenovic, "It makes no sense at all because it didn't happen that way."

"But..."

"Mr. Sharp, if you'd just let us finish. We weren't sent by Thomas Ireland to keep eyes on you. We decided to do it ourselves. We'd been part of the advance security team that arrived in Rome several days ago. Accordingly, we were off duty this afternoon. We followed you on our own time."

If what Djenovic said was true, I remained at a loss.

"Why in God's name would you do that?" asked Greatrex. "What interest could we possibly be for you?"

"Now the story becomes somewhat more complex," declared Andrews. "But first I need to ask, what is your role here? Are you another layer of protection for the secretary?"

I scratched my chin, not really knowing how to respond.

"I suppose, in a secondary sense, yes. Our primary aim is to protect Cassandra Devlin-Waters. She is our friend. Her husband is a former Marine general and we're here at his behest. He'd be here himself if Lachlan Byrn hadn't shot him."

Andrews raised a hand.

"Don't bother asking," I said. "It's complicated. Moving on, the point here is Cassandra's wellbeing, and it's our job to ensure it. To do that, it appears we also need to watch out for Thomas Ireland. Although it sticks in our craw, we are still patriots, and he is still the US Secretary of Defense. We'll do whatever it takes."

"Now, as Jack asked, what interest do you have in us?"

Andrews and Djenovic glanced at each other. Silent communication. They formed quite a team. It took one to know one.

"All right, we are happy to share appropriate information with you. In fact, that's why we're here. But first we must request complete confidentiality with regard to what you will hear."

I didn't like making a promise I couldn't keep. Greatrex would feel the same way. On the other hand, we both loved a good story.

"As long as nobody's life or wellbeing is under immediate threat by what you tell us, you have my word," I replied.

Greatrex nodded.

"Fair enough," replied Djenovic. "I would caution you, when we're done, you may realize more lives are under threat than you had imagined, but you can be the judge of that."

I was blessed with a pretty good imagination, and an even greater curiosity.

"Please, go on," I instructed.

"We were informed we'd be part of the secretary's broader security team about a month ago," Andrews began. "To be honest, we weren't thrilled about it."

"Why?" I asked.

Djenovic responded. "There had been rumors circulating for years amongst the service. Thomas Ireland is difficult to work for. He has a temper, he's erratic in his decision making, and he makes demands that frequently transcend the professional level."

"How so?" asked Greatrex.

"Those who are part of his inner circle are regularly tasked with following, gathering information on, and even wiretapping persons of interest to the secretary," replied Andrews.

"Surely that's not unexpected. Ireland may be an asshole, but he *is* the Secretary of Defense. Our country has many enemies. A component of his job description is to protect us against them. To do that well, he needs intel," I said.

"Absolutely Mr. Sharp, you are correct," replied Djenovic. "Except the majority of people that Ireland is gathering information on are on our side."

"And all too often, the intel collected is of a personal rather than professional nature," added Andrews.

"Are you telling us Ireland is running some sort of J. Edgar Hoover secret files scenario?" I asked.

"Worse," said Djenovic. "He uses the information in the files to get the decisions he wants when he wants them. A diplomat would call it influence. We suspect it's more in the nature of blackmail."

"Why didn't anyone act on this?" asked Greatrex. "If you know about it, so must others."

"Why did nobody stop Hoover?" asked Andrews.

Touché, the power of the files.

"We haven't even begun to discuss his personal proclivities," added Djenovic.

"Do we want to know?" I asked.

"Girls, young girls, barely legal age, often interns. The trouble is they don't always come out of the relationship physically unharmed. I've got to say, to be fair, our suggestion is based on rumor, we have no firm proof. If we did, we would certainly act."

The pain in my body dimmed against the uneasiness in my gut as we found out more about this man. The existence of the files wasn't overly surprising. The general had alluded to it, but hell, this wasn't the nineteen-sixties.

"Okay," I said. "You've provided the background. What's going on now? What prompted your bringing us into this?"

Djenovic leaned forward, his hushed tone almost conspiring.

"We think there's more occurring behind the scenes than people think. The inner circle has been very quiet, verging on obtuse in their response to regular questions relating to possible security threats."

"It's as though they're being dismissive with one hand and over-reaching with the other," added Andrews. "We'd been told that the threat posed by this assassin, Lachlan Bryn, is inconsequential. They described him as just another unhinged lunatic. Yet, the manpower within the inner circle has been doubled. The secretary is never alone unless…"

"He's with a young victim," I finished.

Next to me, Greatrex's forearms tensed, his fists tightening in balls. He didn't like predators who picked on kids.

"We think there is more to the threat from this man Byrn, but we don't know what or why." said Djenovic.

"We can come back to that later," I responded.

Djenovic nodded before continuing. "Ireland ordered his people to focus the security arrangements on himself rather than others in his entourage. It seemed an unusual move. It's certainly not standard protocol. Then we overheard one of his team talking about liaising with the security teams of the other tech company CEOs here at the conference."

"But that's to be expected. Wouldn't it be best practice to have all the security teams working together?" asked Greatrex.

"To an extent, yes," replied Andrews. "The matter of contention is that Ireland's men aren't just liaising with the other teams, they appear to be commanding them. It's as though Thomas Ireland is in charge of this whole tech empire."

"Or wants to be," I commented.

Both Andrews and Djenovic raised their eyebrows, almost comically in unison.

"There's our problem, Mr. Sharp," declared Djenovic. "We hear that President Blake is about to dispense with Thomas Ireland's services. We're told he's had enough of Ireland obsessing with his personal fiefdom. Clearly SecDef doesn't have anything on the president to influence him otherwise."

Andrews took over the narrative. "Given that Ireland is a man whose power needs are greater than most, we believe he has formed a cabal of some sort with the heads of major military technology companies around the world. At least those with a flexible moral compass."

"In other words, most of them," said Greatrex.

"So, consider a situation where a man like Ireland is in bed with all that military capability while wielding the power and influence emanating from his secret stash of personal dossiers." Andrew's brow wrinkled as he spoke. He appeared worried by his own words.

"It's a frightening thought," said Djenovic. "The possibility of military might separating from the control of sovereign states could change the power structures of the world. A man like Ireland in control of such a force without the political restraints of office is unimaginable."

"Ireland isn't positioning himself for a job in the private sector. He's securing a takeover," I said.

"If what we believe is correct, then that's the scenario we're dealing with," said Andrews. "Our problem is the two of us are just low-level flunkies within the system. There are no guarantees that anyone we reported this to wouldn't be part of the plan."

"When we learned of you being involved, at least on the fringes of this conference, and the fact your potential presence irritated both Ireland and Davis so much… we did a bit of our own digging around," said Djenovic. "My regular role is running security for our own intelligence division. It wasn't hard to find things out."

"What sort of things?" I asked, subconsciously wriggling in my chair. Now my discomfort wasn't only physical.

"There is more to the two of you than meets the eye," said Andrews. "It would appear that your own retirement from the military wasn't as complete as you'd hoped, Mr. Sharp. Although we also understand you've thrown yourself into your new life as a professional musician and have actually done quite well, with Mr. Greatrex's support along the way."

Andrews paused, probably for effect. Maybe looking for a reaction. We gave him nothing.

Djenovic chipped in. "My people tell me there have been incidents, unfortunate incidents, Iraq, the Isle of Wight, Paris, Venice, Sudan, even back in LA. Do we need to say more?"

Damn.

He continued. "Suffice to say, those situations were apparently resolved positively, in no small part because of your intervention. Your actions have brought you a modest amount of notoriety in some circles, and from what we hear, a certain measure of influence at some very high levels. Perhaps even President Blake? Certainly, you're well connected with former general Colin Devlin-Waters, a man with a reputation not to be messed with."

You virtually admitted that yourselves when you spoke of your primary mission here to be to look out for his wife," added Djenovic.

Damn again. I remained silent.

"So, to get to the point," said Andrews. "How much information do you have on Thomas Ireland, and how well do you know him? Because you sure have pissed him off."

I inhaled deeply, catching a second to look them both over. There was an element of trust in our relationship now. I hoped it wasn't misplaced. If what they were saying stacked up, these guys were taking a risk even coming here talking to us. Either the cards went on the table now or stayed tight on our chests, permanently. I gave Greatrex a furtive glance. He nodded.

"Okay," I began. "I'd never met Thomas Ireland until today, but we have a shared history."

I could see I had their attention. I told them about the young Marine in deep trouble in the Colombian jungle many years earlier. No one interrupted.

When I'd finished Andrews said, "That's an incredible story Sharp. It's amazing at least one of you made it out alive, but what does it have to do with Ireland?"

I spoke about the bet.

"That's even more incredible. Are you sure your intel is accurate?" asked Djenovic.

"Absolutely, one hundred percent," I replied.

"You've had confirmation from a secondary source?"

"Yes."

"Who?"

"Thomas Ireland," I responded. I told them about the morning's meeting with SecDef.

"Arrogant fool," said Andrews.

"He made an error," I retorted, "but I get the impression he doesn't make many."

Both men nodded.

"Now, about this threat, the assassin, Byrn? Is Ireland exposed there?

"That's probably a bit of an understatement," I said. "The thing is, the other operator in the Colombian jungle didn't die. He survived his injuries under the watchful eye of Chinese intelligence. For two years."

"Shit," said Andrews. "You're not saying....?"

"Yup, Lachlan Byrn was my partner in Colombia."

"Is he as deadly as we suspect?" asked Djenovic.

"Whatever you're expecting, double it. If Byrn wants Ireland dead, the man has little chance of survival," I said.

In the ensuing silence, I considered what these men had said. They seemed genuine, and I had no reason to doubt them. It appeared our US Secretary of Defense was an absolute dirt bag.

I actually wondered if Lachlan Byrn might be the hero in all this.

Again... damn.

Chapter 46

The room buzzed with conversation, voices slightly raised over the quiet hum of background music. The musicians knew this event wasn't about them, at least not until Izzy Galante walked onto the stage later in the evening.

Greatrex and I stood in one corner of the massive St Regis, Ritz Ballroom. Nearly three hundred others spread across the space, filling in the gaps between the crisp white linen and ornate decorations perched on each table. Formal attire, intense discussion and forced laughter. People glanced continuously over others' shoulders, involved in one interaction while eyeing off the next. The search for influence. A game of human chess that would make Garry Kasparov proud. I imagined the characters in the frescoes on the walls laughing at a sight they'd seen a thousand times before.

Thomas Ireland held court amongst a group of guests. Judging from their attire, cash flow wasn't one of their immediate problems. Their static demeanor and concentrated expressions suggested that other, more pressing issues weighed on their minds.

So far, SecDef hadn't noticed our presence, but Wyatt

Davis, lingering near the secretary, had provided us with the filthiest look possible. If it wasn't for Cassandra Devlin-Waters' interference, we wouldn't have been allowed into the gala at all.

I glanced toward the band. It was a small combo: piano, guitar, keys, bass, and drums. They were youthful, and each seemed part mesmerized and part disdainful to be here. A new generation serving an old guard that their contemporaries would eventually replace. Did these young musicians realize how dangerous this old guard could really be?

The band had just finished a playful instrumental version of 'Chain of Fools' when a gong quietly rang behind them and the wait team began guiding guests to their tables. Momentarily, I wondered if the choice of song was an accident or a statement.

They directed the big fella and me to a table in the opposite corner of the ballroom. The St Regis version of being positioned next to the kitchen door. We remained humble pawns in this chess game.

Cassandra sat beside Ireland, just as her role demanded. Earlier in the day, the general's wife provided us with background on the key figures at the conference. Greatrex and I now spent our time trying to identify each of them.

The food, although tasty, did little to quell the boredom as we surveyed the unfolding masquerade.

Eventually, a tall, slender man with an over manicured mustache walked to the podium. He introduced himself as Italy's minister of something or other before welcoming the conference's most important player, the United States Secretary of Defense, Mr. Thomas Ireland. The applause echoed around the room, our fellow pawns saluting their king.

193

Greatrex slouched despondently. I fought the same urge. It's extremely difficult to get the measure of a leader through their public speeches. The words are contrived so carefully to cause minimum offence while selling an image of humble service and grandiose achievement. Jefferson Blake was an exception to that rule. Thomas Ireland was not.

After one too many references about the path to world peace and nations fighting side by side against adversity, I'd had enough. I stood up, pushed back my chair, and headed toward the nearest exit. Fresh air awaited. Apart from the wait staff, Ireland and I were the only two people standing. Our eyes met across the sea of his adoring disciples. He frowned. I smiled smugly before turning around to march out of the place.

Nicholas Sharp, spiteful brat.

I hadn't made it ten paces towards the hotel's foyer before I almost bumped straight into Izzy.

"Nicholas, I hope you're not running out on me. I'm on stage after the secretary's speech and you promised to join me."

I smiled down at her. She looked gorgeous. Ready to captivate the crowd.

"There's no way I'm abandoning you, Izzy. How long until you're on?"

"About twenty minutes," she replied.

"I'll be there, ready for you to call me up."

Izzy reached up and gave me a peck on the cheek.

"Ciao." She smiled before walking away.

I made it to the foyer before spotting another young lady. She stood at the hotel's check-in counter. I could hear the agitation in her voice across the cavernous space. The accent was American, and she was pleading with the concierge.

"There must be a flight out tonight. Please check again. Please."

"I've checked twice signorina. I'm sorry, there is nothing."

I strode up to the desk to see the young woman evidently distressed. Tears trickled down her cheeks.

"Can I be of any help?" I asked.

The girl swung to face me. I realized she couldn't be over twenty. She had long dark hair and a shawl loosely wrapped around her shoulders.

"No thank you, not unless you're a pilot or own an airline," she said.

"Neither of those, I'm afraid. You seem upset, and I hate to see a fellow countryman in distress."

"Well, I'm trying to check out of the hotel and find a flight home," she replied.

"DC?" I asked.

"No, my real home, Clear Creek, Indiana."

"But you're here as part of the conference, I presume. Do you work in DC?"

"I did until tonight. I…"

She stopped short.

"I've said too much. Thanks for your offer of help, anyway." She tried to smile. It didn't work.

"Who do you work for? Perhaps we can contact them and enlist some help." I suggested.

"No… no," a little too insistent.

Before I could reply, footsteps boomed loudly on the hard tiled floor. They stopped right behind me.

"Emma, I'm glad I caught you."

I swung around. The giant of a man had wide shoulders,

close cropped hair and stood as straight as a pole. He may as well have worn a sign that said military security.

"I need you to come with me," he continued. "People are worried."

Emma's skin had developed a ghostly pallor. The girl drew back her shoulders and looked directly into the man's eyes. Defiant.

"Careers and reputations are the only things those people worry about. And you can tell the secretary that from me."

I turned to her.

"You work for Thomas Ireland?" I asked.

"Yes," she responded. "At least I did." As she spoke, her hand shot up, pointing a finger directly in the man's face. "I'm not going back."

As her arm had risen, her shawl fell away. There was a mark above her right elbow. A burn mark. It could easily have been caused by a cigarette butt. Emma noticed me noticing it and quickly covered herself up. The man noticed my reaction as well. He stepped forward and reached for the girl's wrist.

"Come on, we need to go now."

He grabbed her wrist firmly. She struggled to break free, unsuccessfully.

"No... stop," she cried.

He didn't.

"The young lady said no," I said, inserting myself between them.

"Look buddy, just back off. This is not your business, and you don't want to cross paths with my boss." The man tried to elbow past me.

"Let her go, and I'm not saying it again."

In a move he'd probably used before, the guy feigned

backing off before pivoting and lunging directly towards me with his left shoulder. I stepped sideways, brushed the girl out of the way, grabbed the man by the neck, and slammed his forehead against the marble counter.

The concierge retreated in surprise, immediately reaching for the phone. The girl's antagonist staggered back, swaying unsteadily. I swept my right foot under his, and he fell backwards to the ground. I looked down at him. A trail of blood seeped from his nose and mouth.

"Too late," I said. "Your boss and I don't really hit it off, anyway."

I turned.

"Let's go for a walk, Emma. If I didn't need some fresh air before, I certainly need it now."

She nodded, eyes wide in shock. She did, however, allow me to escort her through the lobby and out through the hotel's front door.

Chapter 47

"Thank you, Mr....."

"Sharp, Nicholas Sharp," I replied.

"I'm Emma Moore."

We walked down the Via Vittorio Emanuele Orlando toward the Piazza della Repubblica. For now, she seemed safer out in the public eye.

"Can you tell me what happened?"

Emma stared at the sidewalk ahead. We'd strolled in silence for a few minutes before she answered.

"I shouldn't really be saying anything, but I suppose my career as a civil servant is over now, anyway. It all seems so wrong. Why should I be subjected to such behavior just because I'm female?"

She stopped in her tracks before turning to look up at me.

"No offence meant," she continued. "But why should I need a man to save me?"

"None taken," I replied. "And by the way, I didn't save you. I simply helped you extricate yourself. I suspect that if there is any saving going on here, it will be you saving yourself."

For the first time in our brief encounter, Emma Moore

smiled.

"Thank you."

One more smile before continuing her story.

"I suppose this is really one cliché bouncing into another, but it's all, sadly, true. Let's keep walking while we chat. It's easier that way."

We resumed our stroll toward the piazza.

"I applied for an internship at the Department of Defense. In fact, I applied to just about every government department in Washington. Defense was the only one that gave me a look in. Anyway, I went for the interview, got the job, and started work about six months ago. It was exciting, and I thought it was a great opportunity."

"You don't think that now?" I interjected.

"Most certainly not. I'd been there about a month, and figured things had been going pretty well, when my supervisor called me into his office. He said the secretary is interested in the new interns and sees them as a window to the future. He also stated that Thomas Ireland had requested to see me. Of course, I was gob smacked and immediately agreed. In my eagerness, I hadn't even noticed the sarcastic tone with which my supervisor referred to the secretary. That hit me later. It surprised me when my boss said that I was under no obligation to meet with Ireland. I thought he was crazy, maybe even jealous. I paid no heed to his words."

"But he wasn't jealous, was he?" I asked.

"No, he was trying to warn me, and I didn't listen."

Emma's shoulders seemed to sag, and a little life drained from her eyes. I sensed her frustration.

"Emma, I have a fair idea where this is going, and it is not your fault. If Thomas Ireland is a predator, he should be held accountable. You did nothing wrong."

Emma stopped walking again. By now we stood in front of the Fontana delle Naiadi, in the center of the piazza. The sound of the falling water was soothing, meditative.

"In my head I know that, but my heart hasn't caught up. Everything you have presumed is true. I ended up working directly for the SecDef. Despite him being married, I allowed a relationship to develop. In a matter of two months, it descended from thrilling and what I mistook for love, into a tawdry affair. Then it got worse, the violence started. Only a bit at a time, and never enough to cause me permanent harm. Not physically, anyway. A slap here, a scratch there."

Emma gazed at the running water. Therapy in action.

"Earlier tonight, we hit a new low. The cigarette burns. That was the pivotal moment for me. I saw what he was and what I'd become."

A tear slowly tracked its way down Emma's right cheek. This girl exuded a sense of intelligent strength, even in her most vulnerable moments. I chose my words carefully.

"Emma, the only thing you became was a victim. By definition, for a victim to exist, there needs to be a perpetrator. In this case, the perpetrator is an exceedingly powerful man. You have shown incredible will and strength just to be standing here."

"You are kind Nicholas, but unfortunately, I now find myself in a situation. I need to go home. Suddenly my career seems meaningless."

"Emma, I'm no therapist, but I can tell you this. You shouldn't have to walk away from your career. You should not be the one in pain here. There are people well qualified to help you work this through emotionally, and whether they are in Washington or back home in Indiana, I hope you will allow them to support you."

It became my turn to pause as I considered what to say next. I decided what I shouldn't say and then proceeded to say it.

"I may be able to help with regard to who walks away from their career here."

Emma looked at me, head tilted to one side, confused.

"I don't know who you are, Nicholas, but taking on Thomas Ireland would be a very dangerous thing to do. Perhaps it's better just to let it go. I'm going to find somewhere to stay and then call the hotel for my things. That's a first step."

The rage seeped through my body like a fever. Whatever it took, I knew I'd channel the anger to good use, but not right now.

"Emma, I've got to go back to the St. Regis. I've made a promise to someone that I must keep. In the meantime, there is a lady. She's American, and quite high in the conference pecking order. I'll ask her to spend some time with you. After that, I've got another lady friend you can stay with."

"You don't need to…"

"Emma, I do need to, and not only for you. There will be others that follow you into that office."

"Won't you be in trouble after what happened at the hotel reception, the security guard you slammed against the counter?"

"If he's part of Ireland's team, he's already no friend of mine. Judging from the speed with which the concierge reached for the phone, I suspect I may have some explaining to do when we get back. My guess is that once I've clarified things a little more, the authorities will understand about the angry American security guard who tripped over and banged his head."

As we retraced our steps toward the hotel, I called Cassandra Devlin-Waters on my new phone. By the time we'd reached the front entrance, Cassandra was standing on the steps.

"Emma, I presume," she said in the warmest tone she could muster. "Do you feel you could come with me?"

"If my knight in shining armor here says that you're okay, I'll give it a go. Besides, I don't have too many choices."

I nodded. Cassandra took Emma's hand and led her away. Before passing through the entranceway, the general's wife turned to me.

"I know you Nicholas Sharp, and I suspect I know what you're thinking. Just for a single moment can you calm your innate hot headedness and think this through before you take on one of the most powerful men in the world."

She didn't flinch, like a stern mother.

"Now," she continued. "Your friend Izzy is stalling for time. Can you go and play the piano for a bit, try getting some heat out of your system?"

Cassandra allowed herself a brief grin before turning her back and guiding Emma through the door.

"Ladies and gentlemen, I would like to present my very good friend from the United States. Please welcome to the stage Nicholas Sharp on piano."

Izzy grinned as she spoke. She had already won the audience over with her charm and talent.

I stepped up onto the stage and sat behind the large, black grand piano and began to play. The instrument became a panacea for my anger. As the prearranged arpeggio under my fingers turned into one of Izzy's best-known tunes, I looked up.

The crowd was smiling, all except one.

Thomas Ireland glared at me across the room, his eyes emanating a threatening, glowing, almost manic hatred. It was like he was looking at me for the first time.

Perhaps I was seeing him for the first time as well, or at least seeing the man he really was.

Or more to the point, the man he wasn't.

Chapter 48

"So, you're telling me that your plan is to protect a man you'd like to kill, from another man you'd like to kill, all for the sake of freedom and democracy?"

Greatrex's words sounded unconvincing. The trouble was, they were essentially my words.

We sat in my room, the show with Izzy done and a bottle of scotch on the bar half-done. Emma Moore had gone off to stay with Izzy. The singer didn't hesitate to take her in. Emma seemed mildly besotted having a famous pop star as her chaperone. I figured as two sharp wits, they'd get on pretty well together until Emma was able to make longer-term plans.

"When you put it like that, it sounds a tad nonsensical, but I'm running out of options here," I replied. "We need to secure Ireland in order to protect Cassandra. Ireland needs to be dealt with and I'd dearly love to be the man to deal with him, but allowing a figure with a pivotal role in the elected United States government to be executed just isn't on the table."

"Have you tried talking to Cassandra again? Is there a chance that she would leave the conference and return to DC?"

"I've tried and failed. She's as stubborn as her husband."

"If I'm reading this correctly Nicholas, even if she returned to the States, you'd still want to stay and protect Ireland from Lachlan Byrn?"

Greatrex and I were rarely on different channels, but he seemed to have difficulty seeing my point of view.

"I know this sounds wrong, but we are still Americans. Besides, my own situation with Byrn remains unresolved," I said.

"Funny word, resolved," said Greatrex. "It could mean anything from a handshake to a corpse floating in the Tiber. How do you want this to go?"

"The first seems implausible, and the second untenable. The problem is, I can't see any solution in between."

"And what about Ireland? Surely, we won't let a predator like that escape to pursue another victim?"

Greatrex knew me well enough to know the answer to that question.

"No, you're right. Something's got to be done. Every fiber of my being yearns to tear that man apart, but I'm following Cassandra's advice and trying to step back a little before I do something stupid. Maybe the general has some ideas."

Greatrex leaned into his chair, taking a swig of the scotch glass in his hand.

"You're probably right. The general does subterfuge extremely well." The big fella paused mid-sentence, as though an idea had just occurred to him. "Maybe there is another way."

"Which is?"

"We simply do our job badly, focus on protecting the general's wife and leave Ireland to the gods."

That needed to be said out loud, eventually. The concept had been tormenting my brain all evening.

"We could," I agreed, "and don't think that's an option I haven't considered. But there are a couple of issues."

"Which are?"

"First, would either of us be comfortable allowing a trained killer anywhere near Cassandra Devlin-Waters? One slight miss-aim, or worse, if Byrn used an explosive device. Remember, Ireland is virtually commanding her to be at his side."

"That's not a post event conversation I'd enjoy having with the general," he said.

I continued. "Second, it's back to the previously mentioned US Government leader thing. Could we live with those consequences, the fact we allowed the Secretary of Defense to be assassinated?"

"I can't give you a definite answer on that, but I sure as hell wouldn't mind giving it a try. Either way, you had me with the risk to Cassandra."

"So, we do nothing but attempt to cover everyone's butts," I said.

"I'm thinking of the way Byrn feels about you, and Ireland's men feel about both of us. We should put a little effort into covering our own butts as well."

"Touché."

The night dragged on. I gave up on sleep at around 4am. Coming across young Emma seeded an anger in me that wouldn't resolve with rational thought. I may have been able to consign my own beef with Ireland to the back of my mind. His repulsive bet years earlier had affected my life, and destroyed Lachlan Byrn's, but we were big boys. Emma Moore was little more than a child. The man must be stopped.

The easy answer was to walk away and let Byrn do his worst. Despite my words to Greatrex, and my bid for the higher moral ground, stepping back was still an option.

But what about Byrn? He was one of the most dangerous killers I'd crossed paths with. I shuddered at the idea that at one point we'd walked down the same road. Back then, we'd been following orders, working for our respective countries, or so we were told. What had turned him? Other POWs have survived imprisonment and torture and returned to productive and compassionate lives. Senator John McCain was a prime example.

No, with Byrn, things were different. His years in Chinese captivity had flicked a switch somewhere inside him. Of course, the switch had to be there to be flicked. That was the distinction. Even in our time in the jungle together, I'd sensed he had to force himself to follow rules, it took effort for him to be a conventional warrior.

By the time the sun rose, my thinking had drifted into a muddy void. I was having trouble telling the difference between Byrn's sense of morality and my own. I'd left the Marines because I refused to kill for others. No one would give me orders again. I'd had my reasons, but then again, so did Lachlan Byrn. Good reasons. But I didn't become a professional assassin, Byrn did. I'd made a new start, following my mother's bloodline into the creative industries. Was it possible any two choices of vocation could be more different? Professional musician and paid killer.

My last thoughts before fatigue subdued me were of a clifftop on the Isle of Wight, a ghostly island near Venice, a presidential dinner gone horribly wrong. Finally, there was one wild shot, safely bringing down an aircraft that contained people I cared about. The common denominator, me... and deadly force.

Maybe there *was* no distinction between Byrn and me.

Maybe...

Chapter 49

We all make mistakes.

The next morning, as the piercing sun assaulted my eyes on the steps of the St. Regis, I realized Greatrex and I had miscalculated our strategy. We shouldn't have gone for the second half of the bottle of scotch the night before. My head hurt.

The conference delegates were due to pose in front of the Fountain of Moses. By the time we hit the street, most of the VIPs were there. They had cordoned off part of the Via Vittorio Emanuele Orlando with ropes, so the official photographer would have some room to take his shot.

To take his shot...

We headed towards the ropes, watching everyone jostling for position. There was probably enough money invested in the expensive suits, watches, and jewelry to feed a small nation for a month. SecDef hadn't arrived yet, but his security team stood posted along the route and on each corner. Cassandra was scheduled to arrive with him.

This was one of the two locations Greatrex and I had

identified as likely kill zones. Byrn's murderous task was easily achievable here. Each of the tall buildings lining the street provided a score of hides for an assassin. We couldn't search them all, so we didn't search any. Instead, we focused on scanning selected windows that afforded a direct line of sight to the fountain within a shooter's perimeter.

It didn't help that Lachlan Byrn could fire a weapon at great accuracy further than almost any marksman on earth.

I headed north and Greatrex south. There was nothing we could do to stop the attack if a gun appeared out of one of the windows. We may, however, have time to warn Ireland... and Cassandra.

I knew I wasn't imaging it when each of Ireland's security team gave me a glaring look as I passed. This went way beyond petty professional rivalry, yet clearly they'd been told to back off.

Interesting.

There was a flurry of activity at the Hotel entrance. Two burley men in dark coats stepped onto the sidewalk first. They each spoke into a communication device attached to their shirt cuffs, Secret Service style. The secretary of defense was an important man and America had many enemies.

It occurred to me that perhaps Thomas Ireland had more than his predecessors.

Suddenly SecDef was there, striding up towards the fountain. Two of his security detail walked ahead of him, two behind. Wyatt Davis was two steps behind them. His eyes scanned the building facades, searching for threats. I glanced down the street. Almost all his agents did the same.

"Nothing?" I said into my cell. A futile question, Greatrex would have alerted me to anything out of the norm.

"Nada," came the brief response.

"I'm moving south. I want to be nearer to Cassandra," I said.

"Roger that."

We seemed superfluous to needs, but the big fella and I had promised the general.

Cassandra had already reached the fountain. Ireland's men were directing her where to stand, so she'd be beside him. Her level of tolerance for such a despicable man was astounding.

Although half the width of the street had been closed off, cars and vans now banked up on the opposite side of the road. Between people gawking and the sheer amount of vehicles, the traffic was gridlocked.

I scanned each set of windows methodically, before dismissing them in turn. If Lachlan Byrn made his hit here, we'd be lucky to spot him. I kept searching for an open window, a shadow lurking, a glint of steel, and most of all, a long barrel protruding out of any opening.

Occasionally, I cast my eyes down the busy street. After working so closely with Byrn in a past life, I reckoned I had a shot at recognizing his body language. I got nothing.

Ireland had almost reached the fountain. His smile broadened as he stretched out a hand to connect with other visiting VIPs. His carefully coiffured hair didn't budge in the wind.

The wind. At least that worked in our favor. Byrn would have to account for quite a stiff breeze when making his shot. Yet the wind factor was well within his limits.

Back to the windows.

Suddenly.

"Jack, three buildings from the north-west corner. There's a window open, correction, a door and a window. It's difficult to tell, but I think I've got a figure lurking in the shadows behind. I'm moving in tighter to Cassandra. I don't give a fuck what Ireland's people say. I intend to be within reach."

A pace off the roped off area, one of Ireland's cloned security people stepped in front of me.

"Nobody goes any closer, especially you," he said.

"Go to hell," I replied before stepping around him.

Suddenly, my progress ceased. A tug on my belt yanked me backwards. I swiveled to be greeted by the bruised features of Emma Moore's friend from the hotel reception desk.

"Don't even think about it Sharp. I hate to see you brought down here on a public street when I'm planning to take care of you in private later."

Nice guy, just caring about my wellbeing.

I turned back to get Cassandra's attentions. She was talking to a man next to her on the steps. Distracted.

Pivoting towards my new nemesis, I glared over his shoulder, up at the open window. The figure I'd noticed earlier seemed to move silently in the background.

"Maybe your team should check that apartment out," I said.

"Pathetic," responded the security guy. "I'm not turning around and I'm not taking my eyes off you."

The road noise was building, drivers were becoming tense and frustrated. Roman motorists weren't known for their tolerance at the best of times. A smattering of car horns turned into a cacophony.

I maintained my view over my guardian's shoulder towards the apartment. The shadow was still moving. I squinted into the morning sun. No glare in his eyes to stop him from making his shot.

"Listen dumbass, if you don't check out that apartment, I'm going to lay you flat, right here," I said.

"You and who else? You won't take me by surprise a second time, pissant."

The traffic noise was rising in parallel to my anger. I only just heard my phone ring. Grabbing it out of my pocket, I shouted, "Have you got eyes on the apartment?"

"Yup," said Greatrex. "There's definitely a figure moving inside. I'm looking for an entrance."

I refocused on the window. The figure seemed to be edging toward the open door. Suddenly, the hairs on my neck rose in alarm.

"Jack, he's got something in his hands. It's long and..."

Pain reeked through my wrist as the security guy chopped down onto it. The cell crashed to the ground.

"Stupid asshole," I cussed as I reached down for it.

I'd just wrapped my fingers around the phone when a thunderous impact on my spine sent me lurching forward. Failing to regain my balance, I tripped over a foot. The cement pavement came rushing up to meet me.

"My pleasure," said the CID man.

I rolled onto my back and yelled, 'Cassandra, get down.'"

She wouldn't see me on the sidewalk, but perhaps she'd hear me. I yelled again. I sensed a commotion, but I was more intent on the window. Yet I was powerless to stop what was happening.

"Jack, Jack," I shouted into my cell, surprised that I'd managed to pick it up. "Tell me you're going up there."

"No entrance at the front, I'm trying the back," came Greatrex's terse reply.

We both knew he'd be too late.

I scrambled toward an upright position, only to feel a forceful thud onto my neck. I presumed it to be a foot.

Enough.

I rolled to one side, wrapped my arms around the CID guy's ankles, and yanked. He hit the ground beside me, grunting loudly as his head slammed onto the hard sidewalk.

I sprung to my feet, turning back towards the general's wife. In the chaos, Ireland's men had surrounded him, leaving Cassandra on the outer, totally exposed.

I launched myself toward her, bringing down the flimsy rope barricade. Cassandra Devlin-Waters stared at me, clearly alarmed. Before I reached her, I was taken down by a plethora of hands. SecDef's protection at work.

A long three seconds passed by before an exceedingly pissed off voice said, "turn over slowly, but stay on the ground."

To do anything else was futile. That didn't mean I'd given up. As I turned, a foot came to rest on my chest.

"Look up at that balcony, you morons. Do your freakin' job."

I pointed through a gap in the several large bodies that surrounded me. Two of them turned.

At that precise moment, the figure that had been in darkness stepped forward.

"Cassandra, down," I yelled over my shoulder, one last attempt.

Suddenly, the doorway framed one shoulder and two arms holding a long barrel. The distance made it hard to identify the weapon, but it wasn't a conventional rifle. With one hand supporting it, the barrel swung down to where I'd last seen the general's wife standing.

Defying physical logic, I shoved the foot on my chest aside and pushed myself up. Halfway through the movement, the urge to fight suddenly abandoned me. I felt my shoulders sag in relief. The barrel remained pointed toward Cassandra, but it worried me no more.

I was literally staring down the barrel of a long telephoto lens.

I'd made a fool of myself, but better that than bear witness to a tragedy. I kneeled, fixated on the figure.

As the camera lens lowered, my relief evaporated. Dumbfounded, I found myself staring directly into Lachlan Byrn's tempestuous eyes.

The snappy Roman wind cut like a blade.

The assassin paused for a fraction of a second, holding me in his gaze. I thought I caught a smug crack on his lips before he turned and disappeared back into the shadows.

What the hell was that all about?

Chapter 50

"Well, you're a fool, Sharp, and now the entire world knows it."

Greatrex and I sat in Major Wyatt Davis's makeshift office. He stood behind his desk, an attempt at intimidation. We'd been summoned to attend the meeting after the dramatic events in front of the Fountain of Moses. Davis's people had documented my behavior, and apparently so had half the world's media.

"The secretary has instructed me to inform you we have booked two tickets in your names on the 5.40 United flight out of Leonardo Di Vinci Airport. He expects you to be on that plane."

I sat upright in my chair, squaring up, eye to eye with the man across from me.

"You can tell the secretary that I no longer fall under his command. I have no intention of leaving Rome."

Davis seemed to recoil a little. He wasn't used to being told no.

"I should warn you then that any accreditation to attend conference events that Cassandra Devlin-Waters had arranged for the two of you are now null and void. I expect you to check out of the hotel within the hour."

Davis allowed himself a light sneer.

"In fact, your bags are being packed as we speak."

The nerve of this guy.

"You have no right…" began Greatrex.

"We have every right," Davis interrupted. "They booked your rooms in the conference's name. You are now barred from the event, so… goodbye."

I inhaled deeply. I had no wish to prolong the conversation, but there were matters to discuss.

"Major, I suggest you sit down," I began. "We need to talk about Lachlan Byrn."

Wyatt remained standing, leaning forward with his fists on the desktop.

"That situation has been debated and dismissed. We no longer regard Lachlan Byrn as a credible threat."

"The only person lacking credibility here is you, Davis. I saw Byrn. He stood on that balcony. Thomas Ireland is only alive now because it was a camera, not a gun in Byrn's hands."

This was turning into a repeat of our previous interaction.

Wyatt laughed.

"You have trouble accepting when you're wrong, don't you, Sharp? My team is aware of the 'sighting' of your mythical assassin friend. We're professionals, so of course we looked into it. It turns out the apartment was leased by a press photographer doing freelance for the EPA, the European Press Agency. His name is Claudio Dumont."

Davis opened a tablet that lay on the desk, punched a couple of tabs and passed it over to me.

"Look at this," he said.

217

The tablet showed a photograph. A man in his mid-thirties, unkempt, wavy dark hair. Several days' growth of beard. Penetrating eyes bordering on intense. The perfect description of Lachlan Byrn... only it wasn't Lachlan Byrn.

"That is the fellow you saw. He was briefly questioned before being released. He was simply doing his job, taking photos of world events."

I said nothing.

"It's that easy Sharp, you panicked, over-reacted and saw monsters in the dark. You are the one with a credibility issue."

Davis looked smug. I couldn't really blame him. Could I have been wrong?

"Wyatt, Nicholas Sharp is a trained and experienced sniper. His eyes were the key to his success. If he says he saw Lachlan Byrn, then he saw Lachlan Byrn. Your men have been played. In case your intel isn't up to date, how this has panned out is typical of Byrn's MO."

At least Greatrex believed me.

"Credit where credit is due. You two show tenacity and loyalty, great traits if you were working for me, but you're not. So, get the hell out of my office and the hell out of Rome if you know what's good for you."

A loud banging, followed by raised voices, spilled through the doorway. As the door opened, Wyatt looked up. Secretary Thomas Ireland strode in.

"Wyatt, give me the room please," he said.

"Mr. Secretary, I'm not sure that would be..."

"Now!"

Davis got up and walked through the open doorway. Ireland took two steps toward the door and closed it firmly. He then strolled over to the desk. Instead of sitting behind it, he moved forward and perched on its front edge. Casual, non-confrontational.

"Now Sharp, Greatrex, perhaps we should chat. Things seem to have gotten a little out of hand here."

Chat. My ass.

"I'm sure the major will have delivered my message about leaving the conference. However, I've been reconsidering my position. Maybe the 'get out of Dodge' call was a bit hasty."

Silence. The skeptical kind.

"I've just been having a chat with Cassandra Devlin-Waters. She graciously suggested that you two were really watching out for my, and our country's, best interests, and that maybe I should cut you a little slack."

The secretary paused, searching our faces for some kind of response. He got nothing.

"Look, I'm willing to overlook today's incursion. From what I hear, you're tired and somewhat stressed Sharp. It probably wasn't really your fault you made an ass of yourself."

Pause for effect. Then he continued.

"To be honest, I can also see my way past that small indiscretion regarding your interaction with my man in the hotel foyer last night as well. I understand the local polizia are waiting for a word from me to either charge you with assault or, for the matter to be forgotten about. It could go either way."

That was the moment Thomas Ireland smiled. His mouth widened, his perfect teeth exposed in a warm and welcoming signal. Except it wasn't. It was more like a wolf licking its lips.

I clenched my fingers around the arms of my chair. The aggression had to go somewhere.

"And the conditions for reconsidering your position?" I asked.

"Well, I understand there has been some miscommunication between you and my fellow Miller. He looked out for Ms. Moore because he thought you were threatening her. You understand that Emma Moore is very young and impressionable, and I suppose power can be some sort of aphrodisiac for the young. Anyway, last night I rejected Ms. Moore advances."

"And?" asked Greatrex.

"She reacted badly. I'm afraid self-harm can sometimes be a 'go to' position for the vulnerable. I imagine she showed you the burn marks on her arm, all self-inflicted, of course."

To describe the next few seconds of silence as 'stony' would be like describing a shark's teeth as 'prickly'.

I chose not to speak… at first.

Eventually I stood up, my glare fixed on Thomas Ireland's pupils. His smile widened, but his eyes betrayed his uncertainty. I broke the moment and headed for the door, certain that Greatrex would follow me.

I twisted the handle, pushed, and then stepped aside, allowing the big fella to exit the room first. Pivoting back toward Ireland, I spoke carefully and deliberately.

"Mr. Secretary," I began. "Jack Greatrex and I are Americans. We love our country. We've been fortunate enough to serve the US and other democracies around the globe. We are who we are because we believe in freedom and honor."

I felt Greatrex breathing down my neck. A short grunt suggested his anticipation.

"I think we both fully understand that miscommunication sometimes occurs. Both Jack and I appreciate you clarifying your position today."

Thomas Ireland allowed the grin to spread across his face, slowly but explicitly. This time, the wolf looked satisfied. He'd devoured his meal, his demeanor now relaxed.

I continued. "So, in that spirit I say to you… go rot in hell!"

Within two steps of leaving the room, I'd decided that, in this moment, I wanted to *be* Lachlan Byrn.

Chapter 51

"Sharp," the voice behind us echoed down the street.

As expected, our bags were packed and waiting at the concierge's desk after we left our meeting with the secretary. Greatrex and I wasted no time in getting out of the building. Good riddance.

"Sharp."

I stopped and swung around.

"I'm glad we caught you," said Agent Andrews of the CID. His partner, Agent Djenovic, walked a couple of steps behind.

"Keep moving please," instructed Andrews. "It would be good to put some distance between us and the hotel."

"Read my mind," I responded.

We'd veered left up the Via Parigi before our conversation began in earnest.

"Word has got out amongst the CID team. If you guys were on the outside before, you're considered poisonous now," said Djenovic.

"That didn't take long," replied Greatrex.

"We knew Ireland was heading downstairs to meet with you. I don't think anyone on our team thought that would go well.

"So how did it go?" inquired Djenovic.

"As 'not well' as expected," I responded.

Andrews chuckled.

"So, we're here to offer you a quiet hand if you need it," he said. "Informally, of course."

"Thank you. We appreciate that. But it's probably best we work alone." I responded.

"Best for you or us?" asked Andrews.

I shrugged my shoulders.

"Your call," said Djenovic reaching forward, "but here's a card with both our cell numbers. Call if you need to."

"There is one thing," I said. "When we last spoke, you mentioned that you would move to act on Ireland if you had proof of him abusing young women."

"And we meant it," declared Andrews.

"Well, we have some proof for you, but I think it will take time and luck to make it stick."

I told him all about Emma Moore and her relationship with SecDef.

"Then the rumors are true," said Djenovic. "Crap."

"We'll act," continued Andrews, "and you're right, it will take some time. And some corroborating evidence."

Lachlan Byrn wouldn't need any corroborating evidence.

"Do what you've got to do," I replied. "But please look after the girl. She doesn't deserve this."

I passed over Izzy's contact details.

"What will you do?" asked Djenovic.

"We'll do what *we* need to do," I responded. "We have a plan, and it may even have a chance of succeeding."

"All right, I'm assuming you don't want to share your plan," said Andrews.

"No offence intended, but that's a negative," I replied.

"None taken," Andrews replied. "Best of luck. Remember, we're here should you need support."

"Appreciated," I replied.

We shook hands and went our separate ways.

Ten yards down the road, Greatrex spoke.

"We have a plan?"

I nodded.

"Would you care to share it with me?"

I nodded again, quietly enjoying the moment.

"Hmph."

"Tell me," I asked, "do you enjoy camping?"

Chapter 52

LACHLAN BYRN

Lachlan Byrn stared vacantly into the candescent glare of the bare light bulb before leaning forward and flicking off the switch. He preferred to think in the dark.

His planning complete, Byrn knew to a tee how this would turn out. Only on the rarest of occasions did his plans require modification during execution. It troubled him that Sharp showed some unpredictable traits, but so far, he'd kept one step ahead of the former Marine. Byrn saw no reason for that to change.

He lounged back in his chair. To describe the space as comfortable would be an overstatement. Tolerable, perhaps, spartan certainly. It was the kind of room no one stayed in very long. One chair, one lamp with no shade, a bed, and a tiny bathroom. He supposed the pile of fiber laying on the floor at his feet had once been a rug. Either way, it didn't really matter when the lights went out.

The small apartment in Rome was off the tourist map. Locals in the district kept to themselves and transients such as himself, more so. In a month, nobody would remember Byrn was even here.

The apartment wasn't his base. He never based himself in a city for longer than he had to. His boat acted as his center of operations. The aging thirty-five-foot sloop sat at a swing mooring off Terracina, south of the Italian capital and north of Naples.

The vessel had proved invaluable over the years. He'd painted it and changed its registration more times than he could remember. Even when they saw the craft, no witness ever gave a reliable description. The confusion he created by adding a bowsprit or a stern platform always amazed Byrn. Suddenly, his green thirty-five-footer registered in Athens became a white forty-five-footer registered in the Caribbean. The deception worked for him.

Below the surface, the boat was completely different. He'd created a small workshop with high-level machinery and tools adjacent to the engine room. He could construct, deconstruct, and alter an array of weapons there. He needed no outside expertise; he had the required skills. Although the vessel contained two high powered Yanmar diesel engines, it was also rigged for sail. Between the wind and the solar panels that energized the boat's electrics, Byrn could travel considerable distances without setting foot on shore. Sometimes it suited him to disappear out to sea.

The craft wouldn't get him across the globe in a hurry, so he needed to plan. The boat hadn't been with him in the US, nor England. He'd already made arrangements, through a contact, for it to be delivered and waiting for him at Terracina. Byrn spent the last few days on board preparing his equipment and weaponry. His preferred choice was always a high-range rifle, but being a true professional, he'd long ago accepted the need to adapt to circumstance.

When Byrn completed this mission, he'd return to the boat. The authorities may well be searching airfields, train stations and major ports for a man of his description. No one would think to note a craft previously settled in a remote coastal location for weeks, quietly slipping its mooring and disappearing over the horizon.

As ever, on the eve of a kill, he became morosely contemplative. It remained a habit he couldn't shake. Tired, on edge, and aware he should sleep, he was equally aware that wouldn't happen. An hour earlier, he'd popped some more Modafinil, the Night Eagle. Experience taught him he could go five days without rest while flying on the eagle's wings. He and the boat would need to be away from the harbor by day six. His pattern always the same. One bottle of Stolichnaya vodka followed by thirty hours of dormancy, most of it in a deep sleep.

He was on day four now.

Byrn's contemplation led to reflection. It annoyed him, but he frequently succumbed to the habit.

Many would judge his life to be an abject failure, if many people knew him. Byrn didn't see it that way. He figured most individuals sought counseling to normalize their lives, put them in step with others. Even Sharp pursued some kind of therapy, in the form of his music. If that worked for him, what the hell, why not? Byrn didn't see the need for counseling or being in step with others. He regarded the need to fit in as a weakness. Lachlan Byrn drew comfort from his differences and embraced his irregularities. They made him who he was, who he was meant to be.

Maybe not always. The events of his life led him to this point. Nature verses nurture. Lachlan Byrn figured both had dealt him a twisted blow.

Whereas most people scrambled desperately into the future, attempting to vanquish traumatic memories, Byrn embraced them. The fresher the wound, the greater the pain, and Lachlan Byrn knew that pain was one of life's great motivators. As a twelve-year-old living with his parents, he recalled the Sunday afternoon he'd heard the cries from his sister's bedroom. It wasn't the first time, but the guilt of inaction dictated it would be the last. Byrn ran down the corridor and crashed through the doorway to find his father abusing his daughter... Byrn's sister. For many, that would have been a formidable family crisis. Years of therapy, recovery, alienation, perhaps in time, even forgiveness. The twelve-year-old chose an alternate path. He walked directly out of the bedroom, down the hall to the kitchen and grabbed the family carving knife from the woodblock on the bench. As he strode purposefully back along the corridor to his sister's room, Byrn carefully calculated what he would need to do to achieve a maximum result. He entered the room, leaped onto the bed, and stabbed his father twice in the chest before being satisfied the predator was dead. The first blow was to kill, the second for insurance.

Byrn had never needed a second blow again. Nor had he repeated the experience of guilt induced by inaction.

Nature verses nurture. He'd been driven by his own nature to put an end to his father's poorly nurturing ways. Even as a young boy, he'd entertained no alternative action. The situation was black and white. To Lachlan Byrn, most situations were.

228

The authorities, of course, had found shades of gray. They shipped the violent young man off to a home for treatment. Byrn supposed that the institution had done him a favor. At least when he'd been captured by the Chinese years later, he understood his own levels of tolerance.

Twelve months after his arrival, Byrn had been called into the office of the institution's 'principal.' 'Bad news son, your sister is dead. She killed herself.'

The guilt that racked the young man overpowered his soul. The self-loathing twisted it beyond recognition. Why wasn't he there? What could he have done differently?

In the end, Byrn found no reason to absolve himself. The road to redemption was not his to travel.

When finally deemed ready to return to society, Lachlan Byrn had just turned sixteen. They gave him clothes and enough money to go home. For the first time in years, he contemplated seeing his mother. Then he thought about his sister's empty room. In Byrn's eyes, his mother should have protected her daughter, initially from her father and then later from herself. The young man felt the anger rise within him. Not aimed at his own misfortunes, his fury was leveled at the injustices that befell his sister, and the weaknesses of those who failed her.

There would be no homecoming. The boy assumed the rage would wane, eventually. But it never left. It just reinvented itself every time he saw the strong and powerful betray the weak and vulnerable. The anger simply became part of who he was.

Byrn eased himself out of his chair and flicked the light back on. Pacing would ease his involuntary retrospection. A walk outside wasn't an option. Remaining unnoticed, always vital to his planning, he paced around the room. Three steps wall to wall. He repeated the circuit over and over. A lion caged.

Twenty minutes later, he'd returned to the chair, staring at the light bulb.

As time passed, Byrn grew comfortable living in a state of semi-perpetual fury. Even watching the evening news caused him agitation. Injustice made headlines, headlines sold advertising. Media moguls profiting from injustice. Ironically, Byrn saw that as an injustice in itself.

For some people, alcohol anesthetized their anger, for others the bottle aggravated their animosity. Byrn had tried that approach. For him, the booze didn't even touch the rawness of his rage. He gave up trying. Nowadays he only drank after a job, and then to the point of unconsciousness. A total quelling of the pain.

At one time, Byrn attempted to channel his temper productively. He managed to talk his way into the Royal Marines. He figured that having lived a formative part of his life in an institution, the institutionalization of military service may settle him down.

It didn't take long for his superiors to notice his incredible eye, leading to an astounding accuracy on the rifle range. His tendency to aggression had been quietly overlooked, recorded as youthful impetuosity. Eventually, they recommended him for training in the Special Boat Service. He topped his cohort, despite a few small temper-driven indiscretions rearing their ugly head.

For a brief period, Lachlan Byrn dared to feel faintly optimistic about his future. He sensed he may have a shot with the SBS. Then, after training, he'd been sent on the mission to Colombia with the young Marine, Nicholas Sharp.

Optimism misplaced.

Despite the catastrophic events of his life, deep inside himself, Byrn knew the real problem. Sometimes, in these moments of introspection, he even admitted it to himself.

He enjoyed the moment of the kill.

Once he looked up the definition of a serial killer: 'a person who commits a series of murders, often with no apparent motive and typically following a characteristic, predictable behavior pattern.' Then came the sting… 'usually in the service of abnormal psychological gratification.'

It got Byrn thinking. Could he be a serial killer? He certainly met the criteria. He was at his most comfortable when planning and executing a killing. He sometimes thought of it as his 'happy place'.

Byrn frequently worked for money. That didn't fit the serial killer profile. On the other hand, for him, the money remained inconsequential. They simply paid him for doing what he loved.

Implementing well engineered assassinations.

Byrn knew that the line he drew in the sand seemed extreme compared with most of the civilized world, whatever the hell that meant. He held no issue with stepping outside the law, but he required a reason, justification. People who hired him were informed that despite being well paid for his work, they would have to put a case to the assassin, justifying the need for murder. If a valid case were presented, the injustice clear, he'd do the job. Lachlan Byrn: judge, jury… and executioner.

On a couple of occasions, early in his career, two clients attempted to present a fraudulent perspective. They'd tried to use Byrn's skills to settle their own unjustified vendettas.

Byrn saw only black and white. He killed both clients. No one had lied to him since.

Byrn gradually grew aware that his weakness as a professional assassin was the desire to get close and personal with his victims. He embraced the fear in their eyes and the trembling in their bodies when they faced the inevitable. He also found some satiation when they admitted their actions. He wanted his victims to understand exactly why they would die. Of course, it didn't always work out that way, but they became his preferred jobs.

As Byrn grew increasingly edgy, he felt the drugs pushing his nervous system further out onto a perilous limb. He stood and repeated his pacing. After fifty laps of the room, he dropped for the obligatory hundred push-ups. He poured some water into a dirty glass from a tap in the bathroom before settling back into the chair... and the light bulb.

Propelling himself forward to the current circumstances, Byrn went over his planning, a process regularly repeated over and over before each job. Thirty minutes later, he'd satisfied himself that every aspect and contingency had been covered. The one annoying blemish was the incident in front of the Fountain of Moses.

He'd chosen the apartment across from the fountain carefully. As soon as they released the conference schedule, Byrn scoured the records of all the buildings on the opposite side of the Via Vittorio Emanuele Orlando. Well connected, and always thorough in his research, it had been a windfall to find the apartment owned by a photographer who bore a striking resemblance to himself. A blind payment to the man to take some shots at an out-of-town location over a period of four days allowed Byrn access to the building. He'd seen

Thomas Ireland a hundred times on television, but he wanted to observe the politician close up. Studying body language was a sniper's bread and butter. Even an un-noted twitch, or a tendency to lean backward when laughing, could kill a shot.

The incident with Sharp was a bonus. Byrn knew Sharp and his pal Greatrex wouldn't give up attempting to protect their revered general's wife. But to come face to face, or rather lens to face with him, had been a gift. The downside of Sharp seeing him was it confirmed Byrn's presence in Rome. That information would only heighten Sharp's already overdeveloped sense of danger. Because of the scene Sharp created, the authorities had been quick to connect with Byrn as he attempted to leave the building. Having assumed the photographer's identity, with the appropriate documentation, he talked his way past two polizia who didn't seem to be trying particularly hard. Smoke and mirrors.

As he thought about it, Byrn realized he really didn't care that much. What he did care about was that the encounter hadn't been part of his plan. He'd need to watch himself. Nicholas Sharp remained an unpredictably dangerous force.

Byrn had originally intended to kill Sharp. He held him partially responsible for his incarceration and torture by the Chinese. If Sharp had just killed him, as requested, it would never have happened. But the naïve young Marine hesitated, and Byrn paid the price. He sensed that the general, Devlin-Waters, was a man Sharp respected. That's why Byrn shot him, to lure Sharp out into a circumstance of Byrn's choosing. He'd been genuinely surprised when Sharp told him he'd gone back to the Colombian jungle to look for him, and Lachlan Byrn was rarely surprised. Sharp's story rang true. His captors had told him that there'd been a search party scouring the

233

area for him. Of course, they only informed him to heighten his emotional state, allowing him to sense the closeness of unattainable freedom.

Either way, Byrn believed Sharp, so he let him live. Judge and jury, but in this case not executioner. The two men in England were not so fortunate. The last one, Rogers, had been a good death. The bastard certainly lived long enough to understand why he would die… and to embrace his regret.

Byrn held no regrets. If he was honest with himself, he didn't really understand the word.

He did understand the flame that raged in his belly, a wildfire out of control.

The assassin stood up yet again. He stepped over to the bed and began unrolling the canvas sheets that housed his equipment. Everything would need to be checked and rechecked. It was essential that tomorrow's process of death be clean and certain… and personal.

Chapter 53

NICHOLAS SHARP

The clocks of Rome had not yet struck midnight as Greatrex and I stood on the sidewalk, eyeballing the massive ornate gates of Palatine Hill.

"There's no way we're going over or through those," said the big fella.

"We'll track the fence line south, find a more approachable entrance. And for God's sake, try not to look like a burglar. This is one of the most frequently patrolled areas in Rome."

"Hmph."

It wasn't Greatrex's fault he looked so brutishly intimidating.

We walked south, a small black bag containing our essentials hidden under my coat. Just two tourists out on a midnight stroll. The chilly night air didn't really support our story. We hoped it wouldn't be tested.

"Here," said Greatrex, stopping as we came to a lower part of the wall.

"All right, but be quick," I responded.

I threw the bag over the wall before the big fella hoisted me up. As I padded quietly down on the other side, Greatrex's head appeared above the wall. The man possessed incredibly strong arms and heaved himself over. The landing wasn't the most graceful, nor was the grunt that followed. But we'd made it.

My plan was simple. Breach the Palatine-Forum area by midnight. Identify possible locations where Lachlan Byrn may base himself in readiness to make his play, then conceal ourselves and wait.

Sometimes simple plans are the best, sometimes they are just simple. In this case, it was simply all we had. If Byrn went for a really long shot, neither we nor the secretary would stand a chance. My gut told me that wouldn't be his call.

"We've got a long night ahead of us," I said. "I think we stick with the plan to separate. Let's cover as much of the territory as we can, but Jack, be careful. There is always the possibility that Byrn is already here."

Greatrex smiled. *"I'm* always careful," he said. "It's you I worry about. Stay in contact, message where possible rather than talk."

"Check, let's go to it."

We moved off in separate directions. Jack was to focus on the Palatine Hill area while I headed in the direction of the Roman Forum. Earlier, Izzy's boyfriend, Alessandro, had briefed us thoroughly over a long dinner at the same ristorante on the Campo de Fiori. Both the singer and Emma Moore were there. All things considered, Emma seemed to be doing pretty well. Alessandro offered to come with us. We politely declined. Izzy would never forgive me if something happened to her man. For that matter, I'd never forgive myself.

Both Jack and I had him on speed dial on our phones, and Alessandro insisted on staying up all night to be ready in case we needed him.

Exploring anywhere in the dark can be a little unnerving. Prowling around this iconic location, steeped in such a fascinating yet violent history, was downright unsettling. In the darkness of night, no groups of tourists shielded us from the ghosts of centuries past. The saving grace was the lighting focused on the structures. It meant we didn't have to rely on flashlights, but it also meant we had to cling to the shadows. Fortunately, there were plenty of those.

Alessandro told us the area would be patrolled by guards, but their schedules were tight and repetitive. We just needed to make sure we saw them before they saw us. We were unsure if SecDef's security team would have people here overnight. It seemed unlikely. Their usual operational guidelines suggested they would send a team at the crack of dawn to secure the space. I'd checked in with Agent Andrews. He told me he'd heard nothing different.

The challenge here was huge, but the CID team would be thorough. Alessandro showed Greatrex and me at least half a dozen spots where we could hide as the sun came up. History provided many skeletons in many closets, and Alessandro knew where all the closets were. The CID people would not. Our resident expert assured us we'd be fine. Of course, if the security teams couldn't find us, then they wouldn't find Byrn.

I moved on towards the Forum.

The hill was less lit, but the Forum beamed like a movie set. The rays from the flood lights reached up to the top of the columns. I'd made it half-way along the Via Sacra when I first heard voices. Quickly retreating into the nearest shadow, I slid my way around a column into a deeper darkness. I noticed the beams of their flashlights before catching a view of the guards themselves. Their lights probed the surrounding shadows on either side as the two men walked down the center of the roadway. They didn't seem to pay much attention to where the beams fell.

Once they'd passed and were well clear, I texted Greatrex, letting him know the time and location of the patrol. All I received in return was OK. May as well have been a grunt.

One spot Alessandro instructed us to check was the area beside and behind the Basilica of Maxentius. The shadows rolling behind the structure were long. As I made my way across the Via Sacra towards the basilica, I caught the distant throb of traffic resonating through the night air. It seemed odd to be so close to a busy, modern city, yet feel centuries away. I glanced up. The Victor Emmanuel 11 Monument towered above the skyline, its grandeur only enhanced by its personal light show. As impressive as it was, for me, it stood as an uncontrollable threat. If Byrn got a clear shot from up there, the consequences would be fatal.

I shook the thought out of my mind. Don't try to control what you can't control. The shadows behind the basilica called.

The next two hours were a repeat of the first. Shadows, laneways, and entrance ways to search. Each one potentially a death trap. Greatrex and I texted each other frequently, but neither of us had news. I passed the same patrol on their return journey, only just making it into the darkness in time to avoid detection.

By 3AM I'd listed over ten sights that an assassin may use as a hide, Greatrex slightly less. Our intel told us the secretary would spend more time in the Forum area than on the hill. If nothing else, we both held a stronger picture in our minds of how the next day may unfold.

Thomas Ireland was due to make his statement to the press at 11 a.m. For security reasons, the exact location wouldn't be shared with the press gallery until morning. I figured the man's ego would lead him to choose a spot where he could speak to the history that surrounded him while building his own sense of a leader at the center of world events. That would have to be bang in the middle of the Foro Romano, where centuries before great heroes had delivered impassioned speeches celebrating their triumphs and victories. The venue was made to order.

I messaged Greatrex, suggesting we meet close to our point of entry in thirty minutes. I wasn't sure how much more we'd be able to achieve, and we needed to find a location where we could hunker down for a few hours. At least our midnight foray had ensured our entry to the site. We took it as read that none of Ireland's security people would have allowed us to walk through those gates tomorrow.

My body began sending me messages impossible to ignore. Limbs aching from my earlier beating, my mind ran overtime with different scenarios playing over and over. After three hours chasing shadows, my nerves needed a break. I felt tired as all hell. Time to grab a little shuteye.

Abruptly, all dreams of respite lay shattered when everything around me fell into darkness.

Someone had turned out the lights.

Chapter 54

LACHLAN BYRN

Byrn knew he had little time. Placing a small explosive on the grid supplying the lighting to the Palatine and Forum area had been a no brainer. The grid contained two backup systems, but it would take them a while to realize he'd also sabotaged the secondary system. After that, the tertiary would kick in, probably within ten minutes. He'd be gone by then.

Byrn's task was straightforward. He'd brought equipment that needed to be placed carefully in position. They would search anyone leaving or entering the area in the morning. The resources he required would not make it through the gate, hence the need for the blackout.

He'd made his way over the wall near the Via della Consolazione. With the lights out, he didn't stick to the shadows. The assassin scurried parallel to the Via Foro Romana, past the Temple of Caster and Pollux, toward the Palatino. As always, he'd done his research, and would have known the way blindfolded.

Cautious as ever, that's virtually how he proceeded. Blindfolded. He'd decided not to risk using a flashlight, allowing only the glare of the remaining city lights to guide his course. The patrolling guards wouldn't be an issue. Byrn figured they would have returned to their base to report the blackout and receive instructions. For at least a few minutes, he'd have the place to himself. He could achieve a lot in a few minutes.

He'd almost made it to the Arch of Titus when a brief flash of light caught his attention. Not strong enough to be a flashlight, it vanished as quickly as it appeared. The assassin froze and slid to the ground. He'd move no further until he'd identified the unexpected intrusion. A minute later, the light flashed again. This time, he zeroed in on it. A cell phone. A guard, perhaps, securing boundaries. It was the most probable scenario. But wouldn't a guard use a flashlight?

Staying low, Byrn stashed his equipment beside a stone wall before semi-crawling his way back along the fence line. Halfway along, he found enough coverage behind two pillars to edge closer to the light source. In the overwhelming darkness, he might have moved quicker, but being over cautious had kept Lachlan Byrn alive so far. He didn't see the need to change the habit of a lifetime.

Slowly Byrn edged towards the first pillar. He risked peering around it, the light still too far away. He could just make out a faint shadow of a figure holding the phone. He couldn't tell if it was male or female.

The assassin reached under his coat, withdrawing a Sig P226 pistol. A precaution. He wanted to avoid creating a scene at this time of night. Also as a precaution, he unclipped an extra pocket in his jacket and squeezed the MODX-9 segmented, titanium printed, 9mm suppressor concealed there. The feel of its ribbed surface was reassuring.

241

Pausing to double check the figure hadn't looked up or shown any sense of Byrn's presence, he then slithered around the first pillar. Staying directly in line with the further column, he stepped quietly forward, the soles of his shoes caressing the ground.

Satisfied he'd made the distance undetected, Byrn raised his weapon parallel to his face and slowly peaked from behind the final pillar.

The light from the phone glowed stronger here. The beam showed the person more clearly. Byrn remained unable to identify the figure as a guard. The build, however, suggested a male. This was an unneeded complication.

Just then, the figure spoke. The hushed tones would have been unintelligible, but the breeze caught the sound and relayed it straight back to the assassin's position. Byrn had a flash of recognition. The voice. He peered around the pillar again, searching for giveaway features.

Shit, he should have seen it the first time.

Nicholas fucking Sharp. What the hell was he doing here?

An unpredictable inconvenience had just become a dangerous obstacle to his mission.

Lachlan Byrn leaned back against the pillar, lowered his weapon, and drew a deep breath. Dangerous or not, an obstacle was simply an impediment that required removal. Byrn paused, assessing his options.

Two minutes later, he raised his gun and stepped forward.

Chapter 55

NICHOLAS SHARP

The timing of the power fail couldn't be a coincidence. Not in these circumstances.

I peered into the blackness, my expectations low. Apart from a faint glow provided by the surrounding city, I saw nothing. Fully alert, my sniper's instinct took over.

The cell in my pocket vibrated.

"Jack, are you in shutdown too?"

"Blinded by the darkness," came the reply. "I'm gonna make my way slowly over to your position. The Forum is our most likely ground zero."

"Agreed," I responded. "Just be careful. The idea of Byrn being somewhere close is worrying.

"You think this was his work?"

"Certain of it," I replied.

"Why so?"

"Because it's what I would have done."

"There's some food for thought. I'm on my way. But Nicholas, keep your head down."

I shut down and pocketed the phone. I shouldn't have answered the call. In this darkness, the screen probably shone like a beacon. A calculated risk. Communication in the field is everything, especially when sight lines become non-existent.

As a precaution, I stepped back about five yards. My elbow brushed a column. I slid silently around it. Then I did what musicians do best... I listened.

It took a couple of minutes to filter out the dim hum of the city and focus on the silence of the immediate environment. I strained to make out anything, a footstep, the rustle of clothes, human breaths. Nothing.

The whole thing may have been an overreaction... or not. I listened harder.

Still nothing.

Byrn could be anywhere on the hill or down here in the Forum. But my gut told me he hadn't taken the higher ground.

I stood frozen behind the column for several minutes. The best way for the hunter to become the hunted was to expose themselves through movement. Stillness became my camouflage. Of course, the downside remained that if Byrn was nearby, he'd play the same game. We'd had similar training, similar MOs.

The silence developed a haunting quality. My breathing swept through my head in endless waves. No matter how slowly and quietly I drew breath, it was too loud.

Eventually I decided enough was enough. The power would return at some point, but I needed to be alive when it did. Acutely aware that Lachlan Byrn had spared me once, it seemed unlikely the assassin would give me a second reprieve. Especially now that I'd declared my intentions to impede his plans.

To remain motionless any longer would render me vulnerable. The static tactic had outlived its usefulness. If Byrn had moved position, he would close in quickly.

My left foot rested on a half-buried rock. I used that as a swivel point for the ball of my sole and pivoted around. To move on gravel would be a giveaway. Now pointing ninety degrees behind where I started, I gazed ahead of me, the darkness still blinding.

'Crunch.' There it was, not loud, but loud enough. A small twig or dried leaf under pressure, maybe from a foot. It sounded close, too close, and came from my left.

He was here. I could feel it.

I went low. That would make me a smaller target. My bag contained a pistol, but an opening zipper would be like a siren. So, no pistol.

I estimated the location of the source of the sound to be about ten to fifteen yards away. Then, staying down, I began swinging in a wide arc, trying to work my way around. It was slow going. Move quickly and invite a firefight or go slow in stealth. The tortoise and the hare. A sniper was always the tortoise. I wished to hell I had a shell.

Mid-arc, I heard it. The faintest of clicks, more like a scrape, metal on metal. Instantly, I knew what the noise meant.

I took a deep breath, wondering if it was my last.

Chapter 56

LACHLAN BYRN

Suddenly the cell phone light went dead, and with it, Sharp's silhouette.

Byrn froze. He had every intention of maintaining his status as the hunter here. It took the assassin less than thirty seconds to realize Sharp bore the same intent. Of course he did. But if nothing else, Lachlan Byrn had patience, he would out-wait Sharp. When his prey moved, Byrn would be there.

The silence dragged on, Byrn strained his ears for any hint of movement. He heard nothing. The assassin held no doubt he would win the waiting game on a level playing field, but each second that slipped by tipped the odds. He had a limited window of opportunity before the tertiary systems kicked in and the lights snapped back on. He'd give it five minutes, after that he'd be forced to move. The thought annoyed him. Forced play wasn't his usual style. But then again, Nicholas Sharp wasn't his usual type of adversary.

Byrn counted the seconds. Every action in his world was drawn from either anger or calculation. Usually, the former led to the latter. In this case, his anger at finding Sharp here had subsided. Now it was all about calculation.

When Byrn reached the end of the fifth minute, he stepped forward without hesitation. He'd taken three steps before he heard a slight 'crunch' under his left foot. Amateur mistake. Sharp would now begin figuring out his position, but how would his opponent react? Byrn peered into the darkness. His eyes had grown accustomed to the lack of visibility. In training, they called it 'dark adaptation'. His pupils dilated, and his vision deepened. The Night Eagle added to the effect.

With the edge of his pillar concealing most of his face, Byrn stared ahead, scanning the radius around his position, pushing out in widening circles.

Got him. Sharp was crouching low and advancing slowly, Byrn could just make out his outline. Hell, Sharp moved like a wildcat in the jungle at night. Byrn had noticed that in Colombia. He'd also recognized that when Sharp pounced, he was deadlier than the wildest beast.

Now there was no choice. Byrn reached gently into his pocket and withdrew the silencer. Holding it in his palm, he screwed it onto the barrel of the P226 in slow easy turns. Finally, he eased the suppressor into place, a last turn on the thread and… 'click'. Shit.

In an instant, Byrn knew he'd have to act. Standing up straight, one arm supporting the other, he lined up his target. Sharp stopped, but too late. With his forefinger resting on the trigger, Byrn squeezed ever so lightly.

Byrn felt the anticipation stream through his body. It was an excitement he'd become accustomed to, and one he'd learned to embrace. In milliseconds, the assassin had calculated Sharp's probable course.

For a moment, Byrn sensed a twinge of disquiet within himself. Unexpected and unneeded. He banished the sensation.

The point of the extended barrel lined up perfectly with Sharp's torso. The shot was his, Sharp was as good as dead.

The assassin took one last deep breath, his hand now rock steady.

He squeezed gently... and stopped.

The calculator kicked in. A scene here would be messy, and unnecessary. It would impede his mission. That couldn't be tolerated. His anger had taken momentary control. Lachlan Byrn was a professional. No... Sharp would have to keep for later.

Lachlan Byrn turned and disappeared into the night.

Chapter 57

NICHOLAS SHARP

"He was here Jack. I know it."

"Did you see him?"

"Well, no," I replied.

Three minutes after I'd heard the click, and sensed impending doom, Greatrex had shown up at the edge of the Forum area. I'd been relieved, but also worried he'd set himself up as a target. As it turned out, my fears were unfounded.

Greatrex's figure now loomed before me, a shadow amongst shadows. The lights remained out.

He sighed.

"Nicholas, if you say he was here, then he was here. But just be sure your observations are based on fact. That's the way you've always worked."

"Yeah, I get it. You wonder if I'm losing the plot. The photographer on the balcony outside the hotel, a mythical monster in the dark here," I replied.

"Not for a second do I think you're going out of your mind, but I am aware this guy has haunted you for years. I'm just

249

saying, be careful."

"Point taken, but I'm certain I'm right."

"Hmph."

We held our voices to a whisper, not that it mattered that much. If Byrn had wanted or needed to take me out, he had the opportunity and let it pass... again. That was a mystery I didn't have time to contemplate now.

"We've got a job to do, and the clock's ticking," I said. "Let's compare notes about hides and strategies before we try to grab some shuteye for ourselves."

As I spoke, there was a brief flickering of light before the consistent glare of the floodlights illuminated our world. We headed for the shadows, out of the way.

Greatrex and I exchanged information. The list of locations that a sniper might use within the Palatine-Roman Forum area was overwhelming.

"We can't cover everything," I said. "We're going to need to make choices, split up in the morning, and deal with what we can."

"What would you do Nicholas? If you wanted to assassinate the secretary of defense tomorrow, how would you do it?"

"So, you're wanting me to channel Byrn. Who's losing it now?" Despite my own words, I allowed the cogs in my mind to turn, weighing options, examining scenarios, discarding each before moving onto the next. The big fella remained respectfully silent.

Eventually, I had something to share.

"There is no one certain answer," I said. "You and I both know the possibilities are many. If I wanted to be coldly efficient, I'd go for the long shot. If he gets the right angle, Byrn might take SecDef out from any number of places off-site. I'd be going for the *Monumento Nazionale a Vittorio Emanuele 11,* the 'Wedding Cake'. There is a clear line of sight down to the forum. If Ireland's people hold the presser in the middle of the Forum, the shot is Byrn's to make."

"The variables?" asked Greatrex.

"Like any shot of that length, there are things that could go wrong. The weather, the wind, visibility and, of course, the big one. An object blocking his line."

"An object like a human body?"

"Exactly. Anyone might take a step forward or sideways and block the shot," I replied.

"Anyone who is close to the target."

"Yes," I responded.

"That would mean…"

'Yes, Cassandra Devlin-Waters may well be the one thing standing between Lachlan Byrn and his prey," I said.

"And Byrn won't hesitate to take her out to get to his man."

"Not for a moment."

We stood in the darkness, contemplating those words. Eventually, the big fella responded.

"Shit."

"Exactly," I said.

Five minutes later, we were stalking the shadows, winding our way towards the location Alessandro had directed us to. In reconnaissance, local knowledge was everything.

Twenty-five minutes after that, we pushed down behind two crumbling half walls off the tourist path. The grass was long; we had to feel our way through.

"Here," said the big fella.

I reached my hand forward in the dark. My fingers touched an arc of stone half buried in mud. The arc surrounded a hole in the side of a mound. I climbed in, Greatrex followed, only just squeezing into the darkened space.

"Alessandro mentioned this was probably an original part of the Cloaca Maxima, one of the world's earliest sewage systems," I announced.

"Then we were right."

"Right? What do you mean?" I asked.

"Shit."

Greatrex humor.

"You nap for an hour. I'll keep watch, then we swap over," I instructed.

"Right."

As we crouched there, laying in the shadows of history, I allowed my mind to wander. Was there something to be learned from the ghosts of the past that had lived, fought, and died in these very ruins?

Myth has it that Romulus murdered his twin brother Remus near to where we lay hidden. After that, Romulus developed Rome as his own kingdom. How confronting and brutal would it be to slay your own brother? Did Romulus stare into his brother's eyes as the life drained out of them? Did he find satisfaction in the act of murder, or did he see it as personal revenge for some past betrayal? Could murder be that intimate?

My thoughts froze.

"Jack, wake up."

"I wasn't asleep."

"I was wrong."

"Let me write down the time and place you admitted that. Pray, tell what were you wrong about?"

"Byrn's plan. *I'd* go for the long shot, but he's not going to,"

I said.

"How can you be certain of that?"

"Think about it. How does he kill? Before you answer, I'm aware our intel says that he's used a variety of techniques, all lethal and effective. But when it's really personal for him, how does he take a life?"

"I'm not getting your point. From what you've told me, the man is dehumanized, a human computer. He'll kill with the most efficient method available."

"In most cases, yes, but think about his former SBS commander, the major, Simon Rogers. How did Byrn take him out?"

"In a foxhole, in Wales. Wasn't it either drowning or stabbing?" Greatrex asked.

"Two of the most intimate methods of killing, holding a man under water while he desperately struggles for breath, or plunging cold hard steel into his heart, watching his life evaporate."

"Your point?" inquired the big fella.

"For Byrn, Thomas Ireland's death needs to be up close and personal. He won't shoot from a distance."

"You sound pretty certain of that."

"Positive. I've got proof."

"How so?"

I looked into the darkness where Greatrex half lay, half crouched. I couldn't see his eyes, but I knew they were looking at me.

"I should have figured it out earlier, but I didn't. I let him get to me."

"Go on," said Greatrex.

"If Lachlan Byrn was going to take the long shot, and make

his play from a safe distance away, what the hell was he doing here tonight?"

The light drizzle outside was growing steadily heavier. After several seconds of reasoned silence, Greatrex uttered his response.

"Shit."

Chapter 58

Cloudy with a chance of death.

When Greatrex dragged me from my brief hour of sleep, I awoke to a small waterfall screening the entrance to our refuge.

There's no place like home.

"It actually looks as though it's fining up," said the big fella. "It's been pretty miserable since you nodded off, but I reckon the front is moving on."

"A shame, really," I replied. "If the weather stayed bad, Ireland would have to cancel, and so would Byrn."

"Byrn doesn't strike me as the canceling type."

"I think the first thing on our agenda is to figure out how to stay clear of Ireland's CID team. They'll be going over the place with a fine-tooth comb before SecDef is allowed on deck. Our best bet is to stay here as long as we can."

"Makes sense," replied Greatrex.

My cell chirped. I scanned the ID. Agent Andrews.

"Any news?" I asked.

"Bits and pieces, but we have a time and exact location of the presser."

"Shoot." I probably could have chosen my words better.

As Andrews spoke, the dull thump of a chopper resounded through the valley. I nudged Greatrex to warn him.

"Hang on," I said, "helo overhead."

The beating of the blades gradually drifted away.

"It'll be one of ours. They went up at dawn," said Andrews. "As expected, the time of the presser is 11a.m. Also, as expected, they're setting him up in the center of the Forum, in the marketplace area."

Ireland may as well have issued a personal invitation to Byrn to come and get him. Ego before brain.

"We'll deal with that as we get to it," I responded. "What time are your people combing through the place?"

There was a pause on the line. The conversation had just transcended from casual public information to releasing classified security plans. I wouldn't have blamed Andrews for ignoring the question.

"Their sweep will be complete by 9:30. Djenovic and I are on the team, but not in the immediate close protection detail to the secretary."

"Andrews, you're taking a big risk helping us. Are you sure it's worth it?"

"I met with Emma Moore late yesterday afternoon before she dined with you. I want to see Thomas Ireland face her across a courtroom. It's worth it."

"Thank you." I hung up.

"So now we just wait?' asked Greatrex.

"It's a sniper's lot. Only I guess this time we're more like anti-snipers," I replied.

I smiled, leaned forward, and grabbed a plastic box out of my bag. I ripped the top off the box and passed it to Greatrex.

"Dried fruit, the civilian version of military rations. I love a hearty breakfast."

We ate in silence.

At 9:35 the big fella and I stood ready. Besides food and a couple of weapons, my bag had also contained suits and shirts for Greatrex and me. We wouldn't pass close scrutiny, but from a distance, we could be mistaken for members of the US security team.

"You cut a pretty dashing figure in a suit, my friend," I said.

"No comment. It's certainly not our usual attire in the field, but we've been flexible before," he responded.

"Okay," I began. "We've got to keep checking every location we've plotted. Byrn is here somewhere. He knows the CID people will crawl all over this place. If he's confident he's found himself a secure position, he won't be easy to find."

"So, leave the more obvious locations for the security team, while we think outside the square?"

"Yup," I replied. "But for God's sake, keep a low profile. If anyone from Ireland's detail recognizes either of us, it's all over. Not even Cassandra Devlin-Waters will be able to talk us out. Two armed civilians stalking the Secretary of Defense isn't such a good look."

"Point taken."

We split up. Greatrex circled clockwise, following the area's perimeter. I headed around the other side. We tried to remain inconspicuous but didn't sneak around in the shadows. Hiding in plain sight remained the best option.

By 10:30 we'd met up again behind the marketplace in the Campidogilo area, having had no success. The drizzle had stopped, and patches of blue sky battled to break through the

257

clouds.

"If Byrn is here, he's doing a hell of a job keeping out of view."

For the first time, I began doubting my own theory.

"If he's here. Maybe I was wrong. Perhaps he'll take a clean shot from a distance after all," I suggested.

We looked down at the market area. They had set rows of seats up for visiting dignitaries from the conference. Someone had taped a section opposite off for the press. In between stood a solitary microphone and a small podium.

"X marks the spot," said Greatrex.

"It's like a written invitation to a marksman. Your target will stand exactly here at precisely this time. Please be our guest and take your best shot," I replied.

"Have you noted how many clean lines there are from surrounding locations?" asked the big fella.

"Yup. It makes you wonder whether his team is watching out for him or hanging him out to dry."

"There's something in that," replied Greatrex.

"Yeah, I know. I don't doubt that his inner circle are doing their job, but you do question if others in the detail are trying that hard."

"You mean like Andrews and Djenovic?"

"Exactly. On the other hand, just like those two, and us, those CID people are professionals. There's a right way and a wrong way to do business," I replied.

Greatrex nodded.

The situation contained so many variables I was uncertain how we should move forward. Our number one priority was to protect the general's wife. If that meant looking out for Ireland, so be it. The downside was we couldn't get close enough in to be of any immediate benefit.

Despite my earlier doubts, I remained sure Lachlan Byrn would attack from within. After the damage Thomas Ireland caused him, Byrn's need to make the hit personal would be a fire in his belly. The question was, how much risk would he take to make that happen?

I took my eyes off the view below, turning to Greatrex.

"We're the audience here. There's nothing more we can do but wait for Byrn to start the show. Even then, all we can do is react."

"That's not much of a plan," said Greatrex.

"It's no bloody plan at all."

Below us, the party was beginning. The area taped off for the press slowly filled with the fourth estate. Cameras stood in two shallow semi-circles on each side of the group. Several microphones were now attached to or placed in front of the podium.

That would have been a straightforward strategy, a small explosive device in one mic, enough charge to take off the speaker's head. Ireland's head. I wondered how thorough the CID's vetting process had been. My eyes scanned the faces in the press, searching for any giveaways that may reveal Byrn. It was a pointless exercise. I knew it would be.

Off in the distance, toward the hill, the suits were arriving. Ireland's gray mane identified him as leading the group. All hail to Caesar.

"Jack, you make your way down to the northern side. I'll take the south. Stay low key, but I want us to be as close to the main game as we can get."

"Roger that."

We both moved.

259

"And Jack…"

The big fella turned.

"Keep well away from anyone who may recognize you."

Greatrex nodded and was gone.

Chapter 59

This was all wrong. Everything about it was wrong.

We had no handle on what was going to go down except we knew the target. A professional assassin had scores of accessible means of taking down an exposed mark, and Lachlan Byrn was more than a professional. He was the best. Worse than that, he was driven. A pro would walk away if circumstances became too tight. 'Live to fight another day' was a cliché for good reason.

I made my way carefully down the slope and around the Forum market area, keeping as many columns and ruins between me and the gathering press as possible. I didn't hide nor sneak, but strode forward with intent, as though I belonged.

My aim was to get behind Ireland's party as they marched down the Via Sacra. From there, I could scan the buildings they'd passed, and if Byrn had planned an attack from the rear, I'd be between him and them.

As Thomas Ireland strutted past within twenty yards of me, his features were clear. His hair swept back, jaw jutting out, he carried himself like a general leading his victorious troops.

History repeating itself. Except that being a general wouldn't be enough for a man like Ireland. Emperor maybe.

As his delegates stood, waiting to take their seats, I worked my way around, so I stood just off the road, easy access to wherever I needed to be.

I stayed in the half shadow of a column, but still assumed the stance of a professional security operator, my hands clasped in front of me.

SecDef sat first, the others followed deferentially. One man remained standing. Immaculately groomed, mid-sixties, wearing a dark blue suit, he stepped up to the podium with a confident elegance.

"Ladies and gentlemen, I am Lorenzo Amante, I am the board chairperson and founder of Amante Munitions and Technology. It is my privilege today to introduce to you an astounding man, a great leader, and a humanitarian in the true sense of the word. He is a person who looks to the future, imagines what can be, and then leads us together towards his vision."

The bile rose in my throat.

"Please welcome the chair of the Future Nucleus event. The US Secretary of Defense, Mr. Thomas Ireland."

A smattering of applause from the somewhat cynical press group dissipated quickly into the air.

Ireland didn't seem to notice. He was playing to a much bigger audience than those gathered in front of him. He marched up to the podium, arms high, palms open. His smile, a mile wide, exuded the warmth of a welcoming friend.

I wondered if that's how Romulus greeted Remus the day he murdered him.

"Good morning and welcome," he began, before looking up

to the sky. "I see the clouds are clearing, perhaps symbolic of where humanity now stands in the face of terror and aggression around the planet."

A political start. Scare them first before offering a bold solution.

"Of course, standing here, at the cornerstone where western civilization took root, I wonder what else history can teach us? I think of the brave warriors, centuries ago, who marched victoriously down these very streets, who risked their lives so we could live our own in freedom. What did we learn from them? What would they want to say to us today? What do we owe them?"

This guy was good. He'd played to the cameras, played to the locals, and was now setting himself up as a savior of civilization in one opening salvo.

My bile continued to rise.

"Well, I can tell you that my learned friends sitting behind me here today have joined me in a vision, a quest if you like…"

I didn't like.

I turned my back, deciding to check the outer perimeter of the market area. Anything but listen to that pile of…

"Sharp, you pussy, I knew it was you."

Miller, the security guy from the foyer and the fountain, loomed over me. I didn't need this right now.

"Miller, I'm here for the same reason you are, to look out for the secretary. For God's sake, don't be a fool and get out of my way."

"Get out of *your* way, you smartass prick. The only one getting in the way here is you, and I'm about to fix that." As he spoke, Miller glanced back towards where the speeches were taking place. We were far enough away and out of sight.

He grinned.

He came at me with the weight of his massive bulk behind him.

I stepped to the right, but he'd seen that trick before and followed me around. The big man's shoulder connected with my chest, knocking the wind out of me. We both went down. I gasped while he released a quiet chuckle.

The bulk of his body mass pressed down across my torso. My gasps morphed into grunts of pain as he raised himself on one arm and pounded me with his free fist.

I'd grown tired of being used as a punching bag lately. Summoning all my energy, I thrust myself upward, sticking my left shoulder into his armpit. I gave the move everything I had.

It wasn't enough.

Thugs will always be thugs. He simply head-butted me between my eyes, sending my world spinning.

The great thing about ruins is rubble. No matter how well maintained, there's invariably a rock lying around somewhere. I clawed out with my left hand. Two seconds later, I held a piece of history within my grip. I raised my hand up in the air. Miller hadn't even noticed as he continued his onslaught against my face. I began my swing… to victors go the spoils… and then the first shot rang out.

I thrust my head back towards to where Ireland had been making his speech. The rock half-fell from my fingers, but still connected with Miller. He rolled off me.

Scrambling to my feet, I heard screams and shouting coming from the market center.

Ireland stood erect, bewildered. Not really comprehending. Security agents from either side of him leaped toward their man. They made it halfway.

Two more shots rang out in quick succession.

The men stopped in their tracks as the rounds impacted the dirt around them.

My eyes searched the row of chairs directly behind where Ireland stood. Cassandra Devlin-Waters had turned around, searching for the source of the fire. Two additional shots sent the CID men scurrying backward.

This was all too close to the general's wife. I sprinted forward toward her.

Another shot. This time it splintered a rock almost directly between my feet.

"Cassandra, get down." I felt like the boy who cried wolf. Last time I'd given those instructions, it hadn't gone well.

Cassandra had heard me and ducked down, but she remained dreadfully exposed.

It was obvious the shooter was deadly accurate. I had been completely wrong. Byrn had taken the long shot.

Another round sent me back three paces. He had me pinned down.

I reached for my cell. "Jack, can you get to Cassandra?"

"Already on my way. It's chaotic here."

"Okay. Do what you can."

Years of looking through a sniper's scope had taught me that people under fire react in a variety of ways. Some run. Some just freeze, as though that would make them invisible. Some just stare toward the source, either praying you won't target them or somehow hoping a shooter will respond to their pleading eyes.

Before me, I saw humanity do all the aforementioned.

To get to Cassandra, I'd have to get around Ireland. He

remained static, still standing at the podium, his world suspended in disbelief.

I raced toward him.

Another round stopped me in my in my tracks. This time, two more cracks followed, one of them tearing through Ireland's coat sleeve. He was isolated.

At that point, to my complete surprise, Cassandra stood up and made a beeline for Ireland. When she reached him, she grabbed his shoulders and shook them. Ireland looked around, suddenly shaken out of his stupor. As Cassandra propelled him forward, he pushed the podium aside and ran toward the scattering press.

On either side of him, his security team saw what was happening and grasped the opportunity to intercept him half-way across the open space. No shots intercepted them this time. As true professionals would, they formed a human shield behind their boss, and Cassandra.

The general's wife was one hell of a woman.

Another shot kept the four of them running for cover.

On the right, I noticed Greatrex head straight toward Cassandra's position. He stopped dead when she moved courageously into action.

With Cassandra out of the line of fire, I did what I should have done first, calculate the trajectory of the shots. Within five seconds, it became glaringly obvious where the sniper, Byrn, had positioned himself.

The top of the Monumento Nazionale a Vittorio Emanuele 11w, the Wedding Cake. I should have trusted my original instincts.

Once more, I reached for my cell and dialed.

"Andrews, it's Byrn, and he's on top of the Vittorio Emanuele monument. I'm going after him. Can you send some men?"

"On it, they'll be right behind you. Be careful Sharp."

I started across the open square, ignoring the screaming voices and panicked people running in every direction. Two more gun shots resounded through the ruins. When I realized I wasn't hit, and no puff of dirt had splattered my feet, I looked up to check on Greatrex. He ran in the same direction as me, toward the shooter.

I pivoted around toward Ireland and his protectors. They were still running backward into the center of the ruins. As I looked on, another round almost clipped the heel of one of the agents. In response, he pushed Ireland forward.

With the safety of the secretary of defense and the general's wife now seemingly covered, I turned my attention back towards the shooter's hide. I figured Byrn wouldn't stay there long, so I raced like my life depended on it.

I'd made it to the rear gate of the Forum area, where a guard looked stunned at the stampede of escapees in front of me, when I froze in my tracks. Like a hammer blow to my head, it hit me that for the second time, I'd been witness to one of this assassin's most brazen strategies.

How many times could a man be wrong in a single day?

I turned and ran back toward the forum marketplace, toward Thomas Ireland, Cassandra Devlin-Waters… and if my hunch was correct, toward Lachlan Byrn.

Chapter 60

"Andrews, get your men up to the top of that building. I'm not sure what you're going to find, but it won't be Lachlan Byrn."

"If you say so." The agent sounded unconvinced, but he had little else to offer.

Peering ahead, I saw no sign of Greatrex. He'd disappeared from view, and I didn't have time to call him.

I pocketed my cell and sprinted toward the location where I'd last seen the secretary and his men hasten their retreat.

They weren't there now.

That wasn't surprising. The CID team would keep Ireland moving until he was safe, either secured on the premises or safely away in a vehicle.

Just to make things more difficult, the weather had reversed its trend. Cued by a crack of thunder, the skies suddenly opened. Within six paces, the rain soaked my clothes through. I'd slowed my sprint to a fast jog as I examined the pathways the security people could have used to guide their man away.

Water clogged my eyes as I scrutinized the laneways and buildings. I continuously wiped it away as I searched. At least the secretary and the general's wife were accompanied by two armed professionals with many more searching for him, ready to leap to their colleague's support.

Surely, this would end well.

Suddenly, I lost my footing, tripping on something. After a brief stumble, I regained my balance and looked down. A body lay halfway across the path. Male, in a suit. I reached down to check his pulse. Alive but unconscious. His clothes were saturated, but thankfully not in blood. Beyond his head, the figure's right hand clasped a handgun, a finger poised on the trigger. I leaned forward and touched the barrel. Cold, he never got a shot off.

Apparently, I was wrong… again. No happy ending here.

I looked up, my eyes searching ahead for the second CID operative. It didn't take long to find him. He lay splayed on his back, further along the path. One hand under the flap of his coat, he'd gone for his weapon but hadn't made it. I ran forward and kneeled beside him. Like his partner, he was in a bad way, but alive.

I gazed further up the track, already knowing that with or without the rain, I would see nothing.

My cell chirped.

"Sharp, it's Andrews. You won't believe this, but there is no shooter on top of the monument, at least no human shooter."

"Explain please."

"Our people have found a Songar."

"The sniper drone?" I replied.

"Well, yes, although this one seems to be a Chinese knock-off."

Sniper drones were relatively new technology. Their advent brought a raft of technological and ethical problems. Clearly, Byrn had no issues with either.

"Why didn't the choppers spot it?" I asked.

"Well, there's the thing," retorted the agent. "The drone was concealed under the cannon that forms part of the Quadriga of Unity, the statue on the summit. It could have been there for days, and no airborne craft would have seen it."

Lachlan Byrn. One step ahead, again.

"Alright, that explains the shooting, but we have a bigger problem," I said.

"Which is?"

"Are you getting any confirmation on your radio chatter of SecDef's location and status?"

"Nothing," replied the agent. "We're worried, but we know two of our men are with him. The trouble is they've gone radio silent."

"I'm afraid they've gone more than radio silent. They're both lying unconscious in front of me."

"And Ireland?"

"Nowhere to be seen," I responded. "I hate to be the one to break this to you, but I reckon you can now change SecDef's status to 'currently in enemy hands.'"

"Shit."

"Byrn also took Cassandra Devlin-Waters."

"Shit."

"You're not the first person to say that today."

Chapter 61

Lachlan Byrn now had total control over how this would play out. A concept that sat like a rock in my gut.

I grabbed my cell.

"Jack, where are you?"

"Heading back into the forum area, Andrews filled me in."

"I'm at a loss. Just start looking. Sweep your way westward."

"So, what exactly am I looking for?" he asked.

"Who knows?" I replied, an edge to my voice. "Maybe a Stargate. They've disappeared."

"For God's sake, don't lose it on me now, bud." Greatrex sounded as frustrated as I did worried.

As we spoke, I jogged down laneway after laneway. Every column, every half wall and building I passed received the once over. Each result was the same.

"Jack, I've gotta go."

"Jesus, Nicholas..."

I hung up.

Three seconds later.

"Nicholas."

"Alessandro, I need your help, urgently," I barked into the

phone.

"I'm on my way."

"No time for that, and no time for explanations."

"Okay, what can I do?"

"Please, think carefully. Byrn has made his play. Now he's vanished and taken two hostages with him. How the hell was he able to do that?"

Silence.

"Alessandro?"

"You asked me to think, I'm thinking."

Thirty seconds later, Alessandro spoke.

"He's gone underground."

"He's what?"

"Nicholas, listen carefully. I'll be brief. As you said, there is no time for lengthy explanations."

"Go."

"Rome is a city built on a city," he began. "It is perched on one large archaeological site. For nearly three millennia, Romans built buildings upon other houses. Roofs became foundations as each stratum of the city's history was absorbed to serve the next. Think layer cake if you will."

"Fascinating, but how does that help me find Byrn?"

"It does, but you need to pay attention. The seven hills of Rome have gradually subsided into the valleys where they've accumulated several layers of debris. Ancient communities, once ebbing with life, are now hidden well beneath the earth's surface. Some areas have been filled with earth. Some not."

"Tunnels?"

"Exactly Nicholas. Underneath Rome, there is a vast array of tunnels, caves, roadways, and catacombs."

"Could Byrn have found his way down there from here?" I

asked.

"Of course, although it never occurred to me that your man's research would be that thorough, nor that he would attempt to take captives in this manner. It's not well known, but the emperors had various tunnels and secret passages to take them where they needed to go. It meant they didn't need to mingle with the masses or announce their destinations."

The weight of Alessandro's words bore down on me like the world on Atlas' shoulders.

"Can you get me down there?" I asked.

"Nicholas, I can. But while there are a few select locations tourists may access, you must understand that deeper underground Rome is a very dangerous place. Tunnels collapse all the time, people become lost, some never come out. It is not a journey for the fainthearted."

"Point taken. Just get me in."

"I can guide you to an entrance. After that, you'll have no cell signal and will be on your own. Are you certain this is a place your man would hide out?"

"I'm certain of very little Alessandro, but I can tell you that Lachlan Byrn won't just hide somewhere in that labyrinth. He will use it to escape."

"He'll need to be sure of his way, and dragging two reluctant novices, he'll only be able to move slowly."

"There's my trouble Alessandro. If I don't find them quickly, I'm certain there'll be only one escapee. The other two will end up lost or dead, eternally buried somewhere within the catacombs."

"You must find your way quickly to the Neronian Crypto-porticus. I will give you directions. Head back toward the hill."

As I followed Alessandro's expert instructions, making urgent time, he explained his thinking.

"The Neronian Cryptoporticus is where Caligula, a corrupt, sadistic, and sexually perverse Roman emperor was assassinated. From what you've told me about Lachlan Byrn, the symmetry between Caligula and Thomas Ireland would be too good an opportunity to pass up."

"He's a man who likes to make his point. You could be right," I replied as I scurried along the path as instructed.

"Now Byrn won't use the cryptoporticus to escape. The tunnel is too well known and doesn't currently lead further under the city."

"So why are you leading me there?"

As the words left my mouth I looked down at the path. Stone had given away to a dirt track which had now become mud. Several footprints had formed, as clear as plaster casts, and considering the rain, they could only have been created recently. From the size and shapes of the prints, I figured it to be two males and a female or child.

"Forget that question, we're on the right track, literally."

"Okay, good. I know that there is an entrance nearby to the Neronian Cryptoporticus. It leads to a tunnel that runs parallel and then veers toward the Victor Emmanuelle building. It's a location only really known to professional archaeologists. We don't want tourists impacting it before we know more about it. Besides it's not at all secured. You enter at your own risk."

Two minutes later I found myself staring at a small opening into the side of the hill. It looked more like a drain than a tunnel entrance. Water cascaded out.

"You're sure about this Alessandro," I asked.

"Absolutely."

"And how would Byrn know about it?"

"Unfortunately, we archaeologists are a chatty bunch. Buy us a beer on a hot day and we're yours."

"I'm going in my friend and thank you."

"Take care Nicholas, there will be no light at all. You will only have your cell phone to guide you. Try and take a bearing toward the Victor Emmanuelle. There will be many confusing offshoots. Go carefully."

I couldn't see that I had any choice, so I inhaled deeply, crouched down and climbed through the tunnel entrance.

I didn't know where to go and each second that passed increased the danger to Cassandra Devlin-Waters, and by association to Thomas Ireland.

How could this possibly end well?

Chapter 62

LACHLAN BYRN

It went well.

Byrn had been pleased with the chaotic reaction down at the forum. As expected, everyone assumed he'd been firing from the top of the Victor Emmanuel building and behaved accordingly. It had been satisfying to see Sharp flee the area in pursuit of a gunman who wasn't there.

Controlling the modified Songar from his hide on the hill proved relatively easy. He'd practised it over and over again, picking targets to shoot from his boat several months ago. The drone was an expensive beast. He'd be sorry to lose it, but it was the plan all along. He could afford it. Byrn appreciated the irony that in this situation, his task wasn't to shoot the victims, but to round them up and head them off in his desired direction.

He chuckled to himself. It would really piss Sharp off when he realized he'd fallen for the same ploy twice, first on the bridge over the Potomac and again here in Rome.

Immediately in front of him, Byrn heard Ireland and the

woman sloshing along in the water. Ireland wouldn't be able to tackle him with the woman in the way. It surprised Byrn when she leaped forward to rescue the politician. It was a crazy courageous move. Byrn respected the act but thought it stupid.

Thomas Ireland was simply not a man worth losing your life for.

Still, he'd keep an eye on her.

When he took out the two agents, Byrn brought the woman along. She added another layer of protection. Not that he needed it. Sharp and his mate Greatrex could look around the Forum and Palatine Hill area all day and never get a handle on his location.

Byrn's research had been as thorough as ever. Using the ancient tunnels and catacombs that ran under Rome as an escape route captivated his imagination. He knew his way. He'd done several practice runs. It surprised the assassin that the Roman underground was not better known. A drunken priest with an appetite for archaeology explained to Byrn how the church loved to keep such secrets to itself. It was a bonus to find an entrance to the Palatine near where Caligula had been assassinated. Byrn hoped Thomas Ireland appreciated poetic justice.

Working in the dark wouldn't be an issue. Byrn paced out every relevant section of the tunnel, every turn, every set of steps. Numbers were his thing.

Unless he'd suddenly graduated with a degree in archaeology, Sharp would never find him here.

Chapter 63

NICHOLAS SHARP

There is darkness, and there is blackness.

Twenty paces into the tunnel and all light ceased to exist. No shadows, no outlines, no walls, just plain, simple black. It might have been relaxing if I hadn't been pursuing a crazed, armed assassin with two hostages.

My legs and shoes were soaked. After fifty slow yards crouching painfully, I stopped to listen.

Any semblance of sound from the outside world had disappeared. I strained to hear any sign of activity coming from the tunnel ahead. There was only silence. I pulled my cell out of my pocket, deciding to risk a glance around. Just for a few seconds, and only to get my bearings. Any shaft of light emanating from the cell would also make me a target. Experience learned.

The stone walls arched above. I reached up to touch the ceiling, only about an inch above my head. When I did so, my hands contacted a wet, greasy slime. There was nothing more to see, so I turned off the phone. After waiting another sixty seconds listening intently, I edged forward… to God knows where.

I'd moved quickly after discovering the two unconscious CID men. The instructions Alessandro had provided were given on the fly, yet extremely accurate. I figured Byrn, Ireland, and Cassandra couldn't be more than ten minutes ahead of me. All good so far. The trouble would begin when I came to a junction.

Three minutes later, I came to a junction.

It was the touch of a slight breath of wind on the side of my face that alerted me. I flicked the flashlight app on the phone back on. There it was, coming in from the right, a tunnel virtually identical to mine.

Decision time. Go right or proceed straight ahead. I had no evidence at all upon which to make such an important choice.

I went right.

Nicholas Sharp, may the Force be with you.

I sloshed along as best as possible for another fifteen minutes. How far would Byrn venture with his captives before doing what he'd come to do? On one hand, his prisoners would slow him down, impede his escape. On the other, I felt certain he'd want to square up with Ireland and look him in the eye before killing him. Surely, he couldn't do that satisfactorily in a space this small. Then I thought of Major Rogers and the hide on the training ground in Wales. Moot point.

Of course, then came the worst thought of all. What would he do with Cassandra?

I forged ahead.

Chance begets the unpredictable.

Still crouching and following the tunnel wall with my right hand, the ground underfoot disappeared. Suddenly I was tumbling down, free-falling. Steps. The sensation didn't last long as I crashed onto another floor several feet below.

Bruised but unbroken, I clambered to my feet. At least this space seemed higher. I reached into my pants. I needed to risk one more brief flash of light.

My pocket was empty, the cell phone gone.

Assuming it fell from my pocket during the tumble, I clawed around, the water still swilling at my feet.

Nothing.

Of course, if I had my phone, I'd be able to use the flashlight to search for it. Catch 22.

Decision time again.

Turn around and find my way back to the entrance while the opportunity remains, or stumble ahead in the darkness.

The smart call would be to go back.

I pressed ahead.

Twenty minutes later, I was questioning the sanity of my judgement.

My arms wheeled blindly in front of me, like a helicopter flying sideways. They acted as my early warning system. If the environment changed, I didn't want to repeat the experience of finding out the hard way.

Every ten minutes, I paused for a moment. The only other sensory defense that remained was my hearing. I figured one minute lost in ten wouldn't make that much difference.

Again, nothing.

I'd literally raised my right foot to continue walking when I heard a familiar sound.

Splash. Quiet enough to almost be undetectable but not a splash that I'd caused.

Rats? Possible. Giant man-eating alligator? Highly unlikely. Another human? Probable.

I froze, listening attentively. There it was again. I peered forward into the darkness, as though that would help. Then I realized my hearing had become disorientated. I couldn't tell whether the noise was ahead of me or behind.

Chapter 64

BYRN

"You don't have a chance, man. My people will be waiting wherever we come out of this underground hell. They'll be all over you."

"Thank you for your opinion and observation, Mr. Secretary. For the sake of all our sanity, particularly mine, which, to be honest, sometimes hangs by a thread, I suggest you just stop talking," replied Byrn. It never ceased to amaze him that some people thought they could talk their way out of any consequence. He'd had to make that point, quite brutally, several times in his career.

They were now wading through about six inches of water, but at least they were able to stand upright. The order unchanged, Ireland still led the way and Byrn brought up the rear. The assassin flicked on his powerful flashlight from time to time, just to keep them on track. Byrn wished the politician would shut up, but he knew he wouldn't. Nature of the beast.

"Damn it, I'm going to see you rot in jail for the rest of your days, you son-of-a-bitch."

"Thank you, sir, that's textbook. You're moving this along quite nicely," replied the assassin.

"Textbook. What the hell are you talking about?" Ireland's voice echoed down the cavern. It really began to annoy Byrn.

"Well, Mr. Secretary, there are two broadly accepted points of view on the subject. Some say there are seven phases of grief that we process our way through. I'm a supporter of the more streamlined approach. Five stages are all that's required. You've eloquently slipped from number one, 'denial' into number two, 'anger' in no time at all."

"And what in God's name am I meant to be grieving about?"

"In your case, I don't think it will have anything to do with God's name. Besides, for what it's worth, I've always believed God is just another term for the person holding the gun. As to what you're grieving about, it's the loss of your own life."

"The loss..." Ireland's words trailed off into the darkness... stage three, 'depression'.

Byrn wondered how long it would be until Ireland entered the next stage. Of course, it was a rare bird that went straight into acceptance. Being a politician, Byrn doubted Ireland could bypass some attempt at negotiation, bargaining his way out.

Through the blackness, Byrn noted a drawn sigh. It was the woman.

He reached into his pocket, undid the plastic vial with one hand, and withdrew a couple more tablets before flicking them into his mouth.

Where eagles dare.

Chapter 65

SHARP

Again, a choice. I could quietly go over to the side of the tunnel and wait. If the sound originated from behind, I'd hear the person approach.

The second option: double my pace. Option one meant losing ground. Option two meant I'd be susceptible to an assault from behind.

I went with option two. It bothered me that I had no idea who might be behind me. It was probably nothing. It certainly wouldn't be Greatrex. Even if he'd spoken to Alessandro, he wouldn't have made it to the tunnel entrance in time.

Doubling my speed meant more sound as I displaced the water around my ankles. So be it.

Fifteen minutes later, a glimmer of hope… literally. A faint beam of light lit the passage around a hundred yards ahead. In a second, it disappeared. Either a corner turned, or a light switched off.

My heart lifted. I'd passed two more junctions over the previous ten minutes. Each one required an immediate decision. 'Veer toward the Victor Emmanuelle building' was

Alessandro's instruction. Easy for him to say. For all I knew, I might be heading for Times Square. I'd made each decision instantly and without regret. No point in hesitating. The faint stab of light had been my reward. A real 'stab in the dark', I chuckled. A second later I considered the possibility of someone surprising me from behind. I stopped chuckling.

After a while, the depth of water lessened until it became nothing. Just the odd puddle. The lack of water introduced another problem: the sound of footsteps. I lightened my step without losing too much pace. If I was closing in on Byrn, stealth would mean everything.

I stopped to listen a few times. Wasted effort.

Next time I noticed the flash, it appeared smaller, more distant. Lightening my step had caused me to lose ground. I sped up, fully aware of the hell that decision may bring down upon me.

Chapter 66

BYRN

"That's far enough. Stop there," ordered Byrn.

The sound of footsteps ceased.

"Now, I'm going to turn on my flashlight. Just ahead you'll see some steps. I need you to climb down them carefully."

Under the assassin's guidance, his hostages hesitatingly descended the steps. No one appeared keen to talk. After nearly a mile of traipsing through the darkness, they both seemed intent on catching their breath.

'Grab it while you can,' Byrn thought to himself, before following them down.

Flashlight in hand, Byrn strode across the space. The area was at least four yards wide and six yards long. When he came to the furthest wall, the assassin reached into his pocket and retrieved a cigarette lighter. A quick snap and the flame burst to life. Byrn held the device high against the wall. Suddenly, a gush of flame lit the room, flooding it with an array of light and shadow. He repeated the process on two other walls as the torches fixed to them came to life.

Byrn heard the woman gasp.

"Lunatic," whispered Ireland.

Three walls lined with what looked to be bunk beds appeared out of the darkness. Just like summer camp, only the beds were made of stone. His hostages had reacted when they understood what lay on the 'bunks'. Trails of endless spider webs weaved through the bones. The webs joining the skeletons shimmered in the half-light. In some places, the bones had disintegrated into dust. In others, the lifeless eye sockets seemed to gaze upward.

"Welcome to the catacombs," said Byrn. "I thought this location fitting for our purpose."

"And what purpose is that?" asked Ireland.

"We've covered that, Mr. Secretary," replied Byrn. "I've brought you to your final resting place."

For a time, Ireland just stared absently into nowhere. Byrn sat on a step, relaxed, a man in total control of the situation.

"I don't know what you want, but I can do a lot for you, young man. I have access to money, powerful friends. I can change your life," said Ireland.

"Thanks, but you've already done that."

A flash of recognition crossed the secretary's face when he realized what Byrn was referring to.

Byrn continued, "But good work, anyway. I see we've now moved on to negotiation."

Ireland stared directly at Byrn. The assassin presumed it to be a technique that had worked for the secretary plenty of times. The reflection in the old man's gaze made it seem like the flames were dancing in his eyes. Byrn chuckled. He liked the idea of Ireland burning up from the inside.

"What happened to you was unforgivable, but you were a Marine. War has its costs," said Sec Def.

"Wrong tack, I'm afraid," Byrn responded. "Sending Sharp and me off to Colombia had nothing to do with war and a whole lot to do with your ego."

"I'm sure I don't understand what you mean. You were on a mission. It went bad."

Byrn leaned back on the step above him, shaking his head.

"Wrong again. You and I both know that wasn't a sanctioned operation. It was a personal bet instigated by a maniac with too much power and zero human compassion for the men and women he led."

Ireland leaned forward, his face reddening.

"You talk of compassion while you sit there with a gun pointed at my head. Do you have no belief in your country, in people?"

Byrn paused for a moment. Without a word, he stood up, walked the length of the room, reversed his weapon and pistol-whipped the secretary of defense across his face.

Ireland lunged backward, blood gushing from his mouth and nose.

"How dare you…"

Byrn raised his arm and repeated the action, sending Ireland sprawling on to the hard stone floor. Silently, he strolled back to the steps and sat down.

"I anticipated that would have felt better than it did. Clearly my expectations were too high," he said.

"It's not too late man, you can…"

"Shut up. For once in your goddamn life, listen instead of talking. Your efforts at negotiation, intimidation, whatever the hell you want to call it, are wasted on me. Think of it as though you're speaking directly to a loaded weapon. The fact remains that today you are going to pay a price, not only for what you did to me but also for the young women you have abused, the men you have crushed, and the country you have dishonored."

"Listen to me..."

"Guns can't hear, you pompous fool. It is what it is, and I am what I am. As for you... well, you are currently living the final few moments of your pathetic existence."

"Not if I can help it."

In an instant, Byrn swiveled.

Unbelievable.

Nicholas freakin' Sharp, giant pain in the ass.

Chapter 67

SHARP

Almost imperceptibly at first, they grew louder. Voices in the dark.

I edged my way forward. Gradually rounding a bend, one slow step at a time, I gazed expectantly into the blackness. Halfway round the bend I got my initial inkling of what lay ahead. Another faint shimmer of light reflected off the stone walls. This time it was different. Although I noticed some flickering, the glow remained relatively constant.

I stopped to listen. More voices, slightly louder, but I still couldn't understand what was being said.

When I'd finished rounding the curve, all became clear. About a hundred yards ahead, at the end of what must have been a straight section of tunnel, I saw a luminous glow. It framed the silhouette of a man. He sat low, either on the floor or on a step, his back toward me.

With the advantage of being cloaked in a shroud of darkness, I sidled my way along the wall. The voices grew louder. Halfway down the passage, the first flash of recognition hit.

"Wrong again. You and I both know that wasn't a sanctioned

operation. It was a personal bet instigated by a maniac with too much power and zero human compassion for the men and women he led."

A crack, not a gunshot, but certainly something violent followed Lachlan Byrn's words.

I picked up my pace. When people stop talking, that's when the bad shit happens.

Another crack.

The voices began again. I hugged the wall. If they kept speaking, my footsteps may go undetected.

The words came and went in snippets, but a sharp staccato had replaced what had been a more controlled conversational tone.

I'd made it to within ten yards of them. Byrn was the man on the steps. Ireland lay on the floor, propped up on one elbow, looking expectantly toward Byrn. Cassandra Devlin-Waters perched on a stone bench on the far side of the room.

Byrn's gun was pointed at Ireland.

I withdrew my Heckler and Koch HK45 Tactical from my coat pocket.

The assassin's voice filled the space between us.

"Think of it as though you're speaking directly to a loaded weapon. The fact remains that today you are going to pay a price, not only for what you did to me but also for the young women you have abused, the men you have crushed, and the country you have dishonored."

"Listen to me..."

Five yards. It was a miracle my presence had gone unnoticed.

"Guns can't hear, you pompous fool. It is what it is, and I am what I am. As for you... well, you are currently living the final few

moments of your pathetic existence."

I stepped into the light, my gun pointing at the back of Byrn's head.

"Not if I can help it."

The next few seconds blurred into a frenzied chaos.

Byrn spun around, raising his weapon as he moved.

I squeezed the trigger on the H&K. There was no point in waiting for him to fire first.

In the same instant, a violent force hit the center of my back. Stunned and breathless, I plunged forward down the steps. My shot drove wide as my shoulder took the brunt of my fall. Byrn leaped backwards into the room.

Why hadn't he fired?

Down the tunnel, where I'd just been standing, a huge figure appeared out of the darkness. My first thought was Greatrex, but that made no sense. Then I saw the face.

Miller. The sound I'd heard earlier behind me.

"Miller, thank God."

Thomas Ireland, still on the ground next to where I'd just landed, sounded relieved.

Byrn's weapon had arced around, following my fall. He spun back toward the tunnel.

Miller stood there, bedraggled, clothing torn, anger in his eyes. But his eyes weren't what worried me. It was the service issued M4A1 carbine in his hand that did the trick.

"Mr. Secretary, stay down. Sharp, you're a dead man."

Miller pointed his gun directly at my head and smiled. He squeezed his trigger, just as I had a few seconds earlier.

That was the point the CID agent made his big mistake. In his lust to take me out, he ignored Lachlan Byrn.

The gunshot echoed violently around the stone walls.

Miller froze where he stood. A perfectly formed red dot appeared between his eyes. As the blood oozed out of the wound, he fell backward into the darkness, crashing lifelessly to the floor.

In less than three seconds, control of the room had changed three times. A deadly game of musical chairs, and I was left standing.

Chapter 68

"Well, that was interesting. You don't make friends easily, do you Sharp?" said Byrn.

Ireland groaned and slumped back onto the floor, a man defeated.

My Heckler and Koch had landed a good two feet from my fingertips. I glanced at it. Lachlan Byrn stared at me, his dark eyes saying everything that needed to be said. Reaching for the gun would be suicide.

"Young man, I think we need to talk." The general's wife broke the silence.

Byrn looked up, surprised.

Cassandra returned his stare without flinching.

"You've made your intentions clear," she began. "To be honest, I have no time for this imbecile that masquerades as my country's secretary of defense, either. But killing him in cold blood isn't the right way to end this."

Byrn strolled back to his perch on the steps, his gun still aimed at me. He said nothing, but a lopsided grin appeared on the edge of his mouth.

Cassandra wasn't done. "I will never forgive you for

shooting my husband. It was unnecessary and pointless to put his life at risk. I do, however, acknowledge how this man has wronged you so deeply," she nodded towards Ireland. "Surely there is a better path forward. If you assassinate the United States secretary of defense, you'll be hunted for the rest of your days."

My eyes arced from Cassandra to Byrn. This was her moment.

"Of course, I'd also like to inquire what you intend doing with me, and Nicholas. Over the last hour or so, you have consistently berated and threatened Thomas Ireland, but have made no mention of what you have in mind for me. It may be a little indulgent for me to ask, but if I'm going to die, I'd like to know."

Cassandra was certainly in touch with her inner Hepburn, but it was more Katherine than Audrey at this moment.

Byrn continued to stare at her with what seemed like blank amusement. I knew there was more behind the look. With Lachlan Byrn, there always was.

Then he laughed, a small chuckle at first, but within seconds, it became a full-throated roar. His gun hand didn't falter.

"I'm sorry," he said, "but that was fantastic. I wish I could say you reminded me of my mother, but nothing could be further from the truth."

The assassin paused for a minute. He seemed to search Cassandra's eyes, bemused, possibly confused. That was unusual.

"To be fair, I'm uncertain about you. You're not why I came here, and at this point, your death would be collateral damage. It happens sometimes in my profession. On the other hand, somewhere in the back of my mind there is a lawyer, although

I hate those bastards, and he's currently appealing to the jury on your behalf. Let's see how he goes." Byrn smiled again. A cold smile.

"You are certifiably insane." Ireland spoke for the first time since his one hope of rescue had evaporated.

Byrn looked over at him, almost as though he'd forgotten he was there. He smiled, turned his weapon toward the secretary, and shot him in the upper thigh.

The loud and surprising impact of the gunshot made us all flinch. Ireland screamed out in agony.

"It's best you just be quiet," declared Byrn.

"I'm telling you now, Byrn, if you harm Cassandra, I will kill you, even if I die in the process." I meant every word.

Byrn turned to me. "Beautifully said Sharp. Real matinee hero stuff. The trouble is you'd be dead before I started on her. Whenever I can, I prefer death to be an orderly affair. Must be the military background."

The room lapsed back into silence, punctuated only by some intense groaning from Ireland.

If I couldn't get to my weapon, we needed to stall for time. Surely when I went off grid Greatrex would have contacted Alessandro for more intel regarding possible locations and exit strategies. Eventually, he'd find his way down here. But how long would it take?

"Nicholas, have you ever thought much about the timing of death?"

It was as though Byrn had read my mind.

"Look at that wound," Byrn nodded towards SecDef's leg. "Blood is a bit like sand in the proverbial hourglass. As it seeps out of the body, abandoning its role as a provider of life, it gives notice. Your time is almost up."

As Byrn spoke, sweat beaded on his forehead. For a moment, I thought I caught a small tremor in his hand. That seemed out of character. I wondered if he was sick, or on some sort of medication. Almost on cue, he reached into his pocket, grabbed out what appeared to be a couple of tablets and threw them into his mouth. He must have noticed my expression.

"Mother's little helper," he said.

Again, we lapsed into an uncomfortable silence. Finally, the assassin spoke.

"Now, time to get down to business," announced Byrn. "So, who is going to live, if anyone, and who will call this beautiful environment their final resting place?

No one responded.

"All right. Let's begin with you, Mr. Secretary."

Ireland's groaning seemed to intensify. At least it rose in pitch.

"I find myself consistently conflicted," Byrn began. "As a professional, my work is best done from a distance. It makes for a smoother process and an easier extraction. Yet when the matter is personal, and make no mistake Mr. Secretary, this matter *is* personal, I do prefer to get close with my... er... let's call them the 'nearly departed.'"

Byrn allowed himself a small snicker. It was no villain's laugh, just an acknowledgement of his own wit.

The assassin sat there, his attention focused totally on Ireland. His eyes seemed to stare deep into the politician's soul.

An opportunity. Gradually I eased my fingers forward across the stone floor, a quarter inch at a time. I shifted my body, trying to distract from the creeping hand. My right palm now lay nearly two inches closer to my gun.

"No, Nicholas." In one succinct movement, Byrn turned and fired. The round hit the butt of the gun and sent it skating across the floor. Whatever was wrong with the man hadn't impaired his accuracy.

Again, we all flinched at the sound of the weapon.

Byrn pivoted back toward Ireland as though nothing had happened.

"So, let's talk."

Chapter 69

"How old are you Mr. Secretary?"

"I'm sixty-four. What's that got to do with anything?"

"I'll explain that. Please be patient," replied Byrn. "Now let's see, the average life expectancy for a wealthy white male in the US is around eighty-five years of age. So, if we're talking pure economics, the cost of the life decisions you have chosen is around twenty-one years. I can't guarantee the total accuracy of the calculation, but it's close enough. Eighty-five minus sixty-four equals twenty-one."

"You're insane," said Ireland.

"We've spoken about that. Insane, no, mental health hanging by a thread, perhaps."

The manner in which Byrn spoke was deadpan, with little expression, factual. I glanced across to Cassandra; she stared intently at the assassin, as mesmerized by the conversation as I was.

"So, now it's important to me that you understand what you've bought with this sacrificed time. What has made your life so different from most other people that you have to pay for it in this way?"

Ireland shook his head. "I've been successful. That's not a crime."

"No, success is certainly not a crime, Mr. Secretary. The kicker comes in the manner you achieved your success and what you did with it," replied Byrn.

"I've worked hard, I've earned my prosperity, I've accomplished a great deal. More than a depraved maniac like you could ever imagine."

Byrn waited a moment before responding, as though he was giving the matter consideration.

"Now, no need for insults, but yes, I'm almost convinced that you actually believe that. There's probably been a million small decisions along the way, each time you compromised morality for the sake of moving forward, upward… achieving… digging yourself in deeper."

"Rubbish."

"Let's talk about your secret stash of files."

"That's a matter of national security."

"I don't think so. I believe they are a matter of your own security and mobility. The majority of your files are centered around business and political associates, mostly Americans, but they include plenty of powerful individuals across the globe. Most of them are decent people. Decent people who made mistakes. We all do, you know."

Ireland said nothing.

"Well, of course you're aware of that. It's your line of business. You've used those files to lever your way to wherever you wanted to go, to attain whatever you wanted to. Take that Senator from Michigan. What was his name?… Haggart, that's right, William Haggart. Good man, faithful to his wife, supported his family, loved his kids, adored his grandkids.

300

Picture perfect, really, until he made a single mistake. One drunken night with a hooker in Washington. You found out, put the word on him, threatened to expose him. He was on the appropriations committee, wasn't he? You needed increased funding for one of your, shall we say, covert projects? Being a man of principle, he refused. You threatened to out him with CCTV footage you'd dug up. In the end, Haggart took what he considered to be the only honorable course. He drove his car off the steep side of a mountain road in the Huron Mountains."

Byrn paused, gazing intently at Ireland.

"You did that Mr. Secretary, that and so much more. I'm sure there are many similar instances that we'll never even find out about. Blackmail in its most simple form, really. People get hurt, you get what you want. Now let's discuss your sexual dalliances."

"I'm a happily married man." The weakness in the tone of Ireland's voice belied his conviction.

"My information is that Emma Moore, the young girl Sharp rescued, is just the latest in a line of victims. Some had their careers and reputations destroyed, some, the more unfortunate, were left physically scarred by your fetishes."

"How could you possibly have any proof of these accusations?"

"I have proof. Piles of proof. I do thorough research, and I have friends who are equally comprehensive."

"You'd have no chance in a court of law of proving anything."

"Well, at least we can agree on that. But once again, you seem to have missed the point. I am your court of law. You've been tried and found guilty, so now I'm your executioner, as well. Do you get the idea?"

Ireland slumped down, his chin pressed against his chest.

Byrn continued. "And to you, sir, I say well done. I see you've reached the final stage."

"Acceptance," Cassandra interjected.

"Exactly," Byrn responded. "Besides, if no other proof was needed, I'm sitting here in front of you, the man you condemned to years of captivity and torture, just because you decided to have a half-assed bet. To be honest, I never really required more evidence than that. The rest of the information I gathered just confirmed my view of who you truly are."

Abruptly, Byrn turned to look at me.

"You know Sharp, one thing that perplexes me is how you let this piece of excrement live this long?"

I gazed back into Byrn's eyes, glowing in the flickering light like reflections in a bottomless pool.

I had no answer, so I just shook my head.

"All right, let's move on. My reason for being here with you, and not on some remote rooftop…"

Byrn offered a sideways glance in my direction.

"The reason I'm in this room with you is to hear you say, in your own words, that you understand."

"Understand what?" Ireland wasn't helping with his case.

"Understand that the pathetic, cruel and self-obsessive life that you've lived has expedited your early death."

Ireland tried to prop himself up, but his breathing was labored. He struggled.

"Here, let me help you," offered Byrn. "Sharp, stand up and move over there where I can see you, and keep a good distance between you and your weapon."

I stood up and walked to the far side of the room, eyeing my Heckler and Koch lying on the floor like an elusive pot of gold.

A thousand alternative scenarios thundered through my head, as they always did in times like this. Something would click, some plan or half-baked idea that could bring a bad situation to a close. I was ready to roll the dice… and then I wasn't.

This time, I realized that any move I made would place Cassandra Devlin-Water's life in direct jeopardy.

The cold truth was, Thomas Ireland just wasn't worth that risk.

Byrn stepped forward, gun still in hand. He wrapped his other arm under Ireland's armpits and maneuvered him onto the stone bench a yard down from Cassandra. Ireland cried out in pain but didn't resist.

"There, there, I do believe you're embracing the acceptance of your situation outstandingly well." He then reached down and pressed his thumb directly into the gunshot wound on Ireland's thigh. Cruel bastard.

The secretary screamed out in agony.

"Now," began Byrn, "tell me you understand… and mean it."

"What if I don't?"

"Ask Sharp, he'll explain. He's taken enough lives. There are good deaths and bad deaths. The pain you feel now is nothing to what you will feel if I decide to take my time and prolong the process."

I nodded toward the secretary, but I couldn't help him.

Keeping his eyes on me, Byrn kneeled down in front of Thomas Ireland. The secretary's intense cries were now replaced by a slow sobbing.

Byrn leaned forward, pressing his mouth up to within an inch of Ireland's ear.

"Tell me you understand."

The sobbing swelled to a crescendo.

Byrn placed his gun in his left hand and picked up Ireland's hand. He squeezed it gently. He kept his mouth close to Ireland's ear. Before he spoke, he flashed the weapon in my direction one more time. A warning.

"Mr. Secretary, this is your final chance. Tell me you understand the reason for what's about to happen," he whispered.

A deathly hush filled the room.

Ireland began to speak, so quietly at first, I had difficulty making out the words.

"I understand."

"I beg your pardon."

Then louder. "I understand. I know what I've done. God forgive me."

Byrn withdrew his head slightly, so he could look Ireland in the face.

"He won't."

In a movement so smooth and rapid I hardly realized it was happening, Byrn raised his gun, pressed it against Ireland's temple, and squeezed the trigger.

Needing to do something, I leaped forward, just as the secretary's blood splattered the room. Crimson on stone.

Then I froze.

Lachlan Byrn had swung his weapon back around and now pointed it directly at the general's wife.

Chapter 70

"Don't do it Byrn. It won't end well,"

The assassin turned to look at me. His face appeared drawn, tired. The sweat continued to drench his forehead, his brow wrinkling beneath the sheen. Byrn's gaze shifted, first up at Cassandra and then down to Ireland's body laying prone in a pool of blood on the floor.

"Chances are this won't end well for anybody Sharp."

There was a possibility, if he kept his head down long enough, that I'd make it across the room to my gun. I'd have to be seriously fast.

Praying that Byrn would stay downcast and reflective for a moment longer, I tensed my legs, ready to leap. I could do this... maybe.

Then Lachlan Byrn looked up at me. His eyes appeared dark and lifeless, but surprisingly, his jaw seemed to set itself in resolve. He pursed his lips.

"Don't do it Sharp, I know you want to, but don't. It would be a pointless gesture."

Then, moving with catlike speed, Byrn brought the matter to a close. He leaped on to his feet, wrapped his available arm around Cassandra's neck and pressed his gun to her temple.

"Now, ever so slowly, move behind me and onto the steps where you came in. Again, stay away from your weapon," he instructed.

Cassandra said nothing, nor did she struggle. I had the feeling she sensed the mental health of the man who held her was balanced on a knife's edge.

As I reversed my course back to the entrance of the room, Byrn led Cassandra in the opposite arc. He didn't take his eyes off me. Two animals circling, each waiting to see a weakness in the other, seeking an opportunity.

There was nothing I could do while he held a gun to Cassandra's head. Byrn knew that, but his trust levels remained low to non-existent.

We halted; me where I began, he at the opposite end of the space. Behind him, there was only the blackness of what must have been an exit point.

"It's up to you now, Sharp. I'm going to leave you. Correction, we're going to leave you. This can only go one of two ways. You stay here, allow me time to extract myself, and I'll consider the fate of your beloved general's wife."

"Or?"

"Or you follow, and I'll kill the woman. There'll be a firefight and one, but more likely, both of us will end up dead."

Byrn sighed deeply.

"To be honest, I don't really care that much which way you go, but it's your call."

Keeping his weapon trained on me, his arm tight around Cassandra's neck, he guided his human shield backward into the darkness.

Within a minute, the two of them disappeared from sight.

I stood motionless, the light from the torches on the walls boxing with the shadows across the chamber. At my feet, the United States Secretary of Defense lay impotent in death.

Two minutes after Byrn disappeared, I walked over to where my pistol rested on the floor. I reached down, picked it up, and checked its functionality.

I then strode towards the dark doorway Byrn had used to make his escape.

That was the moment I decided to choose option three.

If the darkness could work for Byrn, it might work for me as well.

As I rounded the first bend, all reflected light quickly disappeared. I trudged through the gloom, one arm directly in front of me, the other gripping the gun. If Byrn heard one footstep coming behind him, he would activate his Plan B, and Cassandra's life would be over.

I stooped down and slipped off my shoes.

Although thankful that the tunnel remained at standing height, rocks and stones lay scattered over the ground. I didn't see them, but each time they bruised or cut into my feet, I felt them. Several times I stumbled into protruding half-walls and other assorted stonework. I fell to the ground more times than I counted, but my main concern was the noise I made rather than the pain I felt.

I pressed on… and on, wondering whether Lachlan Byrn held any expectation that I was stalking him.

Chapter 71

LACHLAN BYRN

Byrn had no illusions about Sharp's intentions. The stubborn fool would follow him. Sharp just didn't know how to take no for an answer.

The whole situation hadn't gone as well as Byrn hoped.

The assassin had been surprised but not alarmed when Sharp rolled up. His presence became a threatening intrusion that required management. The additional entrance of Ireland's man, Miller, had been an interesting but short-lived distraction. Sharp did seem to have a way of pissing people off.

The aspect that concerned Byrn the most was the lack of gratification. There should have been a level of satisfaction in killing Thomas Ireland. He sensed the secretary's admission of guilt was genuine. Experience taught the assassin that death confessions usually were, but even that hadn't been adequate to satiate him.

Job done, move on.

The woman seemed smart. Smart enough to say nothing as

he dragged her along the tunnel. Byrn supposed you'd have to be smart to marry a man destined to become a general in the US military. She probably sensed his edginess.

That presented a problem.

Byrn could feel the Night Eagle wearing off already. The drug had been designed to keep warriors alert in the field for days on end. The assassin wondered if he'd scored a bad batch. His nerves stretched to their limit. When the crash came, it would be big. He needed to be safe on his boat by then. That was non-negotiable.

He had released his hold around the woman's neck when they'd rounded the first bend. Now gripping her hand tightly and pulling her along, they moved more quickly. But if she slowed him down, he'd do what needed to be done.

Byrn knew the way. His extraction from the chamber had been meticulously prepared. The darkness didn't bother him, but it would slow Sharp down considerably.

Not for a second did Byrn underestimate the threat that Sharp posed. The former Marine was a dangerous operator. At least taking the general's wife offered Byrn an edge.

Still, he wondered. Just how far behind them would Sharp be?

Chapter 72

NICHOLAS SHARP

The thought of missing an unseen branch off the tunnel tormented me. I prayed a breeze or change of air pressure might expose any opening. But that was all I could do… hope.

After twenty minutes of stumbling along in pitch black conditions, my chances of catching up with Byrn seemed to fade. Twice I'd fallen down steps I didn't see, and once I'd run straight into a wall when the tunnel, unbeknown to me, had taken a sharp left-hand turn. I dropped my gun in the resulting fall but scrambled around in the dark until I felt the cold metal of the weapon's barrel under my fingers. I returned the gun to my pocket for safekeeping.

To face Lachlan Byrn unarmed would be a foolish mistake.

Every few minutes, I stopped to listen. Byrn wouldn't risk using his flashlight, but I hoped I might catch some footsteps. It wasn't long before hope turned to hopelessness.

LACHLAN BYRN

Byrn worried about their pace.

"Move quickly, keep up with me or I make no promise about your future," he whispered, his tone urgent and intense.

"You've made no promise anyway," replied the general's wife, her own voice faltering as she struggled for breath. "I'm doing my best."

Byrn tugged harder on her hand. Even considering his lack of local knowledge, Sharp would make better time than them if he'd remained on the right path. The assassin mentally kicked himself. He should have put Sharp down at the beginning.

Either way, his human asset was rapidly turning into a liability.

He'd have to decide soon.

NICHOLAS SHARP

I listened attentively, resting hands on knees as I tried to catch my breath. Still no footsteps. There was no point looking ahead or around. I simply couldn't see.

It didn't matter. Too much time had passed, and I'd clearly taken a wrong turn. Byrn would escape. Worse, I'd left Cassandra Devlin-Waters' future in his tremoring hands.

Then I heard it. Water. Running water.

The sound was gentle, not a flowing stream, more like the rustle of a mountain brook. Only this wasn't a mountain.

I pressed forward.

LACHLAN BYRN

Byrn would have to act. They were moving faster, but not

fast enough.

He yanked even harder on the woman's hand. She grunted but followed on. They didn't have too far to go now. The old church crypt that had been his entrance to the underground maze was less than half a mile ahead. He picked up the pace some more. They'd need to run the remaining distance to stay in front of Sharp.

Three steps on, Byrn sensed the ground slip from under his feet. His face slammed into a hard, rocky surface. The assassin gagged as blood seeped into his mouth. A second later, the woman landed on top of him.

"Damn and hell. Must be some sort of landslide," he grunted, pushing his hostage off him.

Byrn reached into his coat pocket, withdrawing the flashlight. He had no option but to risk a quick look around.

The beam revealed a mound of rubble. The roof had collapsed, and a continuous stream of water was trickling in from an upper level. Byrn scrutinized the blockage. Yes, there seemed to be just enough room on top for them to squeeze through. He held the beam steady on the gap.

"You go first," he ordered.

"No."

"Don't make me ask you again."

"No, I'm done. I can't continue on."

"Well, I'm not leaving you here for a happy ending, so climb."

In the half-light, Byrn saw his captive close her eyes tightly. Hesitation.

"Climb or die here." He pulled out his gun and pressed it against her cheek.

Without waiting for an answer, he let go of her hand, wrapped his free arm around her waist, and virtually threw her halfway up the mound. At least the Night Eagle still provided some extra strength when he needed it. The woman struggled up and over.

Byrn flicked the light off. He'd probably let it shine too long. He scrambled up the mound. When he got to the top, he glanced back up the tunnel before launching himself over the peak, rolling quickly to his side as he landed.

The scrape of a passing rock cut into the assassin's cheek just before thumping onto the ground next to him. If he hadn't rolled left, it would have knocked him out.

One more flash of light revealed the disappointment on the woman's face. She had tried and missed. Byrn reached up, grabbed her hand. Turning the beam off again, he led her frantically into the blackness.

"You may have just determined your own future, lady."

Byrn quelled his rising anger. It was still too soon to throw the woman away. She may have one last use.

NICHOLAS SHARP

Seeing the flash up ahead gave me a sorely needed burst of energy. I sprinted through the darkness, the jagged stones ignored.

Within seconds, I'd hit a mound of debris. My hands found it first and cushioned my fall. The coarse edges of the rock cut into my palms. Better than my face.

The light had gone out, yet I felt water streaming over my fingers. The sound I'd noticed earlier. Some sort of underground flow had undermined the stone, and the tunnel had collapsed, blocking the path forward. It was over.

Then the obvious hit me: Byrn and Cassandra must have

discovered a way past.

I scrambled up the rock face, frantically searching for a gap. It took a good two minutes before I found a small space on the left of the mound between the rock and what remained of the tunnel roof. I clambered over.

Rolling down the other side, I was rewarded with more darkness.

Then I heard footsteps.

LACHLAN BYRN

Byrn sensed he had an even chance now. If Sharp was close behind, the mound would slow him down. He gripped his hostage's wrist, thrusting her forward.

Three minutes later, the assassin knew exactly where they were. A slight breeze caressed the right side of his face. Then he smelled the water. Stagnant water.

They were in the lower level of the crypt now, but he would have to be careful. There was only a narrow path around the edge of the huge well in the center of the cavern. Byrn would need to risk using the flashlight again to find the track. His drunken priest had told him that several people had died falling into the hole over the years. He said no one was sure how deep it really was, at least no one who lived.

He flicked the light on, already aiming it in the direction where he thought the pathway would lie. A circular array of cobble stones leading around a large abyss appeared.

Byrn felt the pain a millisecond before he heard the gunshot. The flashlight spun out of his hand and landed on the ground five yards away, its strong beam casting a patchy light across the space.

The assassin swiveled, firing his weapon back into the dark tunnel without thought.

Still clasping her wrist, he shoved the woman to one side as he searched for cover.

There was none.

Not exactly true.

He swung the woman back, released her wrist, and resumed his hold around her neck with his arm. He quickly stepped behind her.

"Take your best shot, Sharp. See how that works out for you."

NICHOLAS SHARP

I'd shot towards the shaft of light.

I'd hoped to hit Byrn, figuring he would be the one holding the flashlight. Instead, I clipped the light, sending it spinning out of the assassin's hand.

It wasn't all bad. With light came hope... and a target.

Byrn reacted like a jackal, spinning Cassandra around, using her for cover.

"Take your best shot, Sharp. See how that works out for you."

There would be no second shot.

LACLAN BYRN

Byrn was confident the situation was developing in his favor. Sharp had no choice but to do as he was told.

"Place your weapon carefully on the ground."

Byrn couldn't see Sharp at all. The ex-Marine remained

recessed into the shadows. But if Sharp fired one more time, Byrn would identify enough muzzle flash to take him out. Except that he knew Sharp wouldn't fire.

But why was he taking so damn long to react?

NICHOLAS SHARP

For the second time within an hour, alternate scenarios rolled through my mind like a slot machine. When a solution finally appeared, I didn't like it at all, but I was desperate.

"You drop your gun, Byrn. We both know you can't find me in the darkness. You can walk away from this."

The bluff.

LACHLAN BYRN

"I'll spell it out for you Sharp. I don't need to see you."

As Byrn spoke, he raised his weapon, placing the barrel against Cassandra's temple.

"Now, do you understand how this will play out? Drop your gun and kick it out into the light. Then you come slowly out after it. And Sharp, I won't say it twice."

Byrn glanced over at the flashlight on the ground. It had landed perched between two large rocks. Taking it out would have been useful, but there was no clean shot. The assassin had decided he didn't really want to shoot the woman; she had courage. He liked that. But given the lack of choice, if he executed her, he'd have a fifty/fifty chance of escaping in the ensuing chaos.

He'd never honestly felt comfortable with collateral damage, despite what he'd said. But he'd vowed he'd do what he had to do.

NICHOLAS SHARP

There was no other plan.

I sensed a familiar coldness envelope me. It always did. Decision time was over. From here on in, everything was a calculation.

Could I do this?

I looked directly at Cassandra Devlin-Waters. She returned my stare as though she knew exactly where I stood.

That was impossible.

"Nicholas, do what you need to do!" she shouted. "End this."

Courage. But she had no idea what I intended to do.

"Sharp!" yelled Byrn.

I raised my pistol level with my eyes and assumed the stance. Left arm supporting right, feet apart.

I took the familiar deep breath.

I steadied my aim. Accuracy was everything.

Byrn shifted on his feet, ready to fire.

Breathe out, one, two, three… I squeezed the trigger… and shot Cassandra Devlin-Waters.

The bullet pierced her right shoulder, unsurprisingly she screamed. More to the point, Lachlan Byrn cursed loudly, probably in surprise as much as pain, as the bullet passed through Cassandra's shoulder and tore into his own flesh.

Involuntarily, he stepped back, but at the same moment, Cassandra crashed forward. Byrn released a shot, which cleared the rear of her head by less than an inch.

I rushed ahead, weapon ready. Cassandra fell forwards into my arms just as I reached her. I shoved my gun around her torso, still primed to fire.

Byrn stood there, unmoving, but at an awkward angle. His eyes open wide, he stared at me. It took me a moment to realize what was happening. I hadn't seen the gaping hole in the ground behind them. A second later, Byrn's head angled upward toward the ceiling as he arched over. I reached out to grab him.

I grabbed air.

For a split second, I could have sworn I glimpsed a familiar grin on the side of his open mouth before he tumbled backward.

There was no scream. Lachlan Byrn just disappeared silently into the abyss below.

Chapter 73

Epilogue

We sat in the ristorante on the Campo de Fiori, the same place Greatrex and I dined with Izzy and Alessandro a month earlier. So much had happened since then. I looked around the dinner table at the smiling, laughing faces. Faces of people I cared about.

Cassandra Devlin-Waters perched at the corner of the long table. Jack and I had stayed in Rome, visiting her in hospital each day, ensuring she received the best possible treatment. She'd graciously forgiven me for putting her there.

No one had ever forgiven me for shooting them before, nor had I sought forgiveness, even from the grave. Perhaps there'd been one exception many years ago in Iraq, but I'd learned to live with that.

At the head of the table, next to Cassandra, sat the general. He'd persuaded his doctors to let him fly over to be at his wife's side. Kaitlin traveled with him and now sat opposite her mother. It had been a difficult conversation, explaining to them both how I'd shot the person they most loved in this world. With Cassandra's support, they came to realize that I had no choice, and my actions probably saved her life.

Next to Kaitlin sat Izzy and Alessandro. Never scared to be the center of attention, Izzy shared an enthralling story about a run in with another local pop star. Without Izzy, we wouldn't have had access to Alessandro and his formidable knowledge. Tracking Lachlan Byrn into his underground labyrinth on my own would have been impossible. Sliding doors moments… the likely outcome of the alternate scenario was unthinkable.

The scene in the crypt after the shooting had been intense. I'd been able to slow Cassandra's bleeding, but I didn't want to leave her down there alone in the dark. Fortunately, within twenty minutes, a tiny light appeared in the tunnel. A short time later, Greatrex and Alessandro strode out of the darkness. Alessandro quickly identified our location, made his way around the cobbled path surrounding the gaping hole, and disappeared upward to find help.

After that, the place crawled with medics and police. When word got out that the US Secretary of Defense had been involved in an incident, the CID team in Rome swarmed the scene.

I had only bad news for them.

Lachlan Byrn briefly became the US authorities' most wanted man since Osama bin Laden. It was a short reign. The local experts quickly persuaded the CID agents that nobody could survive that fall. They confirmed the chasm to be immeasurably deep, and on the few occasions there were records of an accident, no one survived.

Logically, the CID people asked for proof of death. They needed to be certain the killer who assassinated the secretary was definitely, certifiably dead.

The local authorities searched, but it seemed half-hearted.

They knew they would never find the body. At the bottom of the enormous drop lay a series of underground waterways and rivers, most uncharted and all extremely dangerous. In time, the CID accepted that.

The furor across the world's media was intense. Article after article was written about the life of Thomas Ireland. The majority painted him as a patriot and an icon of democracy.

That was disappointing.

At one point, the general pulled me aside. Questions had been asked about my involvement in the shooting, and why I hadn't done more to prevent Ireland's death. Both the general and President Blake quelled the inquiries, saying that if there had been an opportunity to save the secretary, I would have taken it. The naysayers were silenced.

Except for me.

Across the table, Greatrex gazed at me silently. The definitive mind reader.

"Before you say a word Nicholas, there was nothing more you could do."

I returned the look.

"I realize that. The trouble is, Jack, that for one brief moment I wondered if I wanted to do more. I honestly questioned whether Thomas Ireland was worth it. By then, the line between Byrn and I had blurred."

Greatrex sighed, like an impatient teacher.

"I've been over the whole thing a thousand times, but there should have been something I could have done to avert Ireland's death. You and I always manage to pull a rabbit out of the hat at the last minute," I replied.

"Yeah but think about the stakes. How would you feel telling the general his wife had died needlessly because you acted impetuously?"

"I get that too, but…"

"If you're going to tell me again that you missed some-thing… don't. You are not Lachlan Byrn. The way I see it, if Cassandra's life hadn't been under direct threat, you would have responded, no matter what the risk. Byrn knew the general's wife provided insurance. He showed that right at the end, didn't he? He was prepared to take her out to save himself."

"I'm not so sure about that."

Cassandra's voice surprised us both. She and the general had made their way around the table to where we sat.

"Sorry to startle you, but you both looked involved in an earnest conversation. I guessed it might have something to do with my wife," added the general.

I stood up, the general waved me down.

"Okay, yeah, we were getting a little intense," I replied. "But tell me, what makes you doubt Byrn's intentions, Cassandra?" I asked.

"Call it a feeling. But at no time did Lachlan Byrn directly threaten my wellbeing. I got the impression he may have been wrestling with himself about what to do with me."

I glanced over to Greatrex. He shook his head, almost imperceptibly, sharing my skepticism.

"There's more," announced the general, looking at his wife.

"Yes, there is," Cassandra continued. "It didn't really occur to me until the last couple of days. At first, I concentrated on getting through the pain, after that I focused on recovery."

"Go on," I said.

"The thing is, when you shot me, I recoiled backward, toward the hole."

"I'm sorry…"

"Not your fault Nicholas, you didn't even know the well was there," interjected the general.

Cassandra continued. "So, as I fell, of course, I took Byrn with me."

"Makes sense," observed Greatrex.

"It does," said Cassandra. 'But then suddenly I found myself lunging forward, into your arms, Nicholas. "The thing is, I was pushed forward… by Byrn."

Greatrex and I sat in silence for several seconds. The frivolity of the restaurant fading away.

"You're saying…" I began.

"Yes Nicholas, I'm saying the Lachlan Byrn's final act was to save my life."

"God almighty," said Greatrex.

I couldn't have put it better.

The evening wore on. Stories were exchanged, wine was drunk. I was glad to have these people around me, including, perhaps especially, Kaitlin.

I pushed Lachlan Byrn from my mind. Book closed.

Later, as the night wound down, we all stood, still chatting, reluctant to let the celebration end.

In my pocket, my cell vibrated.

I grabbed the phone and glanced down at the message.

Suddenly I felt my gut twist. A knife skewering my soul. I stepped away from the group. Greatrex must have sensed the change in me and followed.

"Want to share?" he asked.

Suddenly, everyone else seemed a mile away.

I took a breath, staring silently across the lights of the

piazza.

"Irony," I began. "It's about the irony."

I turned toward the big fella.

"We've just closed the chapter on a man who defines moral ambiguity. A killer who haunted me like a dark shadow."

"And?" said Greatrex.

"How did we close that chapter? How did I close that chapter?"

He looked confused.

I continued quietly, little more than a whisper. "I shot him, of course. I sent him plummeting down to his death, an un-survivable fall into an inhospitable watery grave."

"What is it, Nicholas?" asked Kaitlin, clearly having noticed something was not right.

I inhaled the night air, searching for a cleansing relief I wouldn't find.

"Who was Lachlan Byrn? Or more to the point, what was he?" I had everyone's attention, but no need of an answer.

All eyes on me.

I continued, "Byrn was a highly trained and highly skilled operator."

"What are you saying?" asked the general.

"Lachlan Byrn was a commando, a Royal Marine, and an experienced special services officer. To be specific, the Special Boat Service. Water was his thing."

I passed the phone across the table to Greatrex.

"Holy shit," said the big fella.

"Read it out," I said. Deadpan.

Greatrex lowered his gaze to the phone and spoke.

'You left me to die once before. This makes twice. Not… ever… again.'

This was far from over.

Afterword

Get your FREE electronic copy of the NICHOLAS SHARP origins Novella PLAY OUT, the latest news about new releases and some other exciting freebies along the way by joining my mailing list at my website: https://mark mannock.com

Although you can begin reading the NICHOLAS SHARP THRILLER series at any point here is my suggested order of reading:

1. **KILLSONG** (NS thriller No. 1-*available on Amazon*)
2. **BLOOD NOTE** (A NS short story-*available exclusively to my mailing list members. I'll send you the link 7 days after sign-up*)
3. **LETHAL SCORE** (NS thriller No. 2-*available on Amazon*)
4. **HELL'S CHOIR** (NS thriller No. 3-*available on Amazon*)
5. **SILENT VOICE** (NS thriller No. 4-*available on Amazon*)
6. **COUNTERPOINT** (NS thriller No. 5-*available on Amazon*)
7. **ECHO BLUE** (NS thriller No. 6-*pre-order on Amazon-out August 2023*)

PLAY OUT-an origins novella (*available exclusively to my mailing list members on sign-up*) can be read at any point. The story takes you back to when Nicholas Sharp left the U.S. Marines.

What readers are saying about the Nicholas Sharp Series:

"I had to keep reading to the end, could not put it away until I had finished."

"I love Lee Child and now have another author who is just as good."

"Jack Reacher's attitude... John Lennon's sensibilities."

"I really enjoyed the sniper-musician-reluctant warrior character..."

"I've read hundreds of books throughout the years and the pandemic has provided me with extra time to discover more reading treasures. Play Out (Nicholas Sharp Origins novella) is one of the best."

"Without a doubt this is a cracking novel... the story then keeps at you in leaps and bounds! Full of action all the way. Just brilliant!"

Reviews are life's blood to an author. If you've enjoyed COUNTERPOINT please consider leaving a review on the book's Amazon page or on GOODREADS.

Acknowledgements

My heartfelt thanks and love to Sarah, Anisha and Jack for your love, tolerance and support. Lachlan, your counsel and wisdom has always been appreciated.

Cover by Anisha Mannock

About the Author

Mark Mannock was born in Melbourne, Australia. He has had an extensive career in the music industry including supporting, recording with or writing for Tina Turner, Joni Mitchell, The Eurythmics, Irene Cara and David Hudson. His recorded work with Lia Scallon has twice been long-listed for Grammy Awards. As a composer/songwriter Mark's music has been used across the world in countless television and theatre contexts, including the 'American Survivor' TV series and 'Sleuth' playwright Anthony Shaffer's later productions.

Mark is presently writing the successful 'Nicholas Sharp' thriller series about a disillusioned former US sniper whose past plagues him as he makes his way in the contemporary music industry. Sharp is a man whose insatiable curiosity and embedded moral compass lead him to places he ought not go. The series is currently read in over 50 countries.

Mark lives in Kettering, Tasmania with his family. His travels around the globe act as inspirations for his writing.

Mark enjoys hearing from his readers, so please feel free to contact him.

You can connect with me on:
🌐 https://markmannock.com
f https://www.facebook.com/markmannockbooks

Subscribe to my newsletter:
✉ https://markmannock.com

Also by Mark Mannock

PLAY OUT
A Nicholas Sharp Origin Novella

Sign up to my mailing list and receive this book for free!

Set five years before **KILLSONG**

A Terrorist attack on the London Underground. Nicholas Sharp doesn't think so.

While on leave from Iraq, the U.S. Marine Sniper finds himself intervening when innocent lives are threatened. He walks away, but for Sharp it's never that easy. Something doesn't feel right. Twenty-four hours later everything is wrong.

The brief solace he finds in his beloved piano is shattered when Sharp becomes the attacker's next target. Step up or step away. Nicholas Sharp doesn't like to kill, but he sure as hell knows how to.

Somewhere between Tom Clancy's *Jack Ryan* and Robert Crais' *Elvis Cole*, Nicholas Sharp may be a flawed hero, but you certainly want him on your side.

"I've read hundreds of books throughout the years and the pandemic has provided me with extra time to discover more reading treasures. Play Out is one of the best." **Goodreads Reviewer-5 STARS**

The Nicholas Sharp origins novella PLAY OUT is sent to you FREE when you join my mailing list at
https://markmannock.com

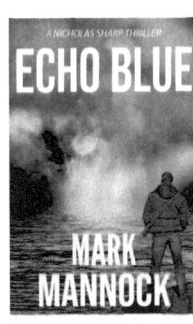

ECHO BLUE
Nicholas Sharp Thriller #6

Are you safe?...

Nicholas Sharp receives a mysterious phone call from Jack Greatrex... then Greatrex disappears.

In a hunt that takes him through South America, Texas, the mountains of Northern Spain and eventually the Middle East, Sharp encounters world renowned environmental activist Dr Deagan Jones from the notorious Crimson Wave. As Sharp uncovers a chain of complex deceptions, Jones' teenage son is kidnapped. The stakes never higher, the ex-Marine sniper turned musician fights to prevent an environmental and humanitarian catastrophe with unimaginable consequences.

Available on Amazon: (August 2023, pre-order now)
http://www.amazon.com/dp/B0BVV25R2F
http://www.amazon.co.uk/dp/B0BVV25R2F
http://www.amazon.com.au/dp/B0BVV25R2F
https://www.amazon.ca/dp/B0BVV25R2F

KILLSONG

Nicholas Sharp Thriller #1

Nicholas Sharp is a killer musician... literally!

Turning his back on the military system that turned him into a murderer when he shot an innocent man, Sharp is grateful to have found refuge in a career as a successful musician. But while he is preparing to back well-known former rock star Robbie West on a USO tour of Iraq, a close friend and her daughter disappear.

In a deadly game of cat and mouse across three continents, Sharp discovers there's more at stake than his own life and those close to him. As relentless shadows from his past chase him down, he faces a brutal choice. Kill or be killed.

"I had to keep reading to the end, could not put it away until I had finished." **Amazon Reader- 5 STARS**

"Jack Reachers attitude... John Lennon's sensibilities." **Goodreads Reviewer- 5 STARS**

Available on Amazon:

http://www.amazon.com/dp/B08CT1FHF5
http://www.amazon.co.uk/dp/B08CT1FHF5
http://www.amazon.com.au/dp/B08CT1FHF5
https://www.amazon.ca/dp/B08CT1FHF5

LETHAL SCORE
Nicholas Sharp Thriller #2

"A great book that has more twists and turns than you can imagine. Pick up and read at all costs." **Goodreads Reviewer 5 STARS**

You can't stop someone with nothing to lose...

Nicholas Sharp is on a tour through Europe, the concerts are sold out and the former Marine sniper turned musician is living in luxury thanks to promoter Antonio Ascardi.

Suddenly it all goes wrong. People are dying along the way and Sharp is blamed. Now a hunted man, accused of terrorist crimes across the continent, Nicholas Sharp must fight for his life and freedom.

Available on Amazon:
 http://www.amazon.com/dp/B08CSYKG18
 http://www.amazon.co.uk/dp/B08CSYKG18
 http://www.amazon.com.au/dp/B08CSYKG18
 https://www.amazon.ca/dp/B08CSYKG18

HELL'S CHOIR
Nicholas Sharp Thriller #3

A goodwill visit to Sudan, what could possibly go wrong?
Nicholas Sharp is performing as part of a political and cultural group representing the US. Suddenly caught up in the middle of a political coup, the leader of the American contingent goes missing and his security staff murdered.

Communication with the outside world is cut off. It falls to Sharp and Greatrex to track their missing leader down.

But then things get really complicated...

"The story then keeps at you in leaps and bounds! Full of action all the way. Just brilliant!" **Amazon Reader-5 STARS**

"Great read and a fun ride." **Amazon Reader-5 STARS**

Available on Amazon:
http://www.amazon.com/dp/B08LRB8CWN
http://www.amazon.co.uk/dp/B08LRB8CWN
http://www.amazon.com.au/dp/B08LRB8CWN
https://www.amazon.ca/dp/B08LRB8CWN

SILENT VOICE
Nicholas Sharp Thriller #4

It's dangerous to be right when the government is wrong...

Hunted down by their government's secret service, the members of protest band Kha Cring flee to Los Angeles to begin a new life. After an unexpected attack, the musicians' safe exile in LA is jeopardized. The desire to fight for their country's freedom undiminished, the band find their soaring popularity and politically messaged music no longer enough to protect them from the evil they escaped.

A deadlier weapon is needed. Nicholas Sharp.

In an instant things go terribly wrong as Sharp finds himself the focus of a network of international conspirators intent on wiping both he and the members of Kha Cring from the face of the planet.

Available on Amazon:

http://www.amazon.com/dp/B08W1V9FWS
http://www.amazon.co.uk/dp/B08W1V9FWS
http://www.amazon.com.au/dp/B08W1V9FWS
https://www.amazon.ca/dp/B08W1V9FWS

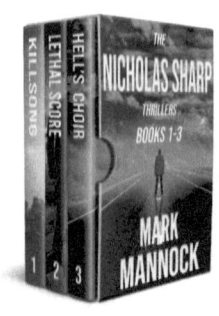

THE NICHOLAS SHARP THRILLERS BOX SET BOOKS 1-3

Nicholas Sharp is a killer musician... literally!

Nicholas Sharp is a disillusioned former US sniper fighting a troubled past and an uncertain future. Seeking solace in his work as a professional musician, Sharp is a man whose insatiable curiosity and embedded moral compass lead him into situations fraught with danger. Nicholas Sharp doesn't like to kill, but he sure as hell knows how to.

Somewhere between Tom Clancy's Jack Ryan and Robert Crais' Elvis Cole, Nicholas Sharp may be a flawed hero, but you definitely want him on your side.

Book 1: KILLSONG
  Book 2: LETHAL SCORE
  BOOK 3: HELL'S CHOIR

Available on Amazon:
  http://www.amazon.com/dp/B08NYLGW1G
  http://www.amazon.co.uk/dp/B08NYLGW1G
  http://www.amazon.com.au/dp/B08NYLGW1G
  https://www.amazon.ca/dp/B08NYLGW1G

BLOOD NOTE
A Short Story Prequel to the Thriller
KILLSONG *(should be read after KILLSONG-available FREE to mailing list subscribers 7 days after sign-up)*

MARK
MANNOCK

Just turn around and walk away. That was all Nicholas Sharp had to do when the mysterious and intoxicating Elena approached him for help.

She knew far too much about him. The warning signs were all there.

Sharp didn't listen to them.

What followed for the former Marine Sniper turned musician, was a harrowing night of violence, deceit and intrigue.

When the sunrise ushered in a new day, Sharp thought it was all over...but it was really just beginning.